MARS ECLIPSED

A Katy Klein Mystery

✦ ✦ ✦

KAREN IRVING

Polestar Books and Raincoast Books gratefully acknowledge the support of the Government of Canada through the Book Publishing Industry Development Program, the Canada Council and the Department of Canadian Heritage. We also acknowledge the assistance of the Province of British Columbia through the British Columbia Arts Council.

Cover design by Val Speidel
Cover photograph by Christoph Burki/Stone

NATIONAL LIBRARY OF CANADA CATALOGUING IN PUBLICATION DATA

Irving, Karen, 1957-
Mars eclipsed

ISBN 1-55192-476-5

I. Title.
PS8567.R862M3 2001 C813'.54 C2001-910863-X
PR9199.3.I688M3 2001

Polestar, an Imprint of Raincoast Books
9050 Shaughnessy Street
Vancouver, British Columbia
Canada, V6P 6E5
www.raincoast.com

1 2 3 4 5 6 7 8 9 10

Printed and bound in Canada by Webcom

To Capt. B. Gordon Irving
October 13, 1930 – March 1, 2001
Good night, Dad.

PROLOGUE

MONDAY, OCTOBER 2
Sun conjunct Moon, opposition Saturn ✦
Mars conjunct Pluto ✦

On the low wooden dock near the boathouse at Dow's Lake, three men stood close together, talking. More precisely, two of the men huddled together, their hands thrust deep into their pockets against the damp and chill. The third, strapped securely into his electric wheelchair, sat, his head bowed heavily. He might have been listening to the other two, whose voices were low; their words did not penetrate the early morning fog that rose from the surface of the brownish water and shrouded the trees and park behind them. Or the man in the wheelchair might have been in a world of his own. It was hard for the casual observer to tell.

A lone jogger passing by observed the group at approximately 6:40 a.m. that Monday morning. At the time, she didn't think much of it. She and her dog, a black Labrador retriever with the seemingly boundless energy of its breed, were headed for the Arboretum, where the jogger planned to let her dog chase his beloved ragged tennis ball for half an hour before she had to take him home and lock him into the kitchen to prevent him soiling the wall-to-wall carpets or eating the arms from her couch while she worked in her downtown office.

Thus, she did not see the man in the wheelchair lift his head in her direction, his out-of-focus eyes turned toward her, as though in supplication. As she passed, she thought she might have heard him utter a single word: "Please!" But she was not sure, at the time, whether he was speaking to her, or to his companions. In fact, she was not even certain she'd really heard him speak. It could have been that her imagination supplied the word to her later, when she'd had the time to develop a deep sense of guilt.

Nor did she see the shorter of the two standing men take a Polaroid camera from his briefcase and snap a picture of the wheelchair-bound man, immediately before his taller, heavier companion squared his shoulders in preparation for the task he was about to undertake. The jogger did not see the taller man walk around behind the wheelchair, flipping the control switch from "Rider" to "Attendant." She did, however, hear the short, sharp yelp that rang out ever so briefly in the misty morning air. And she heard a muffled splash as the chair and its occupant hit the murky, still water of Dow's Lake. She turned back toward the scene she'd just passed, but the restaurant occupying the upper floor of the former boathouse blocked her view, and she hesitated for several minutes before returning to the spot she'd just passed. All three men were gone.

As she told the police later, something about the standing men had given her pause. The taller one wore a suit, but not the kind of standard-issue uniform she associated with her male co-workers in her government office. The jacket looked as though it was made from some kind of animal hide, crocodile perhaps. The pants were shiny, all right for an evening in a cigar lounge but odd for first thing on a Monday morning, on the otherwise deserted dock. The smaller of the two men wore a collarless white shirt under an expensive-looking black jacket, and both men's hair was so short that bare scalp showed through. No beards or moustaches that she could recall. They looked as though they'd joined the US Marines, then thought better of it, and turned to a life of debauchery and high-stakes gambling instead.

The men reminded her, she said, of the skinheads who'd terrorized the patrons of gay bars around Ottawa a few years ago. And there was something in the men's stances, too, the way they leaned in unison toward the wheelchair-bound man, that had made the jogger think twice about facing them alone, even with her large black dog in tow.

Whether her assessment of the men was accurate, or simply a self-justification invented to excuse herself after the fact, makes little difference. The jogger eventually did walk slowly back to the dock, only to find it empty and still. She peered into the water, and saw no evidence of anything untoward — no bubbles as the drowning man gasped his last, no beseeching hand extended upward through the duckweed and algae that clogged the turgid water. Nor, indeed, any sign of the two close-shaven men in their too-flashy clothing.

By the time she had returned to her own apartment, showered and dressed, gulped her coffee, fed and watered the dog, and locked up on her way to work, she'd forgotten about the two men and their companion. She would not think about them again until nearly two weeks later, when the Rideau Canal system was being drained for the winter, and an unfortunate employee of the

National Capital Commission discovered the bloated remains of a drowned man, strapped into a wheelchair, in the suddenly shallow waters of Dow's Lake.

The jogger would see the story trumpeted across the city pages of the local newspaper, and she would be overcome with shame and horror at her own negligence. Why had she not returned to the dock immediately? Why had she not alerted the authorities right away? Why had she allowed herself to forget the incident so quickly and completely?

"I didn't know!" she would exclaim over and over as she was interviewed by a homicide detective with the Ottawa-Carleton Regional Police. "I just didn't know!"

1

THURSDAY, OCTOBER 13
Sun opposition Saturn ✦
Moon conjunct Mars, conjunct Pluto ✦

As a rule, I don't think of myself as a person who has a hard time saying no, even to a friend. In fact, some might describe me as assertive to a fault.

On this particular autumn morning, though, my words kept sticking in my throat, as though they were afraid to emerge into the brilliant sunshine pouring in through the south-facing windows. And when at last I was able to push them out, I wished I hadn't. Not that I really wanted what was being offered, but I wanted to be able to want it, if you know what I mean. It's not like I was facing such a dazzling array of options that I could afford to pick and choose, and on the face of it, I should have jumped at the chance. However, something was stopping me.

I slouched in a buttery-soft leather armchair, enduring the disgruntlement of Greg Chisholm, my former mentor and current friend. At least, I hoped he was still my friend.

"Greg, please. Try to see this from my point of view. Don't be mad." I rubbed my index finger absently along the edge of his polished mahogany desk. "It's wonderful of you to ask, but I just can't work here again. I appreciate your asking me, really. I do. And maybe sometime in the future, I'll be able to imagine coming back. Just not now."

"I don't get it, Katy." Greg pushed his glasses back up his long, thin nose. "You told me, what, eight months ago? At least that long. You told me you'd consider coming back here. I went to a lot of trouble to engineer a consulting psychologist position where you could come in on your own time. You'd have complete freedom, pick your own hours, and you could still do your astrology downtown, if you've got your heart set on it. No one here would need to know what you do on your off time."

"But don't you see? That's just it. I'd be living two lives, always afraid they'd overlap somehow. You can't tell me the shrinks here would be happy to refer their patients to someone who works with all that woo-woo stuff on the outside. I'd be marginalized here, and frankly, I feel quite marginal enough already, thank you very much."

Greg said nothing, but swivelled his chair to face the plate glass window that overlooked carefully groomed lawns and spreading maples. Quite unnecessarily, he adjusted his glasses again. Even though his face was in quarter-profile, I could tell he was frowning.

The coffee mug I'd balanced on the arm of the maroon chair was empty, but I picked it up as though to sip from it anyway, a reflex born of long habit. I put it down again, feeling stupid. The silence prolonged itself, until it grew too heavy to bear.

"Come on, Greg, talk to me. I told you when you asked last winter that I couldn't promise you anything. You knew that, right? It's not like I made you any promises."

He let out his breath slowly, not a sigh but a long, resigned acknowledgement. "Yeah, you told me. I guess

Some of them I knew, some I didn't. Some of them were my fault, some weren't. I can't make them alive again, so what the hell? You know, my mother went through a lot worse in Hitler's camps. I should be able to handle a little bit of the darker side of life, shouldn't I?"

"You know as well as I do, you can't compare traumas — and I'd say that what happened last winter was pretty damn traumatic. For you, for Dawn ..."

"I can take care of myself," I interrupted him. "There's life in the old girl yet." I tried for a jaunty grin. But I could see by the look in his eye that Greg wasn't buying.

"You ever hear of a little thing called post-traumatic stress disorder? Well, you could be the poster child this year, Dr. Klein. Look at you! You're white as a sheet, you're shaking. You need help. Look, I can find you someone ..."

"No thanks," I snapped, withdrawing my hands from his. "I'm fine, Greg. I don't need to see anyone. I'll be okay. Look, can we talk about something else?" I felt chilled, despite the warmth of the autumn sun spilling into the room.

There was another silence. I could feel Greg looking at me, but I didn't meet his eyes.

Finally, he spoke. "Sure. Whatever you say. You're fine. You're a grown-up. You don't need the job I offer you, even though you're up to your eyeballs in debt. You don't need to talk to anyone, even though I can see you suffering. You know best, Katy. I can't seem to offer you much, can I?"

"Greg ..." A lump in my throat choked off my words.

"Never mind. Listen, I've got work to do. We'll go out for coffee sometime, okay?"

I nodded. "Sure. I'll call you." Knowing that I wouldn't. I'd put that off, too, and soon Greg would be like the rest of my life — distant history, a lapsed friendship, another regret.

Pushing my chair back, I hunted around for my

purse. I sniffed back tears. I wasn't going to break down here. I squeezed my eyes shut, forcing the tears back where they'd come from.

"It's on the back of your chair," Greg said, though I'd have sworn he was looking past me, to the Mondrian print on the far wall of his office. "Katy, you know I care about you ..."

"I know," I whispered, trying to hide the tell-tale quiver in my voice. Unfortunately, the words came out as a squeak. I took a deep breath and slung my over-stuffed bag onto my shoulder. "I appreciate what you're trying to do for me. I really do. It's just — no, never mind. Look, why don't we meet next week, okay? It's my turn to buy you lunch."

A small smile played at the corners of my old friend's mouth. "Sure, what the hell. You choose where. Leave a message for me, and I'll be there."

At the door of his office, I paused and looked back at Greg. He met my eyes, and then he seemed to make a decision. Sighing, he stood and folded up his reading glasses, placing them in his shirt pocket.

"Come on," he said. "No one's died of food poisoning at the coffee shop lately. I'll buy you a cup of sludge."

"Now there's an offer I can't refuse." I held out my arm, tears nearly forgotten. He took it, and we walked down the hall toward the elevators. Still friends, I thought with relief. We were still friends. I just needed some time to get myself together, that was all. Time to heal. It would happen, if I just let it. It had to.

✦

If no one had expired yet from the soggy sandwiches and tepid, day-old coffee in the coffee shop, it was purely coincidental. I stood in front of the salad bar, trying to choose slightly less-wilted looking veggies to top my greyish cottage cheese. Greg picked through the cellophane-wrapped sandwiches, but eventually gave it up in favour of a bowl of mystery soup and some soda crackers.

We carried our trays to a corner table, hoping for a bit of privacy. Fortunately for us, it was past one o'clock, so most of the psych patients were already upstairs, attending groups or doing occupational therapy. Greg and I chatted amiably enough, ice-skating over our recent discomfort.

"Now I remember why we usually meet outside the hospital," I remarked, sweeping crumbs and a used straw off the table. "There's just something about the ambience here, a certain *je ne sais quoi* ..."

Greg chuckled. "Hey, don't knock it. This place is the Ritz, compared to the cafe in the basement. So ... what's new and unusual in the life of Katy Klein, Girl Astrologer?"

"I don't want you to laugh at me."

"Katy, would I laugh at you? Come on, tell your buddy Greg. What've you been up to?"

"Okay. You remember I told you about my e-mail friend? Flavia?" He nodded. "Well, she got invited to this retreat next weekend. For astrologers and stuff, you know. It's on this island, Balsam or Sycamore — some tree name — and there'll be about 10 of us, dancing in the spirit or some damn thing. I just hope they don't expect me to take my clothes off."

Greg nodded solemnly, but he couldn't hide the twinkle in his eye. "But I thought you hated things like that. New Agey things, I mean. Auras and spirit guides and angels and stuff ..."

"I do." I made a sour face. "But Flavia convinced me. She's a bit of a fast talker, and she promised me it would be really low-key. I know, I'm a complete snob about everything woo-woo except astrology — call me inconsistent, call me a hypocrite. But she says there'll only be astrologers there, so at least I won't have to deal with anyone channelling Elvis or telling me about their personal guardian angels or anything. My only job will be to help Flavia teach the advanced group, apparently. Besides, we've never met, so this will be the ideal opportunity ..."

"Wait a second!" Greg barely avoided spitting his soup out. "You've never met this woman, and you're going to a retreat with her? On an island somewhere out in the boonies, with someone you don't even know? For a whole weekend?" His eyebrows shot halfway up his forehead, and I had to laugh.

"I'm pretty sure she's not a psycho killer, Greg. We *have* talked on the phone, you know. And besides, I'll be the one driving us there, so if it gets weird, I can just leave, in my nifty rented car."

Greg snorted. "Yeah, right, that would be just like you. If it gets weird, you'll be the first one in line to find out why. I can see it now. I'm going to get a panicked phone call, telling me Mrs. White has killed Professor Plum in the library with the candlestick, and could I please don my superhero outfit and come out to give you a hand. You're becoming the Jessica Fletcher of Ottawa, Katy."

I shook my head vigorously. Unfortunate timing, because I had just placed a forkful of raw broccoli in my mouth, and some of it sprayed across the table. Discreetly, I wiped it up with a paper napkin.

"You forget, Greg. I'm reformed. I'm a new woman. I've learned my lesson. No more butting in for me. And what could happen on an island full of astrologers? We're notoriously non-violent, you know. Besides, I'm sure whoever is putting this show on must have chosen an auspicious date — I think it's supposed to start at some weird time like 2:13 p.m., to avoid a void-of-course Moon. Don't worry, everything will be fine."

Greg pushed his empty soup bowl away and rested his elbows on the table.

"You're right. I should be more trusting. Actually, I'm glad you're going. After all you've been through this year, you need the break. Have a good time."

"I intend to," I said.

There was a long silence, during which we both cast around for something to say — something non-controversial, something that wouldn't further strain our friendship.

"So ... how's Peter doing? I haven't seen his by-line as much lately. Everything okay?"

Peter is my ex-husband, a journalist who writes for the local cat-box liner. He lives upstairs from me, and we are on amiable terms, which is a good thing, since we share custody of our fifteen-year-old daughter.

"Fine, I think," I said. "His editor got all excited about that big piece he did last winter, you know — the five-part exposé — about the religious nuts. So they've had him doing some top-secret investigative piece for the last few weeks. I don't see much of him, and he's always saying things like, 'The walls have ears, you know.' It's getting a bit old, but he seems pretty pleased with himself, so I'm assuming he's been getting the goods on whoever he's exposing at the moment."

Greg nodded. "Good for him. Sounds like his career's on the move."

"Unlike mine," I muttered.

"I never said that!" Greg put his hands up in a defensive gesture, palms out.

"You didn't need to," I said. "I already know it. You

were right, back there. I'm just being stubborn, and I can't exactly tell you why. I don't know, myself. All I know is that I can't jump into anything. I'll think about your offer some more, but I can't make any promises. Okay?"

"Okay." He put a hand on top of mine. "You're the boss."

✦

I walked most of the way back home from my meeting with Greg. It was a longish trek from the Royal Ottawa Hospital to Centretown, but I wanted to get outside, move my legs, clear my head. Even the smell of that place still got to me. Floor cleaner, sweat, and something indefinable — the smell of suffering souls. I just couldn't imagine myself going back, part-time or not.

It had been a beautiful autumn so far. The days had moved from warm to crisp in the last week or so, a change I both loved and dreaded. Loved because the morning air felt fresh and invigorating against my cheek as I walked; dreaded because it heralded the return of winter's darkness. The leaves on the maples lining my street in Centretown were what Dawn used to call "fire trees" — brilliant yellows and oranges that caught and flickered and blazed in the sunlight. They'd begun to fall, creating a thick, comforting blanket over the lawns and sidewalks. This weather was about as good as it gets in Ottawa. And back at our small apartment, Dawn, home from school for lunch, was on the rampage.

For a teenager, she is usually fairly sanguine. She rarely frets over her appearance, which I gather is unusual in a girl her age, and while boys are definitely on the radar, she hasn't evinced much interest in any specific males yet. I figured that whatever was causing her to froth at the mouth today must be pretty serious, on the teen scale of problems. I was right.

"Mom, it's just bloody ridiculous!"

She slammed her book bag down on the kitchen table, almost knocking over the fruit bowl, which currently contained everything but fruit — elastic bands, a screwdriver, several pens missing their lids, three keys that unlocked unknown doors, and two scraps of paper with indecipherable notes scribbled on them. I grabbed the bowl before it could crash to the floor. I opened my mouth to protest my daughter's cavalier behaviour, but before I could say anything, she was off and running.

"It's so completely unfair, I just can't believe it! I'm so mad, I could kill him — wring his little neck with my own two hands. Why should we be the ones who suffer? He's gone, the money's gone. It's just one great big mess! Whoever put adults in charge of the world, anyway? If kids were running things, you can bet something like this would never happen."

"Dawn, sweetie, slow down a bit, okay? What happened? Who are you mad at?"

"Mr. Acres! Our teacher — History of Europe. He's taken a hike, gone on the lam, vanished completely. No one at school knows where he is, and now, if you can believe it, our trip's on hold!"

"What? You mean your trip to Paris? What hap —"

Dawn cut me off, slapping the table in outrage. "Dammit, Mom! We planned this trip for an entire year. I froze my butt off last winter, selling goddamn stupid chocolate bars door to door. I nearly got frostbite, and for what? And Sylvie spent hours helping Mr. Acres do paperwork — all of us worked on this, and now, goddamn Acres just waltzes out of the classroom one day, just like that, and we've had a supply teacher for a week and a half now, and it's like, 'Oh, sorry, too damn bad, kids, the goddamn trip to Paris is toast —'"

"Dawn, please, watch your language." This has been an ongoing battle between my daughter and me. She shook her head impatiently.

"Yeah, I know. I know. Sorry. But this just makes me so damn *mad*!"

She slammed her fist onto the table again, and a couple of books slid out of her open book bag onto the floor. She ignored them, blinking tears out of her eyes. She grabbed a handful of tissues from the box on the counter and blew her nose loudly. I took advantage of her momentary pause.

"And you have every right to be mad, Dawn. It's not fair. Have they given you any explanation yet? Like, where Acres went, or why?"

She shook her head. "Nada. He just took off, right in the middle of class two Fridays ago. I think he might have had a phone call or something — the phone from the office rang, he picked it up, and then he talked to someone for a few minutes, and then he left. We sat there and waited for him, but the bell rang, so we all went to our next class. He never came back, and since then, we've had a supply teacher. Now they say he's left for good, and we can't go on our trip ... Oh, *shit*!" Dawn threw herself into a kitchen chair, leaned on the table with her head in her arms, and sobbed her frustration. I rubbed her shoulders sympathetically.

"Honey, what if I were to call the principal? Maybe they could assign you guys another teacher for the trip?"

Dawn shook her head, and kept crying. It was times like this when I had to remind myself that she was only fifteen years old. Well, fifteen and three-quarters, technically. But still, just a kid. I'd probably be pretty wound up myself, if my favourite teacher had suddenly dropped out of sight, forcing the school to abandon plans for a long-awaited two-week field trip to Paris. And until now, Dawn had worshiped her teacher.

"He really makes you feel like you're there, Mom," she'd say. "You know, you feel like you're in that crowd, just about to storm the Bastille. Or cheering Napoleon as he returns from some battle or another — it's so cool. And he has all these great ideas for places to take us — it's going to be the best trip of my life!"

Now, Acres was gone, the trip was history, and I had a sobbing adolescent on my hands.

"I'm going to call," I said, with a firmness that brooked no opposition. "What harm can it do?"

Dawn quieted some as I dialled the school office — she wouldn't want to miss a word. A secretary put me through to Anne North, Lisgar's vice-principal. She sounded too young to be a teacher, let alone a senior school official, but I let it pass. I've recently begun to realize that I may have a somewhat skewed perspective in the matter of other people's perceived youth.

"I'm afraid there's not much more I can tell you, Ms. Klein." Anne North sounded harried, and I suspected I wasn't the first outraged parent to call this morning.

"Well, why can't the school simply assign another teacher to supervise the trip?"

There was a long, awkward pause. "I don't think that would be appropriate."

"Why not? The kids have all paid their money, the reservations have been made. I'm sure any teacher would jump at the opportunity for a free trip to Europe."

Another pause. "Ms. Klein, there are circumstances that prevent us ..."

"Wait a second." Call me slow, but I was starting to

catch on. "What about the money? The kids are going to get their money back, aren't they?"

"Well ... it's a very unusual circumstance ..."

"You're saying this guy took off with the funds, aren't you?"

Dawn's head popped up like a jack-in-the-box, her eyes wide.

Anne North coughed. "Ah, well ..." She cleared her throat again. "I'm afraid ..."

"Do the police know about this? Are they looking for Acres?"

"We've been in touch with all the correct authorities, Ms. Klein. A search is being conducted. Believe me, the school is dealing with this to the best of our ability. Nothing like this has ever happened at Lisgar before."

No, I guess it probably hadn't. Lisgar Collegiate Institute is one of Ottawa's oldest and most respected high schools, a huge mid-Victorian edifice on the banks of the Rideau Canal. Teachers just did not scamper off with the class trip funds at Lisgar. Not the done thing at all.

"So what are we supposed to do now?" A wave of helpless anger washed over me, and I sat down heavily.

"We'll be calling a meeting for all the families whose children were involved in the trip," Anne said. "Some time in the next couple of weeks. Until then, we'd appreciate your discretion ..."

Ah. "You mean, you don't want us talking to the press?"

"Well, yes. This is a very difficult situation, as I'm sure you can understand. It wouldn't help the students to have it splashed around the media. We're doing our best, but we need the co-operation of all the families."

I reassured her that I wasn't about to call an immediate press conference and hung up, rubbing the side of my nose thoughtfully.

"*He* took our money? Acres took off with all our money?" Dawn looked disbelieving.

"Looks like it. There's going to be some kind of a meeting. For all the good that'll do."

We lapsed into a depressed silence and munched on the cheese sandwiches I'd prepared for our lunch. I'd have preferred tuna, but Dawn showed no signs of relenting on her "meat is murder" rule. She'd decided a couple of years back that we must eschew all flesh in our diet, and she patrolled our cupboards with the enthusiasm of a bloodhound sniffing out contraband. I'd given up trying to hide tins of Spam or tuna or salmon — she always found them, and then I got The Lecture about cholesterol and murdering innocent animals and the inhumane treatment of the poor creatures destined for our tables. Now I just went along with her dictates, and did my meat-eating when I was out of the house. The staff at the local Harveys knew me on sight.

"So. You're still going away tomorrow, huh?" Dawn didn't look at me as she spoke.

"Yep. I'm picking up Flavia at the airport at nine in the morning, and we're going to drive directly to the island. As I've explained to you several times, Dawn. Since your father will still be in Montreal chasing after his latest top-secret journalistic coup, you will be staying with your grandparents. It'll be a nice chance for you to see them before they head for Arizona next month."

"Well, I just thought ..." The sentence trailed off, and she lapsed into silence again. I got up to pour myself a coffee, and waited for her to find her words. Which she inevitably would. Dawn has a knack for finding words.

She spoke softly, her head turned from me. "It's just that I'm so bummed out by this whole thing, Mom. I like going to Zayde and Sabte's, but they'll be all upset if they see me looking sad or whatever. I hate to worry them, you know? I thought maybe you could reconsider ..."

"And let you come with me?" I put the coffee cup down on the counter with a sigh. "Dawn, I know you're disappointed about your trip, but how is coming to some astrology festival with a bunch of middle-aged women going to ..." I stopped myself in mid-sentence, suddenly unable to think of a single reason why my daughter couldn't accompany me and Flavia to the island. And maybe she was really just saying she wanted to be with her mother when she was feeling low. What kind of mother would turn her kid down in circumstances like this?

"Oh, what the hell. Heck, I mean. Sure, Dawn, you can come. It'll be nice to have you along, and I'm sure Flavia will love you. Now, get going. You're going to be late getting back to school. Unlike your teachers, you're not allowed to just disappear when you feel like it."

A weak smile, the first I'd seen from her all day. "Thanks, Mom. I won't get in your way, I promise."

"I wasn't worried about it. We'll have fun. Now, get!"

As she wolfed down the last of her sandwich, gulped some soy milk that looked and smelled like old dishwater, and dashed out the door, I smiled to myself. For some reason, having Dawn come along for the weekend made the AstroFest seem a bit less silly. Maybe things were beginning to look up, after all.

2

FRIDAY, OCTOBER 14
Sun conjunct Mercury, opposition Saturn, square Neptune ✦
Venus conjunct Mars, conjunct Pluto ✦

In a rare splurge, I'd decided to rent a car for the weekend, rather than entrusting ourselves to the Flaming Deathtrap, my ex-husband's ancient car of uncertain lineage. That car had been on its last wheels for years, but now even Peter was admitting that it was terminal. I didn't want to be driving down the highway in it when all the Bondo and duct tape gave way — things were bound to get ugly. So Dawn and I had driven to the airport in a sporty little white Sunfire, complete with a spoiler and CD player that actually worked, and now we stood in the Arrivals area, waiting for someone we'd never met.

To be sure, Flavia had e-mailed me a picture of herself, but picking a middle-aged, height-challenged, self-described "dumpy" woman with long brown hair and glasses out of the crowds that swarmed the baggage carousels was proving no easy task. I'd worn my "Astrologers Against Mike Harris" button as an identifier, and I'd told Flavia to expect someone very tall and big-boned who seemed to be having a perpetual bad hair day, but now I realized how futile all our preparations had been. As I scanned the milling throng, I had to wonder yet again what had possessed me to agree to this adventure.

Lately, all I really wanted to do was hang around my apartment, flipping through the channels on my antiquated television set, or listening to Motown while I worked on my needlepoint. Dawn and Greg, and even Peter, who generally didn't notice such things, had been at me for months now to get out and do things. To oblige them, I'd consent to have dinner out with Benjamin, or I'd tag along with Dawn to the library, where I'd flip idly through magazines while she did research for her term papers or whatever. There. I've gone out. Now, can I go home?

So this trip with Dawn and Flavia, which wouldn't have fazed me a year ago, now seemed like a Big Ordeal. Getting out to the airport, mingling in a crowd like this, looking for someone I didn't know, driving to an island full of more people I didn't know … to be honest, even *Matlock* re-runs would have been preferable.

I felt a hand on my elbow, and I jumped.

"Hey, you wouldn't be some radical hippie weirdo freak astrologer, out to meet her crazy pen-pal, would you?"

Flavia was taller than she'd led me to expect — maybe five-one or five-two, not quite the rotund midget she'd described. Her dark auburn hair was long, thick and straight, and hung down her back like a shimmering curtain; her lively, mobile face, while not exactly pretty, was the kind that drew attention. I think it was the eyes — they were an intense blue, and twinkled from behind wire-rimmed glasses. She was bundled in a wool coat and matching hat, far too hot for a Canadian autumn. The pattern dwarfed her, and she looked like a walking dhurrie rug, the kind you see at the import shops.

"Oh my God! I can't believe it's really you!" I laughed. "You don't look anything like your picture — you're so … cute!"

"Yes, darlin', I'm Flavia! Hey, you're *tall*! And better looking than you said you were. You were holding out on me, honey!"

I laughed. "You were expecting maybe Godzilla?"

It felt awkward to hug this woman I barely knew, even though we'd been in touch almost daily for the past couple of years. In the end, I just squeezed her shoulder. She shook her head, chuckling.

"I always heard you Canadians were standoffish." She opened her arms wide. "Come on, I don't bite!"

So I hugged her. Then I remembered Dawn, who stood a few feet off, watching us with a bemused expression. "Oh, Flavia — this is my daughter, Dawn."

"Hey, Dawn!" Flavia spread her arms again, and Dawn smiled, uncertain what she should do next. I knew how she felt; Flavia was what my father would call a "real live wire." Maybe it was her Texas upbringing, or maybe it really was true that we Canadians are a bunch of emotionally impaired cold fish.

"So," Flavia said, when we'd collected her luggage, loaded it into the trunk of the car, and buckled up. "I got your e-mail about Dawn coming to the island with us. You gonna be okay, spending the weekend with a bunch of flaky old ladies, Dawn?"

I couldn't see Dawn's expression from the driver's seat, but there was a smile in her voice. "I live with my mother. I think I can handle it."

"This is how you thank your poor aging mother? There is no curse like an ungrateful child," I said in my most mournful voice. Dawn snorted loudly behind me, and I smiled to myself. Paying the parking lot attendant some exorbitant rate, I rolled up the window and pulled onto the Airport Parkway.

"So what's the deal with the disappearing teacher?" Flavia half-turned in her seat, to hear Dawn better. "Your mama's been telling me all about it. He just up and vanished? What's with that?"

Dawn shrugged. "No one knows. The admin at my school are keeping it all very hush-hush. You know, 'We don't like to talk about this kind of thing at *Lisgah*.' Of course there are all kinds of rumours, but the bottom line is, Acres just plain disappeared, and so did all our money. It added up to about $50,000, and the school won't even tell us whether we can get it back. Every day this week, though, there've been cops crawling all over the school. It's kind of creepy."

"Have you talked to the police yet? I mean, are they interviewing all the students, or what?" Flavia sounded concerned.

"Nope. What could I tell them? I saw the same thing everyone else did. Acres was a good teacher, and not that old — a lot of the girls in my grade had crushes on him — and he knew a lot about history. Oh, and we all thought we could trust him. That's a laugh."

"Well, what did happen? Did you see him leave?"

"We've got these phones in each classroom, for people to call from the office. You know, if there's a phone call for a teacher, or the principal wants to get hold of someone or whatever. It rang, Acres wheeled over and picked it up. He said something like 'Okay, I'll be right there,' and then he told us to keep working, he'd be right back. We all figured he'd been called down to the office for something. No big deal. Then he left, and that's the last anyone saw of him. And the next thing we know, the principal calls all of us who were supposed to go to Paris down to the office, and tells us we're not going, because Acres has disappeared. And all the money's gone — at least, if it's still around, no one knows where it is. That's the whole story, as far as I know."

"Wow — that sounds like one for the tabloids. Do y'all have tabloids in Canada? I don't read 'em, but I sure do like to read the headlines. 'Man explodes on operating table' — how goofy is that?" She started to unbutton the carpet/coat, having already shed the hat. "Man, I thought they said it got cold up here! Maybe it's just me and my menopausal hormones, but I'm just about coming to a boil, here."

"Common mistake," I chuckled. "At least you didn't bring your skis. Anyway, we do get cold snaps sometimes at this time of year. Mostly October is just ... crisp. Nice and crisp. Hope it stays like this all weekend. You've missed the best of the trees changing colour, but it's still quite pretty, and it'll be nice down on the Rideau Lakes."

Flavia and I chatted about things astrological most of the way to the lake. Dawn, whose interest in astrology is limited to knowing that I make a meagre living at it, sat quietly in the back seat, reading a book on programming in some obscure computer language. Lately she's taken to wearing her Walkman and headphones when we're in the car together, whether to shut herself in or me out, I cannot tell. I think it's just one of those teenage things.

It was not quite noon when we reached Portland, a tiny town on the shores of big Rideau Lake. I parked at the marina, where we had instructions to arrange for a water taxi to Sycamore Island. I sat down on a wooden box on the floating dock, guarding Flavia's suitcase and my own battered knapsack, while she tried to rustle up some coffee at the marina store. Dawn stood at the far end of the dock, tossing pebbles into the water.

The lake was tranquil and glistening in the midday sun, and I sighed and stretched my arms up over my head, easing out the kinks from an hour and a half on the highway. I watched a couple of loons diving for their food not fifty feet from me. They'd paddle along quietly, heads tilted upward, and then suddenly one of them would upend itself, disappear beneath the water, and come up with something in its long black beak. It would toss its head back and gurgle its prey down a long, smooth throat, looking very satisfied with itself. Life must be simple, if you're a loon.

I stifled a yawn; I'd been up at some ungodly hour this morning. Usually, I liked to start my weekends slowly, with plenty of good, fresh coffee, and a leisurely look at what passes for a newspaper in Ottawa, but today I'd foregone all that. I hoped a relaxing weekend on Sycamore Island would make up for sacrificing my weekend morning ritual.

Flavia seemed just as lively and interesting in person as she did online, I thought. I could do worse than to spend a weekend in her company. Maybe some of her enthusiasm and verve would rub off on me. I sure needed it lately. She and I had "met" a couple of years ago, on an astrology chat board, and had been e-mailing one another pretty regularly since then. We'd talked at first about our profession, but gradually our conversations had grown more personal: I knew about her six cats, her part-time job as a caterer's assistant outside Ann Arbor, Michigan, and she knew about my family, and even about some of the more gruesome events of the past year and a half. We considered one another friends, although we'd only spoken on the phone a couple of times.

We'd exchanged pictures, to be sure, but when I met her this morning, I hadn't been prepared. For one thing, while I'm an unadorned T-shirt and jeans kind of person, Flavia's dress code was a little more ... flamboyant. Today, she wore a purple batik dress, upon which turquoise dolphins splashed and cavorted. Her feet were resplendent in gold-painted shoes, and with her long glossy hair straight out of a shampoo ad, and her round John Lennon glasses, she looked very much the astrologer. Whereas when people hear what I do for a living, they tend to be surprised.

"But you look so normal!" is a common response. Guess it depends on what one thinks of as normal.

Flavia ambled back to the dock now, balancing three homemade pastries on two styrofoam coffee cups, and a juice for Dawn.

"Thought y'all might be hungry," she said. "The lady in the store was real nice — said these just came out of the oven. The way I figure it, the conference is supposed to be one of those pure vegetarian things, so we should stock up on sugary stuff and caffeine while we can."

"Thanks." I bit into mine. "Dawn will be right at home there. Maybe she can even give them some cooking tips. This, however — this is decadent, with a capital D. Just what I needed. So — who else is supposed to be coming to this shindig? Do you know any of them?"

Flavia shrugged, rolling her eyes expressively as she chewed and swallowed. "Ten other people, I heard. I haven't seen the registration list yet. I'm supposed to be teaching the advanced class, and there's someone from around here doing the intermediate, I think. I don't know any of 'em, though. Oh, and then there's Cecilia. Everyone knows Cecilia." She wrinkled her nose.

Everyone except me, apparently. "Who's that?"

"She organized this whole weekend. She's got a real gift for getting people to do things — her way, usually. I'm surprised you don't know her; she's supposed to be this big hot-shot spiritual advisor round these parts, from what I hear."

I laughed. "Well, I'm not really up on the spiritual community in Ottawa. I do my job, meet my clients, write their charts, and go home. I've never even had my chakras adjusted, or done past life regression — I just can't get into that end of things. I like astrology as a language of psychology, and that doesn't fit with some people's ideas. Anyway, from the sound of it, I'm not missing much, with Cecilia."

"Oh, Cecilia's all right, I guess. If you like tight-assed controlling bitches. Oh!" She clapped her hand over her mouth, eyes twinkling. "I'm in big trouble now. My karma's gonna sneak right up and wallop me for that one, I can just feel it."

Just then, a shiny new black Jeep roared into the parking lot next to the marina store. The driver applied the brakes rather too forcefully, sending a spray of gravel into the air as the car screeched to a halt. The door slammed, and a tall, slim woman in a lime-green designer jumpsuit sprang out, retrieved a Vuitton suitcase from the trunk, and slammed that door, too. Another woman, much shorter but just as bone-slender, got out more sedately from the passenger side, hauling one of those small suitcases on wheels you see rolling along behind flight attendants at airports.

Flavia raised her eyebrows. Her expression was indecipherable behind her clip-on sunglasses. "Here comes trouble."

"I think they got off at the wrong exit — that jumpsuit won't last five seconds out here. Wonder if we should tell them?"

"Honey, a girl like that doesn't need the likes of us telling her what to do. She'll just get Tonto there to run back home and pick her up another outfit."

"How do you know —"

My question was interrupted, though, as the taller woman strode toward us. The shorter one struggled along with the luggage. Flavia turned away and strolled down to the end of the dock, where she sat cross-legged, watching Dawn.

Green Jumpsuit simultaneously thrust out a long, beautifully manicured hand, and lifted her designer sunglasses to give me the once over. I suddenly felt very conscious of my distinctly unstyled hair and the zit that was starting to make its presence felt on my forehead.

"I'm Amanda," she announced, pumping my hand. Her fingernails dug into my flesh, and I winced involuntarily. "Amanda Weatherburn. You can call me Mandy. And this is my friend, Rowan Healey. But don't call her that. I call her Ronnie. Say hello, Ronnie."

Her friend proffered a hand like a limp fish.

"Hi." Her voice was tiny; I had to strain to hear her.

"Ronnie, speak up! No one can hear you! She drives me crazy, whispering all the time." Then, without pausing, Mandy said, "So ...on the instruction sheet, it said we were supposed to wait for the water taxi. What time is it supposed to get here? I'm starving. I want my lunch, and I want it now." Replacing her sunglasses, she shielded her eyes from the sun and surveyed the lake. "Is that it, that boat over there? Yoo-hoo! Hey! You guys! Over here! Come on, let's get this show on the road!" She started calling out to the two poor fishermen in an aluminum-hulled boat, who looked startled at being thus summoned. One of them lifted a pair of binoculars to his eyes, as though to confirm that Mandy was, indeed, hollering at them. The other pulled his oversize hat further down over his eyes. I couldn't say I blamed him.

"I don't think that's the taxi," I said. "Those two guys have been out there fishing since just after we got here. The people at the marina office said the taxi leaves when there are enough people to take a full load over, and we're expecting a few more, I think."

Mandy snorted. "Huh. Well, I don't know if I can wait that long. Waiting gives me hives — anyone'll tell you that. Ronnie, am I good at waiting?" Ronnie opened her mouth, but Mandy didn't wait for an answer. "Shit, these bugs are godawful! What are they? Oh, God, one just flew into my mouth ... Ptui ... ick, that's disgusting!" She looked accusingly at me, as though I'd set the insects onto her deliberately.

"Just gnats." Somehow, my voice had taken on a laconic drawl. I felt like one of the hick stars of the Red Green Show, doling out wilderness advice to the greenhorn. "It's the season for them. They don't bite." At least, I hoped they didn't. Unless they were planning to bite Mandy, in which case they had my heartfelt approval.

"Well, they're having a sit-down meal on me," she complained, swatting ineffectually at the insects. "I'm very sensitive, you know. God, I hate bugs — totally useless creatures. Ronnie, get me some bug spray, it's in the front pocket of my suitcase. I'd rather stink of some chemical crud than have these disgusting little cooties divebombing me constantly! Oh, shit, get away from me!" She waved her hand in front of her face, to no avail.

"The more you jump around, the worse they'll get," I offered. "They're attracted to sweat."

Mandy gave me a look. Oh, right. People like her

don't *sweat*. They glow. How foolish of me.

Ronnie, searching through Mandy's suitcase, paused and looked up. "Mandy, honey, maybe it's your cologne? Maybe they like the smell of it?"

"What? Speak up, for God's sake! Oh, my cologne. Well, at least they've got good taste. Stuff cost me enough. And now I'm going to have to drown it out with goddamn bug spray—where the hell is that stuff? Ronnie, sometimes I'd swear you're a few fries short of a Happy Meal, darling. How hard can it be to find a bottle of bug spray? Never mind, I'll get it myself." Impatiently, she pushed her friend out of the way, and knelt in front of the suitcase.

"It should be right here, I'm sure I packed it for you. Please, Mandy, let me ..."

"You do that, Ronnie. It's going to be a very long weekend, if we have to spend the whole time looking for things you forgot to bring." Mandy tossed her carefully mussed blonde hair, then noticed the styrofoam cup in my hand. "Hey, where'd you get the coffee? They got any more of those buns or whatever? Not that you need 'em, honey, you look like you could stand to lose a few pounds, if you don't mind my saying so."

I felt myself flush, but propriety prevented me from decking her right then and there.

"I got them at the marina store. The same place I got my ticket for the water taxi." Somehow, even without using my mystical astrological powers, I suddenly had the sense that this was going to be a very long weekend.

"Tickets? We need tickets? For the goddamn boat? Shit, Ronnie, you didn't tell me that! I told you to take care of all that stuff, didn't I? Come on, we'd better go get them. You stay right here and look after our bags, all right? Don't let anyone touch them. We won't be long. Ronnie, where the hell did you put my cell phone? As long as we're stuck in this dump, I might as well give Jimmy another call ..." Without waiting for an answer, Mandy set off up the hill, with Ronnie trailing her like a dispirited puppy.

Contrary to Mandy's order, I walked down to the end of the dock, abandoning her bags to the bugs. Flavia didn't look up as I approached.

"Is she still there?"

"No, she and the little quiet one have gone off for coffee. Although I think caffeine's the last thing that woman needs. Heavy duty sedatives, more like it."

"She's an Aries." Flavia grimaced. "I never get along with Aries people."

"How do you know? Have you met her before?"

Flavia gave a short laugh. "Didn't I tell you, honey? I'm psychic."

"No, seriously —"

But Flavia had turned her head away and was gazing out across the lake. "I wonder if you can see Sycamore Island from here? This is such a beautiful spot — look at those loons."

I could take a hint, if it was delivered forcefully enough. "Well, Mandy's way up there on my list of people to avoid, and I've known her exactly ..." I peered at my watch. "Exactly seven minutes. That's some kind of a record, even for me."

The dock rolled slightly beneath us as a large boat passed by.

"She's a piece of work, that's for sure. Never mind — the island is supposed to be, what, twelve acres? Lots of room to avoid them, if we need to. We can always duck into the can or something. I'll give you the signal if I see them coming, and we can make ourselves scarce."

"Well, they're on their way now, and there's no place to go but into the water."

Mandy strode back toward us, clearly unhappy that I had deserted my post. Ronnie, burdened with the coffee and pastries, jogged to keep up. Mandy had very long legs, and she was obviously a power-walker. She thrust her elbows back and up, and they worked like pistons, in time with her steps.

"Well! Do you really think our stuff is safe, sitting out unguarded like that? Who knows if some local yokel will decide to come and grab my bags. You may not have much worth taking, but I've got a very expensive camera in there, and if it got lost, I'd have to hold you responsible, you know."

I found myself apologizing. "Sorry. I was only twenty feet away, I didn't think ..."

"Well, never mind," she said. "No harm done, I guess. Listen, I talked to some decrepit old broad at the store, and she allowed as how the taxi might be an hour or more, depending." Mandy yawned and rolled her eyes. "Life's too short for that kind of bullshit. So I gave her an extra hundred, and we're leaving in five minutes."

"An extra hundred?" Flavia turned to face Mandy, and her voice shot up an octave. "You mean a hundred dollars? I can't afford my share of that, even if it's only Canadian! You could have asked us!"

"Relax, honey." Mandy peered at Flavia over her dark glasses. "It's my treat. And if it gets us there ahead of time, what the hell? By the way, do I know you from somewhere ... AAAAAAH!"

Mandy let out a sudden shriek, flailing her arms around her head. Flavia and I froze, bewildered. Dawn, at the far end of the dock, turned and started toward us, looking alarmed.

"What? What is it?" Ronnie jumped to her feet and ran to her friend, grasping her by the arm. "Mandy! What's the matter?"

"A *wasp*!" Mandy screamed, and Ronnie gasped.

"Oh my God! Where's your Epipen? Did it bite you? Are you okay?"

Mandy didn't say anything coherent. She just kept waving her arms around and screaming at the top of her lungs. The two fishermen glanced in our direction, started their motor, and began to putt away from us. Briefly, I wished I could join them. Ronnie grabbed her friend's handbag and started rifling through it frantically, tossing used tissues, a gold-plated compact, an alligator-skin wallet, a comb onto the dock.

"I can't see it, Mandy! Where did you put it?" She was hyperventilating too, her face bright red as she tore the purse apart.

Mandy just shook her head, gesticulating wildly, and her screams ratcheted up a notch. I saw no evidence of a wasp. If I'd been any kind of insect with half an ounce of sense, I'd have been halfway to Costa Rica by now.

"Here, give me the purse," I yelled, grabbing it from Ronnie, who was now sobbing in her desperation to save her friend. "Try to get her to stop screaming, okay? I think she's fine."

I was pretty certain Mandy hadn't actually been stung — if she had, the show would have been almost over by now. As it was, she evinced no signs of stopping, or even slowing down, any time soon. I wondered how often this happened on any given day. No wonder Ronnie looked like her nerves were shot.

Ronnie had trouble approaching her friend at first, but she latched onto one thrashing arm and held it until it stopped; then she put an arm around her friend's waist, and spoke softly into her ear. Gradually, Mandy's screams subsided to low moans. She was still pink with exertion, though. I reflected that if she were to put on this performance, say, five times a day, she'd have no need for an aerobic workout.

Dawn, who'd come running at the first scream, and stood wide-eyed throughout, said, "Who's this? Is she having some kind of reaction?"

"Dawn, meet Mandy. She seems to be allergic to wasps, but I think she's fine now. Still, we should get the Epipen out, just to be on the safe side. Where *does* she keep it, anyway?" I had already pawed through several wads of lipstick-stained tissues, with no luck.

"I don't know! But her doctor said if she ever gets stung again, well ... Didn't you read about it in the *Globe*?"

I shook my head. "Don't read it. What was it, an article about anaphylactic reactions?"

"No, about Mandy — it was in the social column, just last week. About the Lieutenant-Governor's garden party. Mandy got stung there, and they had to rush her off to the hospital. The doctors there were really serious. If she gets stung again, that could be it for her. You know." She drew her finger across her throat meaningfully, and Mandy moaned, her eyes rolling back in her head. "Oh, sorry, honey. I didn't mean to scare you."

Mandy didn't seem consoled, but gradually she seemed to realize that she had not, in fact, been fatally stung. I unzipped a pocket in the middle of the purse. Bingo.

"Here's the Epipen." I held it up. "But I don't think she needs it now, do you?"

Mandy shook her head, sniffing. "N-no. I'm okay. It didn't sting me. I just ..."

Ronnie shushed her. "I know, it scared you. But you can't panic like that every time you see a fly or something. My goodness, we're in the country now, you know. I'm sure there's lots of bugs out here. You should keep the pen in your pocket, just in case, so we won't have to go searching through your purse next time, okay?" Ronnie spoke in a low, soothing voice, stroking Mandy's shoulder gently. Mandy nodded.

"I will. I'll put it right here. Don't let me forget it, okay?" She grasped Ronnie's hand tearfully. "I just got so scared ... I don't know what I'd do without you ... Don't leave me, okay?"

Flavia, who had been edging further out onto the dock, past the other two, turned toward me and thrust a finger down her throat. Dawn looked startled. I stifled a giggle and shook my head at both of them. Not now, I mouthed. We'd have plenty of time when we got to the island to dissect the peculiarities of our fellow guests.

3

We were the first to arrive on the island. I couldn't see much from the water — just rocks and pine trees, and I thought I glimpsed the front porch of a large house, high on a hill above the lake. The water taxi, a flat boat on pontoons, piloted by a stoic-looking young man wearing a baseball cap and reflective sunglasses, pulled up at a small dock, and we tossed our luggage ashore before disembarking. I turned to thank the driver, but he'd already started the boat's engine, and didn't acknowledge my smile and wave. Just as I picked up my knapsack, a large, reddish dog of unknown provenance galloped onto the dock to greet us, wagging his tail in feverish delight.

"Hey, mutt!" Mandy knelt to greet him, and he nearly bowled her into the water in his enthusiasm. Dawn came up behind her, eager to meet the dog too. Dawn has wanted a dog for years, but so far I've successfully avoided that issue by claiming that our apartment is far too small to accommodate more than the two of us. Still, whenever we meet a dog, she renews her campaign.

"Rufus! Rufus, sit!" The woman's voice came from up the hill, toward the house, but I couldn't see who was shouting. Rufus, however, sat, his tail thumping rhythmically on the dock, his head cocked to one side.

"What a great dog!" Mandy exclaimed. "Ronnie, you didn't tell me there'd be a dog! What a good mutt ... can you shake a paw? Here, give me a paw ..." Then, in an aside to Flavia and me, she said, "I raise dogs, you know. Bull mastiffs. Purebred. Better trained than this one, pedigrees as long as your arm. Worth a fortune. Ronnie practically had to twist my arm to get me to leave my babies, and I miss them already. This guy's sure as hell no purebred, but he'll do, won't you, mutt? We're going to get along just fine!"

Flavia and I exchanged glances.

"She came, she saw, she conquered," Flavia muttered, *sotto voce*. Dawn, who had been unceremoniously shunted aside in the doggy affection war, looked daggers at Mandy, who seemed blithely unaware that she'd committed any offence.

Just then, the woman who'd called Rufus came half-jogging down the hill toward us, wiping her hands on her jeans. She looked to be in her mid-twenties, with short curly hair and multiple ear piercings.

"Hi!" she said. "I didn't expect anyone for another hour or so, or I'd have been down here to greet you! I'm Cara. Jane and I are on staff here this season. We look after the island, so if there's anything you need, just ask. Why don't we take your stuff up to the main lodge, and we can get you sorted out there."

"Is Cecilia here yet?" Ronnie asked. "She told me she wanted to talk to me and Mandy before we started."

Cara shook her head. "Nope. No one here but us chickens. But people should start showing up soon. This is an all-women's weekend, right?"

Flavia nodded. "It's an astrology intensive. I'm teaching one group, and Cecilia's doing the other. My friend Katy is here to help me out — she's a professional astrologer, so I thought I'd drag her along as an extra resource person. And this is her daughter, Dawn."

Dawn, who was still waiting her turn to greet Rufus, nodded up at Cara.

"And I'm Mandy Weatherburn," Mandy piped up. "I'm in the beginners group. Hey, this doesn't look like as much of a dump as I thought it would! Nothing like country air, is there?" To demonstrate her enthusiasm, she inhaled deeply, drawing herself up to her full height and thrusting her not inconsiderable bosom out like an opera diva's. I refused to meet Flavia's amused glance.

"Oh. And this is my friend Ronnie," Mandy added, as an afterthought. Ronnie flashed a timid smile.

Cara shook hands all around, and led the way up a steep, rocky path to the house I'd glimpsed from the water. It might have been built in the 1910s, with a huge wrap-around porch, complete with wooden deck chairs and tables. I could almost see the original inhabitants, dressed in plus fours and organza dresses, lounging about sipping lemonade and iced tea. I blinked, and the image was gone.

We trooped up the stone steps and deposited our bags, while Cara went inside to find Jane. A motorboat's high-pitched drone sliced through the rustling leaves and lapping waves. It was our two fishermen, out to catch the season's last bass. Dawn waved at them, but they seemed intent on navigating around the rocky point. The boat veered and its wake splashed lazily against the dock, rocking it slowly in the fall sunshine.

"Nice place, if you like that rustic look," Mandy commented, throwing herself into one of the chairs, leg draped over the arm, as if she'd lived here all her life. "Ronnie, where the hell did you put my cell phone? I'm going to try Jimmy again. Stupid bastard, you'd think he'd at least pick up the phone ..."

Ronnie dug in her purse and handed the cell phone over, and Mandy flipped it open and began punching in numbers. There was a pause, and then presumably she was greeted by an answering machine. She tapped a long nail, painted an improbable silver-green, against the phone as she waited for the beep.

"Jimmy? Jimmy, pick up the goddamn phone, would you? It's me. Come on, I know you're there. Stop being an asshole, Jimmy. We have to talk sometime." Apparently Jimmy was able to resist her blandishments, however, for eventually she gave up, snapped the phone shut, and tossed it back to Ronnie. "Bastard," she muttered.

"I doubt he's still in the office — don't you think?" Ronnie ventured. "It's Saturday morning. Doesn't he usually go to the gym?"

Mandy made a face. "My ass. He's hiding behind the answering machine. He knows what I want, and he's taking the easy road out. If he doesn't talk to me about it, he thinks I'll give up and leave him alone. Fat fucking chance."

"Well, maybe you should get your lawyer to talk to him?"

"For all the good that'll do. Look, Ronnie, you don't know him as well as I do. He's going to try to screw me, and I'm not going to let him. That's it, that's all. It's down to him and me, now, hand-to-hand combat. *Mano a mano*." Making a Bruce Lee gesture, Mandy jumped to her feet and trotted down the steps to where Rufus lay sunning himself while Dawn stroked his silky head. "Come on, pooch. Let's take a look around this joint, why don't we? You can show me the sights."

Rufus scrambled to his feet and panted off after Mandy. Dawn gave Mandy a killing glare, but said nothing as the two left. She dragged her knapsack up the stairs, dumped it by the front door, and flopped into an

Adirondack chair. “It’s not fair, Mom. Every time I try to get close to Rufus, she butts in. What am I, some kind of threat to her?”

Ronnie tried to apologize for her friend. “Mandy’s under a lot of stress. She’s not always like this. She and her husband have been having some trouble ...” She shook her head and lapsed into silence.

Dawn snorted and looked as though she was about to say something inexcusably rude. I glanced at her, and she caught the signal and clamped her lips shut.

“So who’s this Jimmy character?” Flavia asked, though she didn’t really sound all that interested. “Is he her husband, or what?”

“Her ex-husband. Or at least, soon to be ex. He’s also my brother. Jimmy comes off a little gruff, but he’s a good guy, a sweetheart really. He loves Mandy to death, but sometimes I think he’s a bit afraid of her. A lot of people are, but Mandy’s okay, once you get to know her. She doesn’t mean anything, she’s just vivacious, and she’s used to getting her own way. Anyway, Mandy decided last week that the marriage was over. Jimmy’s been trying to talk her into coming back to him, but when she makes up her mind about something, she can be kind of stubborn. She’s been trying since yesterday to get him on the phone at work, but he’s not picking up.”

“No kidding. Well, maybe he really is out. It being Saturday and all. Listen, ladies, you’ll have to excuse me for a minute, okay? I’m going to use the facilities.”

Flavia went inside, and I settled myself into the chair Mandy had vacated.

“It must be hard for you, having your brother and your best friend break up like that,” Dawn commented.

Ronnie’s eyes widened. “Not really. I love them both. And they both know that, I think.”

"But isn't it a bit uncomfortable for you, hearing her talk about him like that?" Dawn had found herself a bone, and she wouldn't be satisfied until she'd gnawed it right down to the marrow. However, Ronnie didn't seem inclined to play along. After a few moments of uncomfortable silence, she stood up.

"I should go check our bedroom. Mandy is very particular about the bed she sleeps in — she needs a very firm mattress." She disappeared into the lodge, and the screen door banged shut.

"Geez, Dawn, would you lay off the personal questions already?" I chided her. "You don't even know these people, and this weekend's going to be long enough with Mandy bouncing around the place like Madonna on steroids."

"Well, it just struck me as strange, that's all." Dawn drew a happy face in the dust on the porch, then drew an X through it. "Anyway, I was just making conversation. What else am I supposed to do, now that Her Majesty's taken the dog off, and no one else is even here yet?"

"Don't worry, sweetheart. Once the astrology workshop begins, Mandy will be occupied, and you can have the dog all to yourself."

"Yeah, I guess. But man, what a bitch that woman is! And who's Ronnie — her hired companion or something? She acts like a servant, not a friend."

I shrugged. "There's no accounting for friendship, honey." I closed my eyes, and I might even have dozed off in the chair for a few minutes. The brilliant sun, shining through nearly denuded branches, the soft slapping of water against the rocks, the distant hum of a motorboat all threaded their way through the back of my consciousness, and I felt myself sinking into a peaceful oblivion.

When the screen door creaked open again, I jumped

awake. It was Ronnie, back from bunk inspection.

"Everything looks fine," she said, in that whispery little-girl voice.

"Mandy's lucky you're here to make sure she's comfortable." There was a hint of acid in Dawn's voice. I shot her a warning glance.

"So, Ronnie, where are you from?" I asked, strategically redirecting the conversation.

"Ottawa."

"Really? Us, too. And what brings you here?" I was aware that I sounded like a game-show host, but Ronnie seemed to need prompting. She paused and rubbed the toe of her expensive hiking boot along the well-worn verandah floor.

"Mandy read about this retreat in *Ottawa Lights*. You know — the magazine? She thought it might be fun to see what astrology's all about. So I talked to this lady who was mentioned in the article, and she said sure, come on along. She was really nice about it."

"So this is your first exposure? To astrology, I mean."

"Not mine," Ronnie said. "I've been doing some reading about it, but I'm no expert. Mandy's brand-new. Are you both astrologers? You and ... uh, Flavia?"

"Yep," I said. "I'm from Ottawa, and Flavia is from Michigan, via Texas. I thought ...I mean, I don't want to be rude or anything, but I thought this retreat was for people with some astrological experience."

"I don't know, I guess it is." Ronnie avoided my eyes. "But when Mandy makes up her mind to do something ... and Cecilia was really happy to have us come. She said it would be a great way for us to see astrology in action."

"Well, I hope you get something out of it. There's a lot to learn, but some of the best astrologers are self-taught. Wonder where Cara got to?"

As if in answer to my question, Cara popped her head around the screen door. "I can't find Jane, but you might as well come in and have a bite to eat. I'll show you around, and you can put your bags in your rooms. Where's ..." She searched for the name. " ... Mandy? And Flavia?"

Ronnie gestured toward the lake. "Mandy took Rufus for a walk down there. She's pretty stressed right now, so maybe she needed to walk off some energy. She'll be back soon, I'm sure. And Flavia went to find the washroom."

"Not to worry. It's not that big a place. They'll find their way back. Come on in."

We entered a great room with timbered ceilings and an enormous stone fireplace, with logs laid in readiness for the evening. I inhaled the smell of old woodsmoke combined with furniture polish. The place was an Arts and Crafts afficionado's dream: chairs, settees and tables were placed in cosy groupings to facilitate conversation, and oak bookshelves, stuffed with leatherbound books, lined the walls. There was an elderly upright piano in one corner, with wooden stools arranged around it, probably for sing-alongs. The room might have seemed dark and imposing, had it not been for the huge south-facing windows that allowed the midday sun to stream in. It was a room in which to feel instantly at home, and I did. Dawn came up beside me, and I squeezed her shoulder.

"Nice, huh?"

She nodded. "Yeah. We could fit our entire apartment in this one room. So where do we sleep?"

"You can sign up for your sleeping space on the sheet in the dining room. Oh good, Ronnie, I see you've already chosen," Cara said. "We have bedrooms in the main lodge, but there are also a bunch of outbuildings that we've set up as dormitories. You're a fairly small group, so you'll probably all fit in here, if you don't mind doubling up. We have three bedrooms on this floor, and six upstairs. And the mattresses are all new in the lodge," she added, as though this would settle our choice.

Dawn took all this in without comment, and we followed Cara to the dining room, where two trestle tables had been set for lunch. Ronnie, Dawn and I seated ourselves, and in a couple of minutes, Flavia joined us.

"What happened to Mandy?" she asked, grabbing a piece of whole grain bread from a basket in the middle of the table and buttering it liberally. "I thought she was starving to death — couldn't wait to get here?"

Ronnie shrugged. "She probably got sidetracked. She's like that — she'll start off doing one thing, and next thing you know, she's gone off in some other direction. She'll be back soon, I bet."

Looking out the window, I glimpsed the water taxi returning across the lake, bringing another group of visitors. Cara had seen it too, and was already halfway down to the dock to greet the newcomers. She was joined by another woman, older-looking and sturdy, dressed in a pair of grimy coveralls. That must be Jane, the other caretaker. I watched as the two of them greeted half a dozen disembarking passengers, who began the climb up the hill from the dock.

"Looks like the next contingent is on its way," I announced to the table in general.

"Good," said Flavia. "Time to get this show on the road."

4

A wind had come up, rippling through the last of the golden leaves and across the lake, stirring the ripples on its surface into small waves. Inside the lodge, the newcomers had joined us in the dining room, and we were all enjoying thick slices of tomato and basil quiche, still steaming from the oven, along with a salad of tossed greens and tiny slices of avocado. Mandy hadn't come back, but since we were all here and lunch was ready, Flavia suggested we just go ahead and eat.

"We'll save her some." She shrugged. "She won't starve."

Cara agreed, and lunch was served. All around us, there was animated chat — who had come from where, and who had studied what with whom, along with the nuts and bolts introductions that are common amongst astrologers: instead of name, rank and serial number, we share sun, moon and rising signs. Flavia introduced me to a couple of other women, her former students. They chatted happily together, catching up with one another's lives. From time to time, Flavia tried to include me in their conversation, with minimal success: as always when I'm in a group of people, I felt a little awkward. Still, the food was good and it was fun listening to the fragments of conversation that drifted my way from time to time.

"Not bad, eh?" I nudged Dawn, who sat next to me, wolfing down her quiche.

"It's good," she agreed, around a mouthful. "I'll see if I can get the recipe for this salad dressing while we're here; I bet I could make it at home."

I bet she could, too. Dawn has inherited my mother's gift for inventiveness in the kitchen, and these days, she did the bulk of our cooking. Mainly, she said, to prevent me from shaking extra salt into the dishes, or sneaking in the odd hamburger and fries. Well, I figured I made it up by tolerating tofu.

"Hey!" Dawn put her fork down with a clatter. "There's Rufus! Here, boy!"

The dog, who looked as though he'd been rolling around in a pile of twigs and dried leaves, stood uncertainly at the door to the dining room. His tail was tucked low, and he gazed at us soulfully, as though willing us to forgive him some unknown transgression.

"He might not be allowed in the dining room," I murmured to Dawn.

She scraped back her chair and made her way toward Rufus, whose tail made one slow, uncertain wag before it dropped back to its earlier position. Dawn has been bugging me for a dog for the past year and a half, ever since we came face to face with a killer in our living room.

"A dog will make us feel safer, Mom," she claims. To which I invariably reply, "Yeah, and we can really afford another mouth to feed. And where would we keep a dog? The apartment's bursting at the seams as it is. Not now, sweetie."

It has been a stalemate for months now, but watching her bend her head over Rufus, as she picked twigs and burrs out of his coat, I allowed myself a brief twinge of regret. If only our apartment, and my earnings, weren't so small.

"Mom! Come here!" There was urgency in my daughter's voice. The clatter and conversation of contented diners stopped abruptly, and ten women turned to see what the fuss was about.

"What is it?" I jumped up and hurried to kneel next to Rufus.

"Look — his nose! It's all lumpy and swollen! I think there's something wrong with him!" Sure enough, the dog's muzzle was covered in huge red welts, growing up from under his fur like miniature volcanoes.

"Shit," I muttered. "Dawn, go get Cara, would you? It looks like he's been stung by a bunch of bees or something. He needs a poultice — baking soda and water, I think." At least, that's what I remembered my own mother using, when I got too close to a wasp's nest as a child. It would leach out some of the toxins … Suddenly, the import of my own words came crashing home to me: if Rufus was covered in stings, what had happened to Mandy?

"Ronnie! Has Mandy come back yet?" I jumped up, my heart pounding with a sick sensation of inevitability. Ronnie, who had just opened her mouth for another forkful of quiche, shut it suddenly and shook her head.

"No, I haven't seen her. Why …" The rest of her sentence went unheard as I sprinted through the dining room in search of Cara, whom I'd last seen in the kitchen. As I left the room, Ronnie's voice spiralled up into a thin, reedy scream. I guess she'd figured things out for herself.

It was not going to be an easy task, organizing a group of brand new guests to search Sycamore Island for Mandy. For one thing, only Cara and Jane knew the place, and most of us didn't know one another, let alone the geography of the island.

"Should we call an ambulance?" Dawn asked, quite sensibly, I thought.

"It'll take them at least an hour to get here," Cara said. "They'd have to come in from Smith's Falls, then take the water taxi over here."

"All the more reason to call sooner rather than later," Dawn persisted, so Jane went off to call, while Cara tried to organize an efficient search of the island.

"We should go in pairs," she said. "We need to cover as much area as we can, in as short a time as possible."

Ronnie was sobbing quietly, but she agreed to go with Flavia, while I paired up with Dawn, to cover the southernmost end of the island. Flavia was pale and grim. Before we left, she grabbed my arm.

"There's no rush to find her now," she whispered, out of Ronnie's hearing.

"Why? What do you mean?"

"She's not here. I can feel it."

"Flavia, how can you —"

"Shh. Keep it down. I'm telling you, there's no point to all this. I can't feel her around here anywhere. She's gone."

"Gone where?" I shook my arm free. "Flavia, you're creeping me out. I have to go."

She shrugged, and I took off with Dawn.

"Mom, do you really think she'll be okay?" Dawn asked, as we trotted down a rough path that led to a kind of isthmus, which separated the inhabited part of the island from the wild, overgrown south end. We were heading into densely forested, rocky terrain, and I wasn't sure how we'd find our own way back, let alone track down Mandy.

"No way of knowing." I tried not to think of Flavia's prediction. "She had her Epipen; I saw Ronnie give it to her. But I don't know if that would be enough, if she got stung the way Rufus did. He was covered in bites. Assuming they were together when he got stung, that is. She might be just fine, sunning herself on a rock or something, while Rufus went digging around and found a wasp's nest. We'll know when we find her, I guess."

"If she's sitting on a rock someplace contemplating nature, I'm gonna smack her," Dawn said, as a branch whipped across her face.

I chuckled. "I know what you mean. I have a feeling she engenders that feeling in a lot of people. Come on, let's try down by the water — it looks like there's a bit of a trail there."

The trail was a narrow one, leading us along the perimeter of the island. Across a narrow channel, there was another island, which looked completely uninhabited, brush growing right down to the waterline. We passed a couple of tiny secluded beaches, marked by wooden "Swim at your own risk" signs, and had to climb over protruding boulders and exposed roots to stay on the path. Several times I called, "Mandy!" but there was no reply except the chittering of an annoyed squirrel, who followed us for a time before going back to storing up food for winter.

"What if she went into the woods?" Dawn gestured toward the trees. "We'll never find her if she's in there."

She was right. The underbrush was pretty much impenetrable. Young saplings pushed their way between older trees, and bushes grew in amongst it all. On the other hand, I couldn't imagine Mandy trying to walk through the morass of branches and leaves. She didn't strike me as the intrepid explorer. Might have torn her designer silk jumpsuit.

I stumbled over a root and grabbed a sapling to save

myself from tumbling down an embankment to the rocks and water below us. Just as I was righting myself, I heard the putt-putt-putt of a motorboat, proceeding very slowly through the channel. Probably our fishermen friends, still trolling.

"Hey!" Someone in the boat was calling us.

I turned to get a better look. It was an aluminum boat, the kind you could rent for a day's fishing, and it was piloted by a tall, trim man with a close-cropped grey beard. He looked out of place in his neatly-ironed white shirt and khakis — like someone dressing up to play a role. Preppy Man Out for a Weekend in the Country. I had an easier time envisioning him in pinstripes. He hailed us again.

"Is this Sycamore Island?"

Dawn and I looked at one another. Could it be a paramedic, this quickly? Not that he resembled any paramedic I'd ever seen.

"Yes!" I shouted back. "Who are you?"

Instead of answering, the man gestured to us to meet him back at one of the small beaches we'd just passed. We turned and climbed down to water level, and our new visitor hauled his boat ashore, stepping carefully to avoid getting his new Topsiders wet. At close quarters, he exuded a faint but pleasant odour of aftershave, mingled with the inevitable smell of gasoline from the boat.

"Did you bring a first aid kit?" Dawn wanted to know. "We might have someone who needs medical attention."

The man looked startled. "First aid? I don't know. They didn't tell me when I rented this thing ... Maybe there's one under the seats. You can check, if you like."

"You're not with the ambulance service?" I asked.

He shook his head. "No. I'm here to find someone. She's supposed to be here this weekend, for some astrology thing. I need to talk to her, the sooner the better.

Amanda Weatherburn — have you seen her?"

The expressions on our faces must have given him pause, for he stopped tying the boat to a stump and stood upright.

"What? What is it? Do you know Mandy?"

"As a matter of fact, we're just looking for her now," I said. "She was supposed to join us for lunch. And who are you?"

"I'm James Healey. Her husband." He held out a hand, and I shook it, aware suddenly that I was flushed and sweaty and out of breath, and probably had twigs and dried leaves in my hair.

"Oh, so you're Jimmy," Dawn said. "Mandy was trying to get hold of you this morning. You weren't at the office. She was pretty pissed with you, you know."

"Dawn! What's the matter with you?" I was startled at my daughter's rudeness. She's always been a plain speaker, but this was ridiculous. "I think you owe Mr. Healey an apology."

"Sorry," she muttered. Yeah, she really sounded sorry.

Jimmy didn't look fazed by her boldness, though. "Look, I really don't have time to chat. I have to talk to Mandy in person — it's important. Life-or-death important. You say she didn't turn up for lunch? Where was she last seen?"

I swallowed hard. Should I explain to this poor guy what had made us go searching for Mandy? The same thought was clearly on Dawn's mind, as she met my eyes and shook her head slightly. She was right. There was no point alarming Jimmy unnecessarily. Mandy might be just fine. Hey, it was possible. Not likely, but possible.

"Look, we're just going to check for her down at the southern tip of the island," I said. "Why don't you follow us, and then we'll take you back to the main lodge.

Everyone's out looking for her, so even if we don't find her, I'm sure she'll wind up there."

"Forget it. I need to see her now. No offense," he added. "Who's in charge around here? Just point me in the right direction, and I'll find my own way there."

I shook my head. "No point having two people get lost. You don't know your way around here, and ..."

Jimmy expelled his breath in a snort of exasperation. "Look, I have to see Mandy for ten minutes. And I have to see her now. I don't have time to stand around debating with you, okay? Now, where do I find the guy in charge?"

I didn't bother to correct him. "Okay, but don't blame me if you get lost. Just follow this trail back to the boathouse, and then there's a pathway right to the lodge. It's the big house on top of the hill — you can't miss it. The island co-ordinator's name is Cara. She'll be able to tell you what's what."

Without a backward glance, Jimmy took off at a jog toward the inhabited part of the island, while Dawn and I dutifully resumed our search for Mandy.

When Jimmy was out of earshot, Dawn commented, "I can't imagine what kind of conversation those two are going to have, when he catches up with her. She sounded like she wanted to rip his face off. And he's got this authoritarian thing going — he's almost as bad as Benjamin, for God's sake. Wonder if we should warn the others?"

"What do you think he wants? Ronnie said Mandy kicked him out last week — maybe he's come to beg her forgiveness, or something."

"Huh. If I were her, I'd be grateful to have anyone who'd put up with me," Dawn said. "And if I were him, I'd be down on my knees giving thanks right about now. Yeah, baby, she's gone! I'm free!"

"Oh, don't try to hide how you really feel about

Mandy." I chuckled. "She's a bit on the brash side, I admit. But there's no accounting for love."

Dawn made a gagging noise. We picked up our pace, trotting quickly around the tip of the island and back up to the isthmus where we'd started. We saw no one on our way, but as we emerged from the bushes, I spied Flavia, running through the clearing a couple of hundred feet away. She was waving frantically, gesturing to us. Dawn and I broke into a run and met her at the foot of a set of crumbling stone steps that led toward the main lodge.

"We found her," she gasped. "Back there. Ronnie's with her. I'm going to tell the others."

"Is she okay?" I asked, unnecessarily. Flavia's grim face told me all I needed to know.

"What happened?" Dawn asked, but Flavia had already passed us, and was moving too quickly to answer questions.

"You go back up to the lodge, Dawn. You don't need to see this," I said.

"Mom! No way! I'm coming with you. I can give CPR, you know. We took it in health class."

"All right, but if I say 'stay back,' you do as you're told."

"Promise."

"She must be over here somewhere. Ronnie! Ronnie!" I called, stopping for a second to listen for an answer. There it was, faint but unmistakable. I grabbed Dawn's arm.

"This way." I tugged her toward a stand of birch trees.

Ronnie was crouching near a small hut that might have been used to store maintenance equipment. The door hung open, swaying slightly on rusty hinges. In front of the hut, Mandy sprawled unmoving, her green silk jump-suit torn and stained. Her face was bright purply-red, and grotesquely swollen. Her eyes were squeezed shut, and her lips were puffed up to about twice their normal size. If she hadn't been wearing that lime green jumpsuit, she'd have been unrecognizable. Even from several yards away, I could see the huge welts, and I got that old familiar sinking feeling in my stomach. I was pretty certain she was dead.

"Stay here," I commanded, not wanting Dawn to see. Forgetting her earlier promise, she followed me, and knelt beside me as I lifted Mandy's wrist to check for a pulse. Even her hands were red and rashy looking, and somehow, she'd managed to get splinters of wood imbedded in her fingers and palms, where they stuck out like porcupine quills. I moved two fingers along her wrist, feeling for the slightest sign of life. Nothing. I didn't want to touch that swollen face, but I steeled myself, and pressed my fingers against where I thought her carotid artery ought to be. Still nothing. A lone wasp crawled up her neck, past her ear, and onto her right cheek.

"Flavia says she's dead." Ronnie's child-like voice wavered. She'd been crying, I could see, but now she seemed more resigned than anything. "We can't do anything for her now. Poor Mandy."

"When did you find her?"

"Just a couple of minutes ago."

"Shit." I couldn't think of anything else to say. I hadn't liked Mandy much to start with, but I wouldn't wish this kind of death on my worst enemy.

"Flavia just went to let the others know," Ronnie said. "We need someone to come and take her away."

I swallowed and nodded. I was starting to get that awful sense of unreality again. I pinched my own arm, hard, trying to keep myself here, present, in the here and now. The scene — the three of us crouching around Mandy's inert form, her torn and scraped hands, her hideously misshapen face — spiraled in my brain, and the world began to spin. Suddenly I felt as though I was watching us from somewhere up on the roof of the shed. Stop it, I tried to yell, but nothing came out. My mouth felt cottony dry. Dawn and Mandy and Ronnie whirled further and further away, and there was a high-pitched humming coming from somewhere — like static, or the noise our old black-and-white TV used to make when it was warming up.

I shook my head, as though to rid myself of a swarm of insects. My ears buzzed, and I sat back heavily on the ground, scraping my hands. Insects, swarming. Wasps. There should be more wasps around here, wasps that had stung the woman lying in front of me. What was her name again? And where were the wasps?

Dawn was shaking my shoulder; she peered into my face. "Mom? Are you okay? You're really white."

"Fine," I muttered, forcing my tongue and lips to shape the word, pushing my breath out through them, as though I were speaking for the very first time. "I'm fine, I'm fine. Where are the ... I don't see any insects." Somehow, this seemed important.

"Insects? Oh, you mean wasps. No, I don't see them either. That's funny," Dawn said, suddenly curious. She stood up and peered cautiously inside the shed. "There's one on the door here," she announced. "And another — yeah, there's six or seven of them in here. They're not doing much, though. Just kind of crawling around. I don't see any nest, though." Her feet made a crunching sound as she crept into the shed, exploring. "But there's a whack of broken glass in here. It's all over the place."

"Dawn, come out of there. You don't want to cut your feet."

"Just a sec, Mom. I want to see what's in here."

I forced myself to stand, and though my knees wobbled a bit I was able to walk over to the shed. Dawn was right—there were a few wasps crawling slowly up the door of the shed. They looked slow and stupid, the way they get in autumn, getting ready to hibernate or whatever it is they do during the winter. The cooler air seemed to confuse them, make them sleepy, but they didn't look terribly dangerous to me. Then again, I'm not allergic to them.

"There must be a nest in there somewhere. Come on out before you get stung, too. Or cut your feet or something."

Dawn stepped out, closing the door behind her. Then, as though realizing she shouldn't disturb anything, she opened it again and left it hanging, the way it had been when we arrived on the scene.

"What about Mandy's Epipen?" she asked. Right: the obvious question. Ronnie had tucked the lifesaving equipment into her friend's pocket, back when Mandy had been having histrionics on the dock. I crouched next to the body again, and checked the pocket of her jumpsuit, pulling out the kit. It was unopened, the plastic wrapper untouched. She hadn't even tried to open it.

Ronnie, Dawn and I stared at the Epipen in silence for a few minutes. Somewhere in the distance, I could hear shouts. The rest of the group was on its way.

"She didn't even touch it," Dawn said.

"Maybe she was too flustered?" Ronnie closed her eyes, and fresh tears trickled down her cheeks. "She always got panicked when she saw bees or wasps ... you saw how she reacted ..."

"But to not even try ..." I shook my head slowly. "Amazing. I mean, it's one thing to be scared of wasp stings, but wouldn't you think she'd at least try to open the pen? Or take it out of her pocket? That's pretty basic."

"Mandy was always pretty high-strung," Ronnie said, as though that explained everything.

Like a chihuahua on amphetamines, I thought, but I kept it to myself. Best not to think ill of the dead.

Flavia was the first to arrive, with Jimmy close on her heels. He must have found his way to the lodge, after all. Cara trailed along behind, looking worried.

"Where? Where is she?" Jimmy panted, and some instinct made me move to shield him from the sight of Mandy's body.

"Wait," I said. "You need to understand what happened …"

"Is that her? Oh my God!" he cried, as though I hadn't even spoken. He knelt next to his wife, or ex-wife, or whatever she was, and shook her by the shoulders. "Mandy, it's me! It's Jimmy! Mandy, wake up!" he said, over and over.

Flavia knelt next to him and murmured something. Jimmy tried to brush her off, so she said it again, louder this time. "She's dead. We found her like this. The police are on their way. There's nothing you can do for her now. Let it be."

Jimmy stopped shaking Mandy's shoulders, but he remained next to her, stroking her arm through the stained, torn silk. He didn't even look at Flavia.

"Police? What for?" Ronnie asked, looking alarmed.

"It's what you're supposed to do when you find a dead body," I explained. "Standard procedure." I didn't bother to explain that in the not-too-distant past, I had acquired way too much first-hand experience with the police and dead bodies and such.

"Oh." She looked away, fished in her pocket for a tissue, blew her nose.

"When did you find her?" Jimmy asked me, still ignoring Flavia, who kept glancing at him, then averting her eyes. I suppressed a flicker of irritation: sure, the guy was good-looking, but this was hardly the time for my friend to be making eyes at the newly-widowed James Healey.

"About fifteen minutes ago," I answered. "But I think she might have been here a while. She went off before lunch with the dog who lives here, and he showed up at the lodge about forty-five minutes ago, covered in wasp stings. We spread out to look for her, and this is what we found."

"Unbelievable." He held his head in his hands. "This is just fucking unbelievable."

Well, that about summed it up for me, too.

5

Within half an hour, a couple of OPP constables arrived. Cara led them to Mandy's body, and the rest of us adjourned to the main lodge, where a uniformed constable made a list of our names, addresses and phone numbers. No one felt much like finishing our abandoned lunch, and it would have seemed disrespectful to just carry on with the weekend's planned astrological activities. Cara and Jane went off to the kitchen to make tea, the universal comfort drink, and the rest of us sat in the living room, as though waiting for some instruction as to what we should do next. Dawn sat next to me on the enormous settee, reading from an antiquated volume of Dickens' collected works. At least, she was trying to read. Every few minutes, she'd drop the book in her lap and stare into the empty fireplace.

Flavia and I spoke quietly.

"She must have wandered into the shed for some reason," I said. "And Rufus was with her. Did you see the splinters in her hands? Those are from the door, I'm pretty sure."

"I did. But what the hell was she doing in there in the first place? I thought she was just going to take the dog for a walk. You know, throw a few sticks for him. What would have possessed her to go into a dumpy little shed like that? There's nothing in there but a bunch of old tools and such. Wouldn't she be afraid to get her outfit mussed, or something?"

"Maybe Rufus went in? Uh, maybe after a ... a stick or something. Or a squirrel." I was guessing wildly. "And she went in after him, to make sure he was okay, or to get him to come out, and ... I don't know. Maybe there was a wasp's nest inside?"

"Okay, maybe. But how did she get covered in splinters like that? She must have got locked in somehow. I mean, the woman was no Phi Beta Kappa, but I don't think she was that dim. She wouldn't follow the dog into a grungy little shed, close the door after herself, and then suddenly notice a bunch of wasps — it just doesn't make sense."

"Maybe the door jammed." Dawn didn't lift her eyes from her book.

"Okay. So we've got this woman, who's terrified of any and all flying insects with stingers, going into a shed that's full of the little devils? And then pulling the door shut behind her? I don't think so. Not even to rescue a dog, I wouldn't think. Y'all saw how she reacted when she even thought there might be a wasp, when we were waiting for the water taxi." Irritably, Flavia rubbed the back of her neck.

"Well, what if she didn't see the wasps until she was already inside?" I tapped my fingers against my leg.

"But what could possibly be in that shed to attract her attention in the first place? It doesn't make sense," Flavia complained again.

"It doesn't make sense to me, either, but then we weren't there. We don't know what happened. And you know what? We probably never will. I don't see the point in sitting here dissecting it all — that's the cops' job, not ours."

Dawn looked up. "Mom, don't you think it's kind of natural to wonder what happened?" Her voice was very soft.

"Maybe," I snapped. "But it doesn't do anyone any good. We should let the police handle it. That's their job, isn't it?"

"Mom, are you sure you're okay?" Dawn put a warm hand on my cold ones.

"Of course, I'm fine. Why do you ask?"

She pulled her hand away. "Just wondering. You sound upset."

"Of course I'm upset. Someone just died here, Dawn. I'd say 'upset' would be a good description of how we're all feeling, wouldn't you?" I felt a lump gathering in my throat. Damn. I tried to swallow, and wiped my eyes casually as though the damned tears weren't about to start again.

Flavia intervened, putting a comforting hand on my shoulder. "It's okay, Katy. I understand — it's a shock. And this isn't exactly what you bargained for, was it?"

I shook my head wordlessly. Flavia must have seen the distress on my face, because she gathered me to her in a bear hug. "Don't cry, darlin' — it's gonna be just fine. Everything's gonna be fine. You'll see."

"No, it's not." My voice was muffled by her shoulder.

"Trust me," she said softly. "You're going to be okay. I can feel it. It's going to be hard for a while, but it'll work out."

I pulled away from her embrace, but she retained a grip on my hand.

"Thanks." I felt awkward, and probably sounded ungracious. "I guess I'm just … it's so … I can't seem to go anywhere without something horrible happening. It just got to me for a minute, that's all."

"Don't I know it." She gave a small smile. "I thought I'd have myself a stroke, reading some of those e-mails you sent me last year! But that's all in the past now. This is just a nasty coincidence, and you and Dawn are going to be fine. The question is, what do we do now?"

She looked around the room. The rest of the guests were gathered in small groups, speaking in hushed tones, as though we were already at the funeral. Ronnie sat in an armchair, feet flat on the ground, hands clasped primly in her lap, eyes averted. She looked like a scared schoolgirl, waiting to be punished for some unknown infraction. Now and then, a tear would roll down her cheek, but she made no move to wipe it away. Next to her, Jimmy crouched on a low hassock, speaking to Ronnie in a low voice. I couldn't hear what he was saying, but she wasn't moving. I couldn't tell if his words were penetrating her grief.

"What the heck is he doing here?" Flavia whispered to me.

"He's Ronnie's brother, Mandy's husband. He got here while we were looking for Mandy." I kept my voice low. "He came ashore in a rented boat, and wouldn't wait to come back to the lodge with us. He went tearing off to find Mandy. I can't imagine how he must be feeling right now."

"I know who he is. But why is he here?"

Dawn butted in. "He said he wanted to kiss and make up with Mandy, but I think there's more to it than that."

"Like what?" Flavia looked startled. "What else could he want?"

As though he'd heard us, Jimmy glanced in our direction. Hastily, I looked away, but he stood up and strode across the room in our direction. Without looking at him, Flavia jumped to her feet.

"Pee break," she announced, and disappeared down the hall toward the bathrooms.

Jimmy plopped down between me and Dawn, sighing.

"You're the one who found her?" His voice was flat.

I shook my head. "No, Ronnie saw her first, I think. She was already ..."

"I know. Already gone. If I'd been here half an hour earlier, maybe ..."

"Can I ask you a personal question?" Dawn leaned toward Jimmy, who looked a bit startled. Maybe he wasn't used to forward adolescents. However, he recovered quickly.

"Shoot."

"Well, I know you and Mandy were having some troubles, but why were you in such a hurry, coming here to see her? I mean, couldn't you have talked by phone? She did have a cell on her, and she kept leaving messages on your machine to call her back. It just doesn't make sense to me."

Jimmy gave her a hard look. Then he studied the floor, seeming to search for words. "It's ... well, it's hard to explain. I just felt like, you know, if I could talk to her in person, we could — well, there's a chance we could work things out. She's ... that is, she was a real go-getter, and when she made up her mind to throw me out, I knew she meant it. But we were married for fifteen years. You don't just let that go without a fight. At least, I don't. She meant a lot to me." He blinked several times, and finally a tear trickled down his cheek, losing itself in his close-cropped beard. I resisted the urge to offer him a tissue.

"Mom, I need some fresh air," Dawn announced, throwing down her book. "Want to come for a walk? It's getting stuffy in here."

The abruptness of her gesture startled me, but I, too, was feeling a bit claustrophobic. "Sure, honey. Let me just get my jacket."

The cop in charge had no objections, so we wandered down to the front dock and stood a while, staring out across the lake. Finally Dawn broke the silence.

"That man is the biggest fake I've ever seen in my life."

"What? What are you talking about? The guy's lost someone close to him. Why wouldn't he be upset?"

"Huh." Dawn picked up a stick and started tracing zigzag patterns along the dock. "So you believe him? I think he's full of shit. That fake crying thing made my stomach turn."

"Dawn, you don't even know him. How can you judge him?"

"Forget it." She was quiet for a while. Then, as though thinking aloud, she said, "Mom, it's just not right."

"You mean ... all this?" I gestured around us. "Mandy dying and all? No, it's not. She's way too young ..."

"Mom!" Dawn sounded exasperated. "Are you being obtuse on purpose? What's got into you? You're acting like, oh, this is sad, but oh well, nothing we can do now ... Mom, someone killed that woman. I know it."

I drew a deep breath, and expelled it very slowly. "Dawn. You don't have any way of knowing that. And besides ..."

"Mom, please! Use your head. When we found Mandy, what was different about her?"

"Uh ... she was alive before, and now she's dead?" Clever, Katy, very astute.

Dawn made a dismissive noise. "Don't be ridiculous. She had wood splinters all over her hands, under her nails, sticking out of her palms, the whole bit. Her nails were all torn up, and the tips of her fingers were bloody. And didn't you see the scratch marks she left on the inside of the shed door? She was stuck in there, but when I closed the door, it was easy to open it again. Someone was holding that door shut. From the outside."

"Oh, come on, Dawn, who would do that? Mandy said herself that she didn't know anyone here; she was coming here because she'd never met any real astrologers. The only person I can think of who might have wanted to do her harm would be her ever-lovin' husband, and he got here too late. Remember, Rufus was covered in wasp stings long before Jimmy showed up."

Dawn scowled. "I don't know who did it. Doesn't matter; someone did. And whoever it is, they're still on this island. No one's left, have they?"

"Oh, for heaven's sake! You sound like an announcer on a cheesy detective movie trailer. 'Alone on an island — with a killer on the loose!' I'm sure there's some explanation for what happened to Mandy. And even if there isn't, you know what? It's really none of our business."

"Huh." My daughter sounded distinctly put out. "I don't know what's wrong with you these days. Aren't you even curious about what happened?"

"Nope. Not in the least. We only met Mandy a few hours ago. I didn't care for her much, but I'm sorry she's dead. The bottom line is, I just don't want to get involved."

"You're still freaked out about last winter, aren't you?" Dawn didn't sound accusing, just matter-of-fact. I would have preferred accusing — then I could have responded angrily. As it was, tears sprang unbidden to my eyes, and I turned my head so she wouldn't see.

"It's fine," I lied. "I'm fine."

There was a long moment of silence between us. I didn't usually talk about what had happened last winter, for good reason: I still couldn't think of any words to express the horror, the shock and grief of that time. I'd made a sensible decision to put it all behind me, but somehow, it just wouldn't let me go. I still had dreams of blood on the snow, and it had been more than nine months now. Maybe

Greg was right — maybe I did need to speak with someone. What I didn't need was to get involved in another mysterious death. But I couldn't say any of this to Dawn. She needed a mother right now, not a sniveling basket case.

Fortunately, Rufus came to my rescue. He stood on the rocks above the dock, like a sentry on duty, barking a warning. The baking-soda poultice that Cara or Jane had smeared on his snout hadn't stopped it from swelling up, and he looked a bit like a woofing platypus: his poor nose was twice its normal size. But that didn't stop him from dancing up and down along the rocks, barking and wagging his tail as the water taxi buzzed across the lake toward the dock where we stood.

The same young man who'd ferried us across the lake was driving again, but this time he had only one passenger, an older gentleman dressed in a dove grey suit, a bit rumpled, but still dignified-looking. The taxi idled alongside the dock as the man stepped ashore, quite nimbly, given his apparent age.

"Where are the police officers?" he asked me, without preamble. "I need to see the body."

"Why?" Dawn asked, as though he hadn't just ignored her.

He stopped, peered at her, pulled out his glasses and set them on his nose. "Because, young lady, that is my job. I am the coroner. Now, which of you would care to escort me to the police officers?"

"It's this way." I took over, heading Dawn off at the pass. She has been known to be a bit touchy about adults who even think about condescending to her. Best to leave that avenue unexplored, as I didn't know how strong this old guy's heart was.

We led the coroner to the shed where we'd left Mandy. The area had been transformed into a crime scene: the two OPP officers had strung yellow police tape from tree to tree, sealing off an area around the shed, and now they were conferring together. They looked up as the three of us approached.

"The coroner is here," I announced, suddenly realizing that the guy hadn't actually told me his name.

"I can handle it from here, madam," the elderly gentleman informed me. "I'm very well known to these gentlemen."

And indeed he seemed to be. They greeted him without much enthusiasm, as though they'd had dealings with him before, and found them less than satisfactory. I turned and tugged Dawn's arm, letting her know it was time to go back up to the lodge.

"Just a moment, ma'am," one of the officers called out.

I wheeled around. "Yes?"

He was a youngish fellow, probably in his early thirties, with a plump face that gave him an earnest look. His bushy blond moustache, probably intended to lend some authority to his baby-face, looked as though he'd pasted it on for a costume party and forgotten to remove it. I decided it would be impolitic to try to tear it off for him.

"Constable Hendricks, ma'am." He shook my hand, then Dawn's. "Could we ask you a few questions?"

"I suppose so," I sighed, then corrected myself. "That is, yeah, sure. What do you need to know?"

"First, could I get you to give us your name again? Just for the record." He pulled a notebook from his jacket pocket. When he'd written Dawn's name and mine down, he motioned me over to a fallen log, outside the crime scene tape. He and I sat, but Dawn remained standing, one hand on her hip, listening attentively.

"You and your daughter were second to arrive on the scene, is that right?" Hendricks asked.

I nodded. "Flavia and Ronnie called us over. We'd been running around that end of the island, looking for Mandy." I gestured back over my shoulder. "The south end, I guess. I don't have my bearings here yet."

"Looking for her? Why?"

"Well, we knew she was allergic to wasp stings. And when Rufus — that's the dog — came back to the lodge all covered in stings, we were pretty sure Mandy must be in trouble."

"I see. When did Ms. Weatherburn first leave your sight?"

I looked at Dawn for assistance. She shook her head — she wasn't sure, either. "I'm not really sure. We'd only been here a few minutes. And it was before lunch. Maybe … quarter after noon? Twelve-thirty?"

"Okay. And who was with you at that time?"

I thought back. It seemed like days ago. "Uh … Ronnie was there. And Flavia, and Cara …"

"No, Mom, they went inside," Dawn interrupted. "Don't you remember? Flavia had to go to the can, and Cara went to see if she could find Jane. And then Ronnie had to go check Her Majesty's bed arrangements."

Hendricks gave her a sharp look. "Who's Her Majesty?"

Dawn, realizing she might have trod over some unspoken line, flushed. "Mandy. The, uh, deceased. She had Ronnie running around at her beck and call, like she was some kind of royalty. That's all I meant."

Hendricks was scribbling busily. "So how long would you say Ms. Jerome was gone?"

Ms. Jerome? Oh, he meant Flavia. "Not too long. She came into the dining room a few minutes after we did."

"Which was when, exactly?"

"It's really hard to say. I wasn't exactly keeping track, you know? Um, I'd say she was out of our sight for maybe twenty minutes."

"What about Cara Medeiros?"

"Even less than Flavia. Maybe fifteen minutes," I guessed. "The thing is, I kind of dozed off, but not for very long, I don't think."

"I was awake," Dawn offered. "Mom's right — none of them were gone for long."

"Okay. And how long would you estimate Rowan Healey was gone?"

"Maybe ... ten minutes, max," I said.

Hendricks nodded, still writing. "So you all went in for lunch, and then the dog came back?"

"Sort of. First, a whole boatload of people arrived. Other astrologers, for the weekend retreat. There must be about nine or ten of us, I think. I didn't count."

"And then the dog came in, and you realized there was a problem."

"That's right. So we broke up into pairs, and set out to search the island. We'd been out maybe fifteen minutes when Dawn and I met Jimmy, Mandy's husband. At least, her soon-to-be ex-husband."

Hendricks held up a hand. "Whoa, hold on a minute. Back up. Ms. Weatherburn's husband is here? When did he arrive? Do I have him on my list?" He fished a piece of paper out of his shirt pocket and studied it.

"You should have him there. I saw the other cop write his name down. He came by boat, while we were searching for Mandy," Dawn interjected. "He saw us, and asked if Mandy was here. When we said she was, he parked the boat and went running off to look for her. We didn't even have a chance to tell him about Rufus and the wasps, or anything."

"Okay. And then ...?"

"We came back around to where we'd started, without catching sight of Mandy. So we were heading back up to the lodge, when Flavia called us over, and we found … this. Her. Just the way you see her."

"So no one touched anything at all?"

Dawn shifted her weight a little, and looked down apologetically. "Well, I did go into the shed to see if there were any wasps in there. And I closed the door, then opened it again. Just to see if it worked."

Now, if I'd said something like this to Benjamin, the cop I've been dating, he'd have crawled up one side of me and down the other. Disturbing a death scene? Horrors! But Hendricks took a more sanguine approach.

"But you didn't move anything? Disturb the victim in any way?"

"No," we answered in unison. And then I added, "Except that I did take her pulse. Radial and carotid. Just to see if she was … you know. If she had a pulse. But I put her back carefully. Listen, can I ask you a question?"

"Sure." Hendricks looked mildly amused.

"All this tape — these questions — am I correct that you're treating this as a crime scene?"

His expression changed to one of gravity. "We sure are, ma'am. At least, until we find anything to convince us otherwise."

"See?" Dawn turned on me. "I told you someone killed her!"

"What makes you say that?" Hendricks asked.

"Well, isn't it obvious? She's allergic to wasp stings, but she went into a building full of wasps? Not! And the door on that shed works fine now, but somehow she wasn't able to get out while she was being stung to death and panicking? I don't think so. Plus, I looked around in the shed. There were a few wasps in there, but no nest. And the place was full of broken glass. What were the wasps doing there? I think someone shoved her into the shed, tossed a bunch of wasps in a jar after her, and held it shut while she got stung. Then, when it was too late for her, they let go of the door, and she staggered out and collapsed here. That's what I think."

Dawn ended on a note of finality, then watched Hendricks closely for confirmation of her hypothesis. She was rewarded with another tiny smile.

"Ms. Klein, you've got a sharp young woman here. She should consider going into police work. That is, if she can remember not to touch anything at a potential crime scene." Hendricks grinned at Dawn, who smiled back, happy to feel appreciated. He snapped his notebook shut and tucked it away again. "We'll call you if we need anything else from you. And remember, if you recall anything at all, no matter how small, don't forget to let me know, okay?"

"Sure." I turned once more to go. But Dawn wasn't ready to leave.

She watched curiously as the coroner made notes in his own book. "What's he doing here?" she asked Hendricks. "Isn't it obvious that Mandy's dead? Why does he need to be here?"

Hendricks gave a short laugh. "Doesn't matter. It's his job — he has to come and pronounce the death. The victim could be a skeleton, and he'd still have to come in and tell us, 'Hey, this one doesn't have a pulse. Doesn't even have a heart. Guess it's a goner.'"

Dawn giggled. "That's a bit silly, isn't it?"

"Yep," Hendricks agreed. "But it's just the way things go in police work. There's a set of rules, and we all play by them. We cops like things orderly. Guess that's why we got into the business in the first place." He grinned, and Dawn grinned back.

6

The AstroFest had pretty much fallen apart before it had even started. By the time Dawn and I got back to the lodge, Flavia was sitting on the steps of the front porch, conferring heatedly with one of the other guests, a tall, gaunt woman whose silver hair was gathered into a thick knot on the back of her head. I took this to be Cecilia, and I was right.

"Oh, for God's sake, Cecilia! We can't just pretend nothing happened here," Flavia was saying, as we approached. "A woman died here, for the love of Pete! Okay, so none of us really knew her all that well, and she wasn't one of my favourite people, but she's still dead. We have to cancel the event." Flavia was flushed, her voice raised.

"What, and send all these people home?" Cecilia's voice was low-pitched and perfectly modulated, as though she earned a living narrating those soporific meditation tapes. "You know as well as I do that some of these women made special arrangements to get here, not to mention paying good money for the workshop. We owe it to them to carry on. We could have a circle to commemorate Mandy and work through some of our feelings about her death, don't you think?"

"A circle?" Flavia snorted. "Like that would make it

okay? You're dreamin', honey! This is supposed to be a retreat, a place where we come to renew our spirits — and Mandy died here! In fact, there's talk now that she might have been murdered, did you know that? That's not exactly what I'd call restful, unless someone's got a real sick sense of humour ..."

But Cecilia was just as adamant, though her voice never rose above its calm murmur.

"Death is a part of life, Flavia. It's all part of the great cycle, and all we can do is try to honour that. Mandy passed over to the other side, that's all. She didn't stop existing, it's just that now she's on a different plane. We don't have to stop everything — in fact, don't you think it would send a strange message if we were to say that one person's death was enough to prevent us from celebrating life?"

I had to hand it to her, Cecilia had a way with words. Strange ideas, but good execution.

"Excuse me," I said, and the two women noticed us for the first time. "Can I make a suggestion? Why don't we get the group together and discuss this whole thing? Do it the old-fashioned way, by a vote?"

Flavia nodded, but Cecilia pursed her lips in my general direction. "People don't necessarily know exactly what it is that they need, at a time like this. Sometimes those of us in a position of leadership need to step in and show the way. I do have training in grief counselling, you know."

Yeah, and I have a doctorate in psychology, but it hasn't helped me worth a tinker's dam lately, I wanted to yell at her, but I stopped myself. I didn't want to get into a pissing match with this woman.

Dawn raised her eyebrows, but diplomatically said nothing. I was grateful. Flavia, however, did not have diplomacy on her mind.

"Bullshit. Cecilia, that's just crap. Katy's right. We need

to call a group meeting. Good ol' democracy in action. American way, and all that. I'll go let people know."

Cecilia's mouth tightened — the first sign of anything resembling irritation on her part. "Flavia, you're not in America at the moment."

Flavia paused, and had the grace to look embarrassed. "Yeah, right. Sorry. Well, no matter. I still think a vote's the way to go."

Cecilia stood up slowly and gracefully, and gave a small nod. "Very well. Have it your way. I'll join you in a few minutes." She disappeared through the screen door, letting it slam shut behind her.

"Whoa, who the hell was that?" Dawn sat down where Cecilia had been.

"She's the retreat coordinator. Cecilia. She used to be this big high-society matron, but she chucked it all to go back to the land. She lives in this neck of the woods somewhere, in some kind of ashram or something, led by this whacked-out guy, Bawa or Boohoo or something. They make candles and wait for the aliens to land. She's a bit of a control freak, and she hates my guts — always has."

"Where do you know her from?" I asked.

Flavia grimaced. "I don't remember where I first met her. It seems like every time I go to anything like this, there she is. Like the proverbial bad penny. Speaking of filthy lucre, I think she's just worried the participants are going to ask for their money back, and she'll be in the hole. Don't know how she's going to explain that one to Bow-wow or whatever her guru's name is."

"What, she financed this thing herself?"

"Oh, no. But the deal was that her ashram would front the money, and then the instructors would split any profits. She'll be in deep shit back at UFO Central if she doesn't show up with some cash in hand. They tolerate her astrology stuff, because it helps keep them afloat financially. And think about the math here — ten women at six hundred bucks a pop ain't chicken feed, even split up. Anyway, no matter. Where've you two been?"

"We took the coroner down to the crime scene," Dawn said.

"Crime scene? They're calling it a crime scene now?" Flavia looked startled.

"Well, they're saying someone killed Mandy," I put in. "I hate to admit it, but it sure looks that way to me."

Flavia's face grew pale. "So Sheila was right. I thought it was just gossip. What makes them say it's murder?"

Dawn recounted our conversation with Hendricks, emphasizing the part where he'd called her clever. "But what I'd like to know," she finished, "is this: who had that much of a grudge against Mandy? I mean, I can see where she might have pissed some people off, but killing her seems kind of extreme, don't you think?"

"Dawn, that's not very nice," I said. "What's with this tough girl attitude you've had lately? It's getting a bit tiresome, you know."

Dawn did not deign to answer me, but Flavia jumped in.

"That's the sixty-four-thousand dollar question, all right," Flavia said, as if I hadn't spoken. "Who dunnit?"

"Exactly." Dawn sounded relieved to be speaking with someone at least marginally sensible. "And I intend to find out."

"Good for you," Flavia said. "Hey, here comes the law now. Wonder if they've figured it out yet?" She gave us a shaky smile.

As it happened, they hadn't. Or if they had, they weren't telling us. But Hendricks did want to take a statement from Flavia.

"And Ms. Klein, I'd appreciate it if you'd find Rowan Healey and send her out to see us," Hendricks said. "We'll talk to her next. Then her brother, James."

We were being dismissed, no doubt about it. I caught Flavia's eye, and she nodded. "Go find Ronnie, Katy. I'll just talk to these fine gentlemen for a bit."

Inside the lodge, Cecilia had apparently decided to take charge of the democratic process. She stood in front of the fireplace, addressing the group in the sitting room. All eyes were on her.

"... So there you have it. One of our number has passed into the light, and it's our task to help her on her way. Now, are there any questions?"

No one said a word, but a couple of people shuffled uneasily, and someone coughed. I scanned the room for Ronnie's small, pinched-looking face. She wasn't here. However, Cara stood by the door to the dining room, so I skirted around the cluster of women, Dawn following in my wake.

"Have you seen Ronnie?" I murmured.

"You mean Mandy's friend? The little one? I think she went for a walk with that guy, Jimmy. How'd he get here, anyway?" Cara twisted a corner of her T-shirt.

"By boat. Did you see which way they went?" Dawn asked.

"I don't know. Maybe ... down toward the south end of the island? Last I saw, they were headed off that way." She motioned toward the path Dawn and I had taken earlier, in our search for Mandy.

"Okay, thanks. Come on, Mom." Dawn made for the back door, pulling me after her.

"Come on where?" I demanded. "Dawn, what do you think you're doing?"

"They're heading for Jimmy's boat," she threw back

over her shoulder at me. "We're going to stop them, before they take off."

"Very funny, Dawn. Ha-ha-ha. No, we're not. We're not going anywhere." I dug in my heels, and Dawn, who'd been tugging me along by the arm, skidded to a halt. Sometimes there are advantages to being on the heavy side — when I put on the brakes, there is no moving me.

"Mom! Come on, what are you waiting for? I bet you anything they're going to leave the island." Dawn tossed her head impatiently.

"What makes you think so?"

"Where else would they be? Don't you think it's just a tiny bit coincidental that Jimmy shows up literally minutes after his soon-to-be ex-wife dies? And we both heard Mandy say he's after her money, didn't we? That's motive and opportunity, right there. Now, come on!" She tugged my arm, but I still held back. "Mo-o-o-m! They're going to take off, and the cops want to talk to them. We'll be doing the police a favour!" Dawn wailed.

"No. Absolutely not. Now you listen to me, kiddo. We're not playing Thrilling Detective here. If you think Ronnie and Jimmy might have left the island, we'll just let the police officers know. They can handle it a whole lot better than we can. That's their job."

"There's only two of them, and they're busy interviewing Flavia!" Dawn said, impatience ratcheting her voice up several notches. "Mom, come on! If we don't stop the them, they're going to get away!"

"Dawn, I said no. No way. We're not chasing them down. Besides which, you don't have any proof that they didn't just go off for a quick walk to clear their heads. Jimmy's lost his wife, and Ronnie's lost her best friend and sister-in-law, you know. They're both in a state of shock. Maybe they needed a bit of space, away from everyone else. Family time."

"Can't we just check and see if the boat's still here?" Dawn begged. "I promise, if they're still on the island, I'll let it go, and I won't say another word about it. And if they're gone, the police will need to know, won't they?"

I paused for a moment. On the surface of it, Dawn's argument made sense. Somehow, all her arguments did. It annoyed the daylights out of me, sometimes.

"Oh, for God's sake — okay, fine. We'll go for a nice walk, and we'll just check quickly to make sure the boat's there. And then you'll shut up about it, right?"

"Promise." Dawn pretended to zip her lips with a finger. Ha. That would be the day. Nevertheless, I trudged next to her down the path toward the end of the island, for the second time that day. As we passed the taped-off crime scene, I couldn't help glancing toward Mandy's body, now neatly covered with plastic sheeting, guarded by one of the OPP officers. A drop of rain splashed on my cheek. Funny, I hadn't even noticed it clouding over — the grey sky just seemed to have crept up on us.

I understood why the police had covered the body — not out of any sense of decency or gallantry, but simply to keep any evidence from deteriorating in the rain, as her body grew soggy out there on the damp ground. Now there was a charming thought. I pushed the image from my mind.

We walked in silence through the woods this time, keeping our heads down to protect us from the branches and the rain that had begun to fall more heavily. Dawn pulled up the hood of her windbreaker, which gave her some protection, but my jacket had nothing, so I turned my collar up and hunched my shoulders to protect my neck a little, and grumbled to myself. There was no point in going back now — either way, we'd be soaked.

"Are you sure we haven't already passed the beach where the boat was?" I called ahead to Dawn. I had the feeling we'd been walking in circles, but that was probably because I was paying more attention to where I put my feet than where we were heading, now that the ground was getting slippery with mud.

"No — at least, I don't think so," Dawn amended. "I thought it was just up here, past this tree trunk ..."

"Well, I don't see the boat. Let's go back."

"No, wait! What's this?" Dawn leaned down and picked something up. It was a scarf — a pink scarf with black edging, sodden with rain. "This wasn't here before, was it?"

"I don't know, Sherlock, I wasn't looking for scarves before, I was looking for Mandy," I said acidly. "Better put it in an evidence bag. Watch out for fingerprints."

"Mom, knock it off, would you? It's not funny. I think this is the one Ronnie was wearing, before. Besides, you'll notice we haven't seen Ronnie and Jimmy yet, right? So I was right — they've taken off."

"Okay, Dawn, you win. You were right. They've done a bunk. Vanished. Escaped. Disappeared. We'd better go back and tell the law, don't you think? They'll want to rustle up a posse and head on out to look for them."

Dawn favoured me with a ferocious glare, but something distracted her.

"Just a sec ...what's that? Down there ..." Dawn started to climb down toward the tiny beach. I followed, and in a moment I could see what had drawn her attention: it was Ronnie. She was propped up against a log, staring blankly at the raindrops as they splashed into the lake. When I called to her, she didn't move a muscle, didn't even look in my direction. I believe I might have uttered a curse word or two as I slipped and scrambled down to the beach.

Dawn knelt and I crouched beside Ronnie, shaking her by the shoulder. Her skin was waxy, her eyes vacant, and she didn't even seem to notice the rain that streamed from her limp hair down her cheeks.

"Ronnie! Where's Jimmy? Which way did he go? What happened?"

Slowly, she turned and looked at me, but her eyes seemed out of focus, the pupils huge. "Out there. Inna boat." Her voice was vague and slurred. She waved a limp hand toward the water, and then her head lolled to one side. Was she drunk? I couldn't smell anything on her breath.

"What do you mean, out there?" Dawn asked. "Did he leave?"

"Yup. Tol' me to just sit here like a good girl. He hadda go ... do something. Somethin' important. Just lef' me here, all alone. Me an' Mandy. Poor Mandy." Ronnie giggled mirthlessly. "Just the two of us now. An' she's dead. Me next." Then she flopped to one side, with a weak sigh.

"We're not going to get any sense out of her," I told Dawn. "Let's just get her back to the lodge. She must be stoned or something. Drunk, maybe."

"She doesn't look the type to succumb to reefer madness," Dawn said, but she agreed that we had to get the other woman back to the lodge. We hoisted Ronnie between us, and started the long walk back. She wasn't heavy, particularly, but if you've ever tried to lug a hundred pounds of dead weight up a muddy embankment, then along an overgrown path, stumbling over roots, getting whipped in the face by branches, in the middle of an autumn downpour — let's just say that by the time we got Ronnie back up the hill to the lodge, I was not in the best of moods. Ronnie didn't say a word the whole way. Her head flopped like a rag doll's, and her feet dragged along the ground behind us.

We'd been gone perhaps forty-five minutes, but the place had been transformed by the time we got back. For one thing, several more cops had descended upon the island. I guess Hendricks and his partner had called for reinforcements, because everywhere I looked, I saw another OPP officer. There were four or five of them down at the crime scene, huddling under a tree conferring among themselves while someone took pictures of the area. A couple more sat in the otherwise empty dining room, sipping coffee and discussing something that was apparently top secret, since they abruptly shut up and stared at us as we passed by the doorway.

Hendricks was still interrogating Flavia, which was just as well, since Ronnie, who was next up at bat, was not in much condition to answer any questions.

To my surprise, no one asked us what we were doing as we half-carried, half-walked Ronnie through the living area and down the hall to the bedroom she'd chosen earlier. I guess everyone was preoccupied. Cecilia did give us a peculiar look, but then seemed to lose interest.

Dawn nudged the door open with her knee, and we dropped Ronnie onto one of the single beds. She flopped onto the chenille spread, and let out a loud snore. The room was a large one, with four beds neatly made up, like a barracks — only prettier. A vase of dried flowers sat on the antique bureau, and each of the beds had a different wrought iron frame; they looked like original antiques to me, not the cheap reproductions you see these days. I looked around for an extra blanket and threw it over Ronnie, while Dawn found a towel in the bathroom next door and started rubbing the woman's wet hair.

Ronnie lay on her back, completely oblivious to our ministrations. She was down for the count.

"I didn't notice her drinking, before," Dawn whispered.

I grimaced. From long experience with an old friend, I knew that it wasn't necessary to actually witness someone drinking — practiced alcoholics could slip a little nip in any time, anywhere. "I didn't either. But she's certainly not sober, is she?"

Dawn sniffed Ronnie's breath. "Nothing. I was thinking maybe she's been taking downers. She's got the classic symptoms. We learned about it in school."

Drugs? Ronnie? She seemed like such a straight arrow, I had to admit the possibility hadn't occurred to me. Although prescription drug abuse is not exactly unheard of among women of her age and social class.

"Well, she can tell us herself, when she wakes up. I'm going to go get a hot bath, and get changed. You should, too. We're a couple of drowned rats, and I don't want either of us catching cold."

"I'm fine. So — where do you think Jimmy went?" Dawn waggled her eyebrows at me meaningfully. "He skipped out awfully fast. You'd almost think he didn't want to talk to the police, huh?"

"Oh, Dawn, who knows? Maybe he figured there was nothing more he could do, so he went home." I sighed in exasperation. I didn't want to talk about Jimmy, or Mandy, or people getting killed, or suspects, or anything even remotely related to all of the above. And Dawn seemed determined to talk about nothing else.

"Oh, sure, Mom, that's really likely. Uh-huh. His wife, this lady he's supposed to love so much, is dead, and the cops think it's a murder — and he just decides, well, what the heck, that's it, I'm outta here. Sure. I'll buy that.

Thousands wouldn't, but I'm gullible. Plus, don't you think he'd have to tell the cops where he was going, first?"

God, this kid can be a pain. I rubbed my temples, which had started to throb. "Okay, all right. So it does look a little odd. Who knows, maybe Jimmy did her in. But I'm sure the police have ways of handling things like this — they'll probably track him down and bring him in for questioning, and that'll be the end of that."

"Well, I'm going to go tell Hendricks about this. At least we can give the cops a head start. I mean, how fast can that little boat go?"

"You do that, Dawn." My hand was on the door handle. "And then, get yourself a bath, okay? Your father would kill me if I let you die of pneumonia out here."

To my surprise, the lodge seemed to have an abundant supply of hot water, and before long, I was immersed to my chin in a huge old-fashioned clawfooted tub. I put my head back and closed my eyes. I needed a rest. Oh, God, how I needed a rest. It wasn't just the day's events, which had been pretty damned awful so far. Somehow, the sight of Mandy's lifeless, swollen face kept getting superimposed with other, older images, ones I just couldn't shut out of my brain. There had been too many deaths, too much senseless killing, and somehow, no matter where I went or what I did, it kept following me around, like some kind of curse. I wanted to cry, but although the tears lurked somewhere deep inside me, they wouldn't come to the surface. More than just my body felt chilled, and it was going to take more than a hot bath to thaw me out.

Maybe I should have listened to Greg's advice. Maybe I really did need to talk to someone. This frozen, dead feeling inside me wasn't getting any better, and it had been almost a year since ... since I'd watched someone I loved blow themselves to smithereens, out there in the snow. There. I'd allowed myself to think The Thought. Despite the steam billowing around my face, I felt a chill run through my body, and I started the damn shaking again. This was getting ridiculous. First thing when we got back to the city, I was going to give Greg a call, and let him set me up with some shrink. I'd been stupid to think I could handle this myself.

7

When I finally emerged from the bathroom, so wrinkled I could have auditioned for the California Raisins, Dawn was already deep in conversation with Hendricks in the hall outside the room where we'd stowed Ronnie. The fact that I was standing there in my robe, with my head swathed in a gigantic terrycloth turban, didn't seem to faze them a bit.

"Mom! I was right — they're going to arrest Jimmy." Dawn looked triumphant.

"Whoa, there!" Hendricks held up a cautioning hand. "I never said we were going to arrest him. I want to have a word with him, that's all. We aren't anywhere near charging anyone, not until we have a better idea about what's going on."

"Yeah, well ..." Dawn wasn't about to be put off so easily. "Why would he run away then, unless he was guilty? And you know he *could* have killed Mandy — don't you think it's kind of convenient, how he just happened to show up just minutes after she died? I think he killed her, then hopped in his boat and came around to the other side of the island and met us. I didn't like him from the minute I saw him. He's way too smooth, you know?"

Hendricks looked amused, but said nothing.

"Dawn, you can't arrest people just because you don't like the look of them," I said. "Besides, I'm sure the police have the situation well under control. Right?"

Hendricks inclined his head. "We're working on it, ma'am. Right now, I'd like to talk to Rowan Healey. Your daughter here says you brought her up from the beach earlier on?"

Wordlessly, Dawn opened the door and motioned Hendricks into the room where Ronnie still lay, sleeping deeply.

"We found her down there like this," she said. "Leaning against a log, completely stoned. I think Jimmy drugged her or something."

"Dawn!" I cautioned her. "We don't know anything of the kind."

Hendricks tried to shake the sleeping woman awake, but she didn't budge. "How long has she been like this?" he asked over his shoulder.

Dawn and I looked at each other. "About an hour and a half," I estimated. "We had to drag her up here from the little beach on the other side of the island ..."

"The one where Jimmy had his boat," Dawn put in. "He left her just sitting there, getting soaked in the rain. For all he knew, she could have died, too!" Righteous indignation filled her voice. "What kind of man would do that to his own sister?"

"You should have told one of the officers," Hendricks began, but Dawn cut him off.

"I did," she said. "Right after we brought her in here. That old guy — the coroner or whatever. He said he'd tell someone."

Hendricks rolled his eyes. "He's not a police officer, he's a retired doctor who happens to have the job of coroner in this county. Well, no matter. Probably wouldn't have made much difference."

"Is there any way to tell what she's on?" I asked.

"We'll check it out when she wakes up," Hendricks said. "Might as well leave her for now. Were you two planning to sleep in this room tonight?"

"Um ... actually, I'd sort of thought we might go back to Ottawa," I said.

But Hendricks shook his head. "Sorry. We're going to be here questioning people for a while yet, and we might need to talk to you again. I was going to say that if you were planning to sleep here, I'm going to have to move you. We'll need an officer to stay and watch Ms. Healey until she wakes up."

"Then I guess we'd better find some place to crash," I said. "Where's Flavia?"

Hendricks pointed up the stairs. "Last I saw, she was stomping off in that direction."

Stomping? I raised an eyebrow, wondering what had transpired between Flavia and the police, but Hendricks didn't bother trying to enlighten me.

The room under the eaves was much smaller than the one where we'd left Ronnie, and had three iron-framed single beds crammed into a U-shape along the walls. Flavia slumped on the middle bed and greeted us unenthusiastically when I cleared my throat.

"They think I killed Mandy," she said, without preamble. "I can feel it. They think I killed her. Or at least that Hendricks guy does."

"What? How could you have killed her? And why? That's ridiculous." I crossed the room in one stride and sat cross-legged next to Flavia. "What makes you think you're a suspect?"

"They told me not to leave the island."

"Oh, that! That's nothing — they said the same thing to us."

"Well, and they made a great big deal about me being an American. Like I snuck up here just to kill some loud-mouthed broad with more money than taste! Oh, and they kept asking me over and over again what I was doing when I was out of your sight, you know, when we first got here. Like I would have had time to sneak out, find that woman, kill her, and come back to the lodge, all in the time it took to go to the bathroom."

"Well, you were gone quite a while," Dawn said, unhelpfully.

I glared at her. "Dawn, don't be ridiculous! That's a terrible thing to say ..."

"It's okay, Katy." Flavia sighed. "I know I was gone a while. I had ... you know, business to attend to. In the bathroom, that is. My gut always gets tied up in knots when I travel. But what am I supposed to say — I can't prove I was in the can because my digestive tract was acting up, can I? It's not like I had witnesses in there."

"I guess not," I said. "But why would you kill Mandy? That's just plain stupid. You never even met her, until today. And yes, she was obnoxious, but that's not exactly grounds for a death sentence."

Flavia studied the floral print on the threadbare bedspread. "Actually, I think I might have met her before." Her voice was so soft I nearly missed her words.

"What? When? What are you talking about?"

"Don't jump down my throat, Katy. I'll tell you, just hold your water."

Dawn perched on an adjacent bed and leaned forward to hear Flavia's story. Flavia seemed to shrink into herself, and I had to strain to hear her words.

"Well, it was like this," she started. "My parents were

poor as dirt — Daddy worked as a handyman on a ranch, and my mother stayed home with all us kids. There were seven of us. And it wasn't one of those 'we were poor but happy' stories, either. Daddy was a drunk, and he was a mean drunk; and Mama wasn't far behind him. The only place I ever remember feeling happy was at school, even though we were living out in the boonies. The back roads of east Texas ain't exactly the culture capital of the western world, but I had a couple of good teachers who really liked me. In my last year of high school, one of them started putting the screws on me to go to college. Now, you have to remember, Daddy never got past Grade 4, and Mama might have had Grade 6, so the idea of me going off to a college was about as foreign to them as if I'd decided to grow wings and fly.

"Anyway, this one teacher decided I had a brain in my head, and he wanted me to get the hell out of east Texas, so he helped me fill in all these scholarship applications to different places around the country. Colleges I'd never even heard tell of — Bryn Mawr, Brown, places like that. When I got the letter back from Bryn Mawr, you could have knocked me over with a feather. I'd never even been north of Arkansas, where my mama's family came from, and now I was supposed to go to this exclusive liberal arts college for young women? I don't think so! I dug in my heels, but that teacher dug in his harder. He even came with me to tell my parents. If he hadn't, I don't think I'd have had the guts to do it.

"My daddy was a mean bastard, but he was still a bit intimidated by this teacher, so I wound up going up north to college. I felt like I'd landed on a different planet — this little college town in Pennsylvania was like nothing I'd ever seen before. And there were all these other girls my own age, but it seemed like they all came from these rich families, who could afford to send them care packages and money — the most I ever got from my family was a Christmas card. I was so lonely and isolated that first year, I thought I'd die. But I didn't. I started studying psychology and social work and stuff, and gradually I started to adapt. In the summers, rather than going home to Texas, I took a waitressing job in a high-class restaurant in town. It gave me a bit of extra money, and kept me busy.

"Well, one night I was serving this group of people, and I realized I knew some of them. There was this one girl, not pretty exactly, but obviously rich, and full of herself. She was drunk, and you could hear her from the kitchen, she was talking so loud. I knew her from biology class, but she didn't let on that she'd ever seen me before. She was draped all over this guy, a real cute one, and she was making this big show of him being her boyfriend. I didn't think much of it, but a couple of times I caught him looking at her like she was something he'd found on the bottom of his shoe — a real nasty look, y'know? Made me wonder about their relationship, but I figured it was none of my business. I was just the help, invisible to them, anyway.

"But after that night, this same guy came back to the restaurant a couple of times, and he always sat in my section. At first I didn't think anything of it — people choose a place in a restaurant, and that's it, that's their place. But every time he came in, this guy would kind of make conversation with me. Turns out he was a southern boy too, from Mississippi. He was engaged to this girl I'd seen him with, but he wasn't happy about it. He wanted to call the whole thing off, but I think he was too scared of what his girlfriend might do. So one night, he'd had a few to drink, and he calls me over to the table, and asks me out. I didn't exactly laugh in his face, that would've been rude, but I turned him down. He was engaged, for Christ's sake! I mean, sure, he was cute and all, but I wasn't dumb. I didn't want to be his diversion, something to keep his mind off his girlfriend. I told him that, and he got kind of quiet. Next time he came in, he told me he'd broken off the engagement, and asked me if I'd go out with him now. I let him ask me a few more times, and finally I agreed to go to a movie with him.

"Well, one thing led to another, and next thing you know, I was pregnant. Sure, we had birth control back then, but I was young and stupid and figured I couldn't get pregnant if we didn't go all the way. Yeah, right. Well, anyway, I broke the news to this feller, and he just went pale. Said he wasn't ready for a family, and no, he wasn't about to marry me, and well, I guess he'd about had enough, because that was the last I ever saw of him. Next time I saw him, it was on the front page of the social section of the newspaper. There he was, all dolled up in a tux, next to this same girl he said he'd broken off with, having an engagement party. I cried a little, and got a little bit depressed, and then I pulled myself up by the bootstraps and decided I was better off without him. The bastard."

"So he got married to her? And that was Mandy, right?" Dawn guessed.

"Yep," Flavia said. "That was her. I didn't think it could be, when I first saw her today. For one thing, this whole story happened twenty-five, thirty years ago. People change a lot. But as soon as she opened her mouth, I knew. There wasn't any mistaking her — Mandy had a certain style, if you know what I mean." Flavia smiled mirthlessly.

"Do you think she recognized you?"

"Me? Naw. Mandy wasn't the type to pay attention to the help. Plus, even if she was, I've packed on more than a few pounds since then. And you know, I don't even know if she knew about me and her boyfriend. He was pretty quiet about it — kept me in his back pocket, brought me out when he wanted to have some fun, you know?"

"So ..." Dawn paused. "This is kind of a personal question, but what happened? With the baby and all? If you don't mind telling, that is."

Flavia twisted a piece of the bedspread between her fingers. "No, I'll tell you, it's okay. I had my little girl the next spring, right after final exams. And I never saw her again — the social services people took her away before I could get attached to her. They said it was better for me that way. I wanted to die. It took me a long time to get over that."

"That's awful!" Dawn looked shocked.

"It's the way things used to be done back then, honey," Flavia said. "They thought they were doing me a favour. I don't hold it against them. It's funny, but that experience put me right off social work. I dropped out and joined a commune in upper New York state. That's where I started learning about astrology."

"So — what happened to the guy? It wasn't Jimmy, was it?"

"Good lord, no! I don't know what happened to the guy. But a lot can happen in thirty years. They probably parted ways years ago. This fella never had a good word to say about Mandy when I knew him, and I can't imagine they had a happy marriage. In fact, I'd bet you the farm they were both miserable, if they even wound up getting married at all. I'll tell you, that thought sustained me through a lot of pain!" Flavia grinned suddenly, and I chuckled.

"Yeah, there's a lot to be said for knowing that your enemies are suffering," I said.

"Flavia, did you tell all this to the police?" Dawn asked.

"More or less. I told them I thought I recognized her from college, years ago. I didn't tell them about the guy or the baby — then they'd think I offed her, for sure! Not that I didn't want to, at one time. Kill her, that is."

"Oh, shit." The words were out of my mouth before I could stop them.

"What? Katy, it all happened so long ago. I'd never even think about such a thing now. Don't you know me any better than that?"

"Well, let's just hope they don't find out you didn't tell them the whole story, that's all I can say. It won't look good at all, especially if you were withholding information that could be a motive for murder."

Flavia grimaced. "I know. But I just couldn't — it's hard enough for me to tell you guys this, and I think of you as my friends. A stranger, and a cop to boot? I don't think so."

"But ..." I stopped myself before I said something unnecessarily judgmental. Flavia hadn't killed Mandy, so what was the big deal if she wanted to keep her personal life to herself? She wasn't hurting anyone, was she?

Dawn was obviously on my wavelength. "Listen, Flavia, my mom and I have had to deal with the cops a couple of times, and one thing we've learned is that if you keep stuff back from them, it sneaks up on you afterward. Maybe you should go to Hendricks, tell him what you just told us. It's better that he hears it from you, you know?"

Flavia planted her feet on the floor beside the bed and rested her elbows on her knees. She stared at the pine planks for a while before she answered.

"You're right, I guess. But no one except you knows the story. Who else would he hear it from? And it really doesn't have anything to do with Mandy getting stung to death, does it?"

Dawn shrugged. "Who knows? I don't want to rat you out, but still ..."

"I told you that story because I trusted you." Flavia raised her face and stared at each of us in turn. Her face was pale. "I can still trust you, can't I?"

"Sure you can." I darted a look in my daughter's direction. Come on, Dawn, cut the woman a break. Dawn, who had opened her mouth to speak, shut it again.

"Yeah, you can trust us." She didn't sound happy about it.

8

We hadn't eaten much at lunch, and it was now well past the supper hour, with no sign of a meal being prepared. I guessed it was every astrologer for herself, so I went off to forage for food in the kitchen. The place was empty — Cara and Jane, who would normally have been preparing the evening meal, were still being interviewed by the police. However, there were big bowls of fruit on the counter, and I did find some bread, so I toasted three slices and spread them with peanut butter and honey. I couldn't find a tray, so I put the toast on a large plate and tucked three apples into the crook of my arm for the trip back upstairs.

I tried to cut through the living room, but it had been drafted into service as a police interview room. A middle-aged cop with a paunch sent me back toward the sleeping quarters, but not before checking out the various foodstuffs I was balancing in front of me.

"There's more where this came from," I told him. "You can get some in the kitchen."

"Sorry, ma'am, I really shouldn't leave my post," he said, but he looked mournfully at the food, then at me.

Oh, for God's sake. I sighed inwardly, handing him two pieces of toast and an apple. "Never mind, I'll go back and make more," I said.

To save time, I returned to the kitchen the back way, by the staff doorway. As I stood waiting for the toaster to disgorge the slices I'd just cut, I kicked idly at the baseboard.

"How can you say a thing like that?" A female voice wafted plaintively into my consciousness. "No one deserves to die that way. God, how horrible!"

I blinked and looked around, trying to locate the source of the voice, but there was no one in the kitchen. Then I realized: the person who was speaking was sitting directly under the pass-through window to the dining-room. I leaned across the counter, curious now.

"I didn't say she deserved to die," came another voice. "I just said it wasn't a big surprise that someone would want to kill her. She specialized in jerking people around — you know it as well as I do."

The second voice was familiar; I searched my memory banks for a match, but I couldn't place it.

"What do you mean?" Voice Number One sounded genuinely puzzled. "I didn't know her that well, but I've heard she was into about a zillion charities — homeless women, AIDS, animal shelters, you name it. I heard she had a bit of a temper, but that's really about it. Why would someone want to kill her? I mean, she never hurt anyone I know."

"Probably just never occurred to her," the second woman said. "And don't think for a minute that she was doing all that charity stuff out of the goodness of her heart — it was all optics. Probably for the tax benefits. Mandy took very good care of Mandy. And what she wanted, she got."

"How do you mean?"

"Oh, come on! Don't tell me you haven't heard the stories? She had all the society hostesses in Ottawa quaking in their Guccis — every time she went to a party, she'd wind up snagging someone else's husband. Not that she ever kept them — use 'em and trash 'em, that was Mandy's motto. But she certainly had a reputation. Believe me, I've heard it from some good sources."

"How come I never heard this? No one ever said a word to me ..." Now Voice Number One sounded positively aggrieved at being left out of the gossip loop.

"Probably because you're not married any more. You'd have known if she'd ever turned her eyes on Frank, believe me. He'd be a little puddle of jelly on the floor. Anyway, I guess she just pushed someone a bit too far, that's all. I'm betting on dear old Jimmy. He had plenty of reason, and he had to have known about her sleeping around. I heard she made him sign a pretty nasty prenuptial agreement, so he wouldn't have seen much of her money, if they'd actually divorced. As it is now, I bet when the police check out her will, it won't be too long before they put a warrant out for his arrest. It's too bad, really — I always liked what I heard about him."

"But to actually kill her — for what? The man's loaded as it is; why would he need her money? I just can't believe anyone would go that far. I heard her skin went all black and purple from all the bee stings. And she was puffed up like a balloon, you know. I can't think of a worse way to go! Would Jimmy really have done that? He always seemed like such a nice guy to me. I saw him at the tennis club a few times."

"I didn't see the body. Ronnie did, though. And that big woman and her kid — you know, the ones who came with Flavia. And now Ronnie's off with one of her 'fainting spells', I hear. Well, I guess as Mandy's acolyte, she's pretty much obligated to put on the damsel in distress routine. Even if she hated her guts, it would be kind of tasteless to act like she didn't care that her alleged best friend was about to be pushing up daisies."

"Cecilia! Don't be cruel," the first woman giggled. "By the way, is it true Ronnie has ... you know, a problem?"

"Don't ask me. I don't associate with her any more. But I wouldn't doubt it."

Cecilia. Of course. But where was the calm, judicious, New-Age voice she'd used with Flavia? This new version of Cecilia struck me as just a tad on the callous side.

"Anyway, I'm not being cruel, just realistic," Cecilia said. "Come on, let's go see if there's anything to eat in this joint."

I gave a guilty jump. I didn't especially want Cecilia and her buddy to know I'd been spying on them. Well, there was nothing for it: they were on their way into the kitchen. I busied myself slathering more peanut butter and honey onto the toast, and greeted them as they came through the doorway. They looked startled. I took the innocent approach.

"Cara and Jane are off giving their statements to the police," I said. "But you can fix yourself a quick snack, if you like. I don't know what they're planning to do about dinner."

Cecilia narrowed her eyes at me suspiciously, but I smiled and sailed past her and her friend. I practically jogged down the hall and up the stairs, and by the time I reached our room, I was breathing heavily. I really do need to get more exercise.

Flavia and Dawn had booted up my laptop computer and were sitting side by side on one of the beds, discussing something in earnest, intense tones.

"Hey, you guys," I said. "What're you doing?"

"Oh, good, you're back," Dawn said. "I'm starved. We were just having a quick look at Mandy's birth chart. It's really interesting, Mom."

Flavia nodded agreement. "I haven't figured out how to get transits and progressions on your astrology program yet, but the birth data itself is pretty fascinating."

"Oh yeah? Where did you get the data?" Forgetting all about Cecilia, I handed out apples and toast all round, then joined them on the bed, which creaked alarmingly under our combined weight.

"All the participants filled out forms," said Flavia. "Dawn here just went and got Mandy's. Thought it might be interesting, you know, to see if the chart could tell us anything about her death. I've been doing some work lately on the Arabian Parts, the Part of Murder, Part of Suicide, and so on."

"What have you got?"

"Sagittarius Sun, Aries Moon, Aquarius rising, for starters. Fire and air — not someone to weigh her options carefully before she acted. And she didn't really give a flying ... uh, fig about how she came across, either." Flavia glanced at Dawn, who grinned.

"Don't worry, Mom's always on my case about swearing," she said. "I can take it."

"She doesn't need any encouragement, though," I told Flavia. "So, what's the final dispositor? Have you figured it out yet?"

"No final dispositor, but the chart signature is cardinal fire — I'd say Aries. That fits, too, doesn't it? And look at all these oppositions." Flavia pointed to the screen.

"Mom!" Dawn groaned. "You guys are talking astrology-speak! What the ... what are you talking about? What's a cardinal fire? Sounds like a little red bird that got too close to a candle!"

"Sorry, Dawn. It just means that she has a lot of planets in cardinal and fire signs, so it's like she's an Aries, even though her Sun is really in Sagittarius. And Aries people are known for being straight-ahead, me-first people who don't always stop and weigh the consequences before they do or say something. Okay?"

"Right. Sure. Whatever you say. That does sound like Mandy, for sure."

"She's got Mars conjoining the Ascendant, too," Flavia pointed out. For Dawn's benefit, she added, "That means Mars is especially strong in her chart. We already know she had a big mouth, and she'd just say anything that came into her head, without thinking about how it might affect anyone else. This Mars thing means she had a hard time co-operating with anyone else, because she'd say or do something, and alienate them just like that." Flavia snapped her fingers. "Mars is the planet of action, the warrior god — he just goes ahead and picks a fight, and damn the torpedoes. People with this placement don't have any trouble telling the world where to get off."

"Yeah, that makes sense," Dawn said.

"But what about this Moon-Neptune opposition?" I said. "That shows a bit more sensitivity and impressionability, doesn't it? So she wasn't a complete bulldozer, underneath it all."

"True enough," Flavia said. "Usually when I see a connection between the Moon and Neptune, I ask the client about her relationship with her mother. I find people like that seem to have a hard time getting hold of who their mother really is ... sometimes the Mom is an alcoholic, or maybe she's just kind of vague. And the relationship with her mother could get played out in her other relationships with women — like Ronnie."

"So she chose Ronnie for a friend because she reminded her of her mother?" Dawn was getting into this.

"Or maybe," I said, thinking aloud about the conversation I'd just overheard, "she chose Ronnie because of Ronnie's pill addiction."

"How do you know she's got an addiction?" Flavia asked.

"Heard it through the grapevine." I smiled enigmatically.

Flavia looked quizzical, but didn't pursue the matter. "Well, I'll bet you dollars to doughnuts, she doesn't see Ronnie as she really is."

"Eeenteresting. Very interesting," Dawn said. "So, you think under the little girl act, Ronnie might actually be, like, Zena, Warrior Princess?"

Flavia laughed. "Could be, honey, could be. Hey, look at all these squares to the Moon — Mandy might have seen her mother as suffering, somehow. Maybe she didn't want to end up like her, so she adopted her louder-than-thou thing. That would make sense, wouldn't it?"

"Well, we can't exactly ask her about it now," Dawn said. "What about her husband? Anything in there about how he bumps her off?"

"Dawn ..." I started to reprimand her, then stopped. She might not be the only person who thought Jimmy had done the evil deed, and he *had* left the island in an awful hurry. I had no real reason to think he was innocent of his wife's death. Plus, it was none of my business. Silently, I repeated my new mantra: "Not your concern, Katy, not your concern."

"She has Pluto in the seventh house," Flavia said. "The seventh rules marriage, and Pluto is the god of the underworld, so she attracted a husband who's as strong-willed and domineering as she is. He'd need to be, or the poor guy'd get squished like a bug."

"Pluto's in accidental detriment in the seventh house," I said, "so for Mandy, it was either dominate or be dominated. But that doesn't prove anything. Tons of people have that placement, and they don't get killed by their husbands."

I caught the look in Dawn's eye. "Look, Dawn, all it means is that marriage plays an especially important role in her life. When I get a client with that placement, I say they're looking for someone with a powerful personality, and that makes sense in Mandy's case. I can't imagine her being married to a milk-toast kind of guy, can you? She'd need someone who could match her own energy, or she'd be bored out of her skull. It's not like we got a chance to know Jimmy, but he struck me as the kind of guy who could fend for himself against someone like Mandy."

"Well, her chart doesn't prove he *didn't* kill her, does it?"

"Dawn, has anyone ever told you you're like a dog with a bone? You know perfectly well that a birth chart can't tell you who killed someone. Besides, this isn't our problem to solve," I said. "I'm sure the police are right on top of it, as we speak. I bet they've already caught up with Jimmy, and if he did it, it'll come out soon enough."

"Hah," muttered my daughter. Her mouth was drawn down at the corners, and she kicked absently at the bedframe. "We could have caught him, if you hadn't been such a chicken."

"Hey, you two, check out this Venus-Uranus opposition." Flavia was trying to distract us. It worked, on me at least. Dawn looked unconvinced.

"Venus opposing Uranus — relationships made her feel confined. She'd have sought out partners who were a bit offbeat, maybe eccentric. People who could help her shore up her own self-image as a unique person. It sure bears out the self-centredness thing, doesn't it?" I said. "And I've noticed that people with that placement tend to go through relationships at a pretty good clip, haven't you?"

"Well, it shows she's on the distractible side when it comes to relationships, that's for sure," Flavia said. "Always on the make. I tend to think of it as a fear of rejection, like 'I'm going to hurt you before you hurt me.' I wonder if that's why she was about to dump Jimmy — she thought he was about to do the same to her, and she wanted to get there first?"

"Or ..." Dawn's eyes narrowed in concentration. "Maybe he was going out with someone else, and Mandy caught wind of it, and decided to ditch him, but he killed her before she could?"

"Objection!" I said. "Calls for speculation, Your Honour. Come on, you two, we can't piece together what happened to Mandy from her birth chart. You know that, Flavia, as well as I do. Even if we can't convince Sherlock Hemlock over there."

They laughed, and Flavia munched on her apple. Food — that reminded me again of the conversation I'd overheard in the kitchen. Mandy as devourer of unsuspecting husbands, Ronnie as doped-up pill popper. It was not a pretty picture

"So Flavia, what's with this Cecilia person?" I asked. "I heard her and this other woman when I was downstairs, and she didn't sound at all like the New Age Priestess she was playing when she talked to you outside. In fact, she was being downright nasty about Mandy."

Flavia swallowed her mouthful of apple and grimaced. "Not one of my favourite people in the world, if you really want to know. When she sent me the invitation to teach here, I nearly swallowed my teeth. Every time I've met Cecilia, I've had the distinct impression she didn't care for me, but I guess she thought I was a fair to middlin' teacher, and she'd be able to charge the students a bit more if she could claim she was importing a real live astrologer with a radio program in the good old US of A. That's my theory, anyway."

"You've got a radio program?" Dawn was impressed.

"Sure do, for my sins. It's one of those call-in shows, you know? People call me and say they're a Pisces, and their husband is a Leo, and should they get a divorce, or what? I take a quick peek at their charts, tell them to hang in there, and take the next caller. It's no big deal."

"Wow, Mom, you should do that! I bet they'd pay you good money!"

I groaned, and for a while the discussion of Mandy's killer was dropped in favour of Dawn's career plans for me. That led to Greg's offer of a consulting job at the hospital, which I soon wished I'd neglected to mention. Flavia and Dawn turned on me as one.

"Mom! I can't believe you'd turn down an offer like that! Come on, you're the one who's always saying we can't afford this, and we can't afford that — and then when someone drops a high-paying job in your lap, you say no thanks? That's just ..." Dawn searched for the correct expletive. "It's just *dumb*, that's all," she said finally. "No, it's perverse. What's with you, these days?"

I didn't bother to answer that one.

Flavia agreed with Dawn. "Wouldn't it be a handy thing to have on your business card?" she pointed out. "'Katy Klein, Ph.D, Psychologist and Astrologer'? You have to admit, it has a ring to it."

"I can say that on my business card whether or not I go to work at the hospital," I said. "I earned the degree, and so far no one's come by to demand my diploma back, just because I dabble in the dark arts. But I just don't think I can deal with the kind of work Greg has in mind for me. Forensics. It wouldn't be all dealing with loony killers who think the aliens are telling them to hack their mothers' heads off with chain saws, but I just don't need the extra aggravation. It would be a lot of stress, you know?" I sounded whiney, even to myself.

"Look," Dawn said, as if she were explaining something to a three-year-old. "I know you're upset about last winter, but ..."

"Dawn!" I snapped. "That's quite enough. Just let it drop, all right?" Tears suddenly swam behind my eyes, and I turned my head, not wanting her to see. "How I feel after last winter is no one else's business, not even yours. And the work I choose to do is my own affair, too, contrary to what you seem to think. It's not up to you, and I've already made my decision. And now, if you don't mind, I'm going to go get ready for bed."

Dawn looked as though she would have liked to say more, but something about the set of my shoulders must have stopped her.

"Fine," she muttered.

Flavia looked puzzled for an instant, but covered it by stretching gracefully. "I'm bushed, too. If the cops aren't planning to arrest me tonight, I think I'll turn in and get a bit of sleep."

Later, I lay still in my narrow bed under the eaves, listening to my roommates' breathing gradually slow and turn to gentle snores. The police were still downstairs, and now and then I heard a door open and shut, or a toilet flush. The rain had stopped, and outside my window, a branch scraped against the side of the lodge, back and forth with the wind. Beyond the lacy curtains, clouds obscured the stars and even the moon. The darkness in the room was almost complete.

The day's events seemed distant, as though I were remembering something that had happened several years before, yet still I couldn't allow sleep to overtake me. Every time my eyes closed, I saw Mandy's purple, swollen face, that lone wasp crawling up her cheek. And when I was able to shove that out of mind, I saw a snow-covered field, blood spraying out, freezing to my hands ... The early morning sun had begun to edge along the horizon before my eyes finally shut, and I slept uneasily for an hour or so. My dreams were full of red insects that swarmed and stung my face and neck; finally, desperate to escape their burning stings, I clawed at my face, scraping away both the tormenting insects and my own flesh, which had turned black and hung in shreds from my claw-like fingers.

I woke myself, trying to replace the skin and flesh I'd torn from my own face. I wasn't sorry to be awake.

9

SATURDAY, OCTOBER 15
Sun conjunct Mercury, square Neptune ✦
Moon conjunct Saturn ✦
Venus conjunct Mars, conjunct Pluto ✦

The room was empty. I lay still, my sheets damp with sweat, trying to get my bearings. The light trickling in through the dormer window was grey and cold, and rain splattered intermittently on the roof. A familiar smell tickled my nostrils — coffee. And something else, too. Maybe pancakes? My rumbling stomach reminded me of the inadequate dinner we'd had last night, and suddenly all of yesterday flooded back into my consciousness. Mandy, lying dead, shrouded in plastic. I wondered whether the body was still down by the tool shed — surely they must have moved it by now. It would be in the morgue, cleaned and chilled, draped in white. I shivered.

Resolutely, I pushed the image away, swung my legs over the side of the bed, and fumbled for my clothes. Just as I was pulling my sweatshirt over my head, the door opened.

"Mom? You up yet? Geez, I thought you were going to sleep all morning! I brought you some coffee."

The last of any residual irritation I'd felt toward my daughter melted away, and I gripped the mug in chilled hands, inhaling the steam that rose from the delicious dark liquid.

"You know you were always my favourite daughter." I gave her a grateful smile.

"Mom, I'm your only daughter."

"Well, you're still my favourite. So what's going on downstairs?"

"Breakfast is nearly over. I helped Cara and Jane make pancakes and french toast. You'd think these people never saw food before. They tore into it like a pack of wolves. We made a lot, though, so there might still be some left."

"Well, if our experience is anything to go by, no one around here got much to eat last night either. Are the cops still here?"

"Oh, yeah. Some of them have left, and I think I heard one say they'd taken the body back to Ottawa. Oh, and Ronnie is up, but she didn't come into the dining hall. I saw her in the hallway, and she looked like hell, too. Hendricks is talking to her in the front room now, and I hung around for a bit, but all I could hear was her crying. And calling for *Jimmy*." Dawn spat out the name with distaste.

"What — you were eavesdropping?" I tried to sound shocked. Conveniently forgetting, of course, that I'd done just the same thing with Cecilia, not twelve hours earlier.

"Not exactly." Dawn looked impish. "I just happened to be standing in the hall, waiting to use the can, when I saw them going past. And I can't help it if she was crying loudly, can I?"

I sat on the edge of my bed, sipping my coffee. "Where's Flavia? Does she still think the cops are after her?"

Dawn shook her head. "She went for a shower a while ago. But they haven't asked her back in to talk, or anything. They're concentrating on Ronnie this morning, I guess. I don't think Flavia has anything to worry about. Do you?"

As if on cue, there was a light rap at the door, and Flavia came in, a damp towel wrapped around her head. "Hey, you're up! I'd just about given you up for dead ..." Her voice trailed off. "Shit. Sorry. Bad turn of phrase."

Ignoring her gaffe, I drained the rest of my coffee. Already, I could feel the caffeine pulsing through my veins, easing the ache in my head, helping me force my eyelids open. I know, I know, it's an addiction, but as a non-smoker and very light drinker, I can't get too worked up about the dangers of my coffee habit. Even Dawn, who used to nag me about it, has eased off some of late, especially since I gave up poutine. The supreme sacrifice, in the name of my arteries.

Dawn and I left Flavia to dress. I wanted something to eat, and I wouldn't have objected to another coffee, either. If one had had this salutary effect on my alertness and attitude, imagine what two could do. On the way to the dining room, we passed the front room where Hendricks was still with Ronnie. The cop with whom I'd shared my toast and apples last night sat outside the door, thumbing through an elderly copy of *Time* magazine. He barely glanced at us. I could hear the murmur of Hendricks' voice behind the closed door, followed by a short silence.

"No, no, no, *nooo*!" Then something crashed to the floor, and a woman screamed. It must have been Ronnie, but I wouldn't have associated this shrieking with her usual kittenish voice. "That's not true! It's not! You're trying to make me crazy! How can you say something like that? She was my best friend!"

Dawn and I exchanged glances. "What the hell is going on in there?" Dawn whispered. "What's he saying to her?"

"Sounds like a Haldol moment," I said. "Hendricks has probably broken it to her that her brother is wanted for questioning. This falls under the heading of none of our beeswax, Dawn. Come on, let's get out of here."

Dawn hung back, but the cop outside the door put down his magazine and started to stand up, a warning look on his face. I grabbed Dawn's arm and dragged her, spluttering and fuming, to the dining room.

Six women sat at the end of one of the long tables, poking at the remains of their breakfasts, carrying on a murmured conversation amongst themselves. A couple of them glanced our way as we came in, nudged the others, and suddenly, six pairs of eyes turned our way. Not hostile eyes, but not welcoming, either.

I didn't really know any of our fellow guests, and I wasn't keen on imposing Dawn and myself on their breakfast discussion, but it would have seemed churlish of us to sit at another table, so I picked up a clean plate, helped myself to a few slightly deflated pancakes, poured another coffee from the urn, and joined the group. Dawn trailed along behind me.

"Hi, I'm Katy Klein," I said. "And this is my daughter, Dawn."

There was an awkward silence, that stretched for a good minute. I regretted my choice, but there was nothing for it now — I couldn't very well just pick up and move. Stupid conversational openings flitted through my head: *What brings you here? How are the pancakes? Too bad about the stiff, huh?* Wordlessly, I poured syrup on the cakes and began to dissect them with my fork and knife.

"You're one of the astrology teachers, right?" The speaker was a slight young woman, her pale, drawn-looking face framed by ultra-short hair that had been moussed or gelled into a reasonable facsimile of a porcupine being electrocuted. I couldn't tell whether her pallor was a result of yesterday's events, or a cultivated look. You know, the Dying of Consumption look. Apparently it's popular now, among a certain demographic.

I nodded and swallowed my pancake morsel. "Sort of. I came to assist one of the teachers. Which group are you in?"

"Group?" She laughed through her nose, not an attractive sound. "Haven't you heard? There aren't any groups, not now. I don't know about the rest of you, but we've just decided: we're all getting the hell out of here, the sooner the better. Cecilia can take her —"

"Allison!" Another woman, this one older, interrupted. "We agreed we weren't going to cast around for someone to blame. It's no one's fault, it's just one of those things."

"Well, if Cecilia hadn't got greedy and decided to rope in Miss Rich Bitch, none of this would have happened," Allison persisted. "We all know why Amanda Weatherburn was invited here. Don't try to pretend Cecilia's motives were pure, okay?" She dropped her fork onto her plate with a clatter and scraped her chair back. Her back was poker-stiff as she stalked outside. No one said a word, or watched her go.

Dawn gave me a quizzical look, and I shrugged. None of our business, I tried to convey, shaking my head slightly. Dawn had her own ideas, though.

"I don't want to be rude," Dawn asked the remaining women, "but what was she talking about? Why *did* Cecilia invite Mandy here?"

Glances were exchanged, and then the woman who'd tried to rein Allison in sighed, perhaps lulled by Dawn's youth and apparent naiveté into being less than discreet. "I suppose it's not exactly a secret. Cecilia is trying to start an accredited New Age college, and of course, in her position, it's natural to think about people who might be persuaded to become sponsors ..."

"You mean, she wanted Mandy to donate money to get her college off the ground?"

I kicked at Dawn under the table, but she paid no attention. I suppose I should have been used to that by now, as she'd been ignoring me a lot lately. Frankly, it was starting to tick me off.

"Well, yes," the older woman admitted. "At least, that's what we presume. Of course, Cecilia had no idea what would happen to Mandy ..."

"Well, it must take a lot of money to do something like that, right?" Dawn asked.

The woman nodded. "Mandy was known for supporting certain causes. She had the resources to do it, you might say."

"She must have been really rich, then."

The woman smiled for the first time. A thin smile, but a smile nonetheless. "Very."

"So what happens to all her money now? Did she have children, or anything?"

"No. No children. And I really couldn't say what the terms of her will might be. None of us knew her very well, and it's hardly the sort of thing one asks, is it?"

By now I was glaring darts at Dawn. They would have been lethal, had she bothered to glance in my direction.

"Well," she said brightly, "if I were the police, I'd be wondering right now about that soon-to-be-ex-husband of hers, wouldn't you? I mean, he shows up half an hour after she dies, and then disappears again before anyone can question him too closely. And if he stood to gain a lot of money from Mandy's death, doesn't that make him a prime suspect?"

This speculation seemed to strike a chord with the group. There were nods and raised eyebrows all around. Time for me to take a stand, here.

"Come on, people, let's not get too carried away." All eyes turned on me now. "We don't know who killed Mandy. It's not up to us to try and convict some guy in absentia, is it? Everyone is stressed out about this, and that's natural, but if we go overboard and start throwing those kinds of accusations around, without any actual proof" and here I paused to glare pointedly at my daughter, "we're just letting our own fears get the better of us. The police are investigating, and I see no reason to believe that they won't figure out what happened. Do you?"

A couple of the women shifted uncomfortably in their seats, and the older one who'd challenged Allison nodded her agreement. "I think we all need to get off this island as soon as possible. The sooner we put this ugliness behind us, the better. I think this place must have some kind of bad karma."

Flavia slipped into the room, looking subdued in a grey fleece tracksuit. "You're right," she said. "We should go home. Has anyone seen Cecilia this morning? I think we need to let her know that this retreat just isn't going to happen."

"Who's going to tell her?" someone asked.

Flavia shrugged. "I might as well. I'm already in her bad books. Can't get much worse."

"What about the police?" Dawn wanted to know. "Are they finished with all their questioning and stuff?"

"I met one of them out in the hall on my way here,"

Flavia said. "He said they were just wrapping things up. Said we'd be free to go, as long as they can contact us if they need to. We can probably call the water taxi and reserve spots starting in a couple of hours, I think. I'll get Cara to look after it."

And so the retreat ended, not with a bang, but more of a waterlogged fizzle. The taxi arrived around noon and carried the first batch of would-be astrologers through the autumn fog and drizzle to the mainland. It was decided that since Flavia's airline reservation was for Monday morning, she'd stay at my place for the next day and a half. She mustered polite enthusiasm at Dawn's offer to show her the sights of Canada's capital city.

As Dawn, Flavia and I sat on the front deck, watching the first boat leave, the screen door opened, and Ronnie took a few hesitant steps toward us. She looked terrible. Her hair hadn't been washed or even combed since yesterday, and she wore no make-up; her face was pasty, her eyes sunken.

Flavia jumped to her feet and offered the woman an arm — she looked as though she might fall over, without support.

"Geez, are you okay? You look awful!" My daughter has a knack for stating the obvious.

Ronnie shook her head, but didn't answer. Flavia helped her to a seat, and for a few minutes we sat in silence, watching the rain. I glanced at Ronnie a couple of times. She wasn't crying openly, but now and then a tear would find its way to her cheek. She didn't bother to wipe them away, but just let them straggle down her face. I offered her a tissue, and she took it, but didn't use it.

"Ronnie, you want to talk about it?" I asked. "You might feel better if you get some of your feelings out." Hey, you can take the girl out of the shrink biz, but you can't take the shrink out of the girl.

At first she didn't answer, but after a few seconds, she sighed. "It's … I don't know. I can't make any sense of it. That cop was trying to get me to tell him things … bad things, awful things, and I just couldn't. He's wrong, I know he is."

"Bad things? Like what?" I encouraged her.

"Oh, you know. About Mandy. Who killed her, all that. They asked if Jimmy could have done it, and I kind of freaked. I mean, he's my brother, for heaven's sake! He took good care of Mandy, better than she deserved sometimes. But they wouldn't listen to me." She smiled bitterly. "What do I know? I've only known both of them practically all my life, right?"

"They have to ask questions, Ronnie," Dawn explained, the pro educating the novice. "It's part of their procedure."

"Well, I didn't like it. And I didn't know anything. How could I?"

I changed the subject. "Ronnie, what happened yesterday?"

"Um, I hope you don't mind, but … Mandy was the only person who ever called me Ronnie. My real name is Rowan."

"Oh, sorry. So … yesterday? When we found you on the beach? You were really out of it."

She stared at me blankly. "What do you mean? On what beach?"

"You don't remember? Dawn and I noticed that you'd gone off with … that you'd disappeared, and we were a bit worried, so we went after you. You were sitting on a little beach on the other side of the island. We had to practically carry you back, and then we left you to sleep it off."

There was another long pause. "Oh. I wondered how

I'd made it to bed. I don't know — I was so totally freaked out, you know, finding Mandy and all ... Jimmy said I needed some fresh air, so we went for a walk, down by the water. That's the last thing I remember."

"You didn't — you know, take anything, did you? To make you relax?"

Ronnie's — that is, Rowan's — eyebrows furrowed. "No, I don't think so, why?"

"Well, you just seemed like you were a bit under the weather. Like someone who's taken a bit too much Valium or something."

Rowan flushed. "That's silly! I never take drugs. Not even aspirin. Why would I —" She broke off and closed her eyes. "God, I have such a headache. When is that boat coming?"

The trip back across the lake was a sombre one. No one felt much like making casual conversation. At the marina, Rowan stood on the dock, looking anxious and uncertain.

"What's up?" Dawn asked.

"Oh — well, we drove out here in Mandy's truck. But I don't have the keys for it, and I don't think I'm allowed to take it away anyhow. It might be evidence, or something. I don't know what to do." Her lip trembled, and tears filled her eyes again.

"Never mind. We'll give you a lift back to Ottawa," I volunteered. "Come on, Dawn, give me a hand with this luggage, would you?"

We piled our stuff into the trunk of the rental car, and drove home through the fog and unremitting drizzle. Rowan had us drop her off at a posh condominium in New Edinburgh, and from there it was a short drive to my own much more modest Centretown abode. It felt like we'd been gone for weeks. It had been a bit more than 24 hours.

10

My apartment looked even smaller than it was, dark-ened by the clouds outside. However, tiny or not, I was glad to be home. I dropped my overnight case at the door and sagged into the chair next to the phone. The answering machine light flicked frantically, telling me that seven or eight people had wanted to talk to me while we'd been away.

First came Peter. "Hi, ladies, it's me, the erstwhile man of the house. I'm in Montreal right now, following up some interesting leads, but I just wanted to call and see how things were there. Katy, I had a call on my machine from your mother, asking me to dinner. I don't think I'll be able to make it, but could you apologize and give her a hug for me? Dawn, I miss you ... guess I'll see you when I get back. I should be home tomorrow or the next day, depending on how things go here."

My mother does not particularly trust new-fangled technology, and she is especially not fond of answering machines, so it was a real surprise to me to find she'd left a rather long message on mine. Granted, she was probably responsible for the four hang-ups that preceded her message, so perhaps she was getting desperate.

"*Mamaleh,*" she said, with a slight catch in her voice. "Are you there? I know you have such a busy life, it's hard for you to remember to call your parents on *shabbos,* but now I'm worried. Not a lot worried, just a little, but a little worry is as much of a curse. Where are you? ... .What's that, Bernie? I can't talk now, I'm on the phone with Katy's machine ... Oh." There was a few seconds' pause, and then she resumed. "Your father says you're out of town for the weekend. That's right, I'd forgotten. But then, I'm not as young as I used to be, and at my age, you forget a thing or two. Call me back, *mamaleh.* I just hope you're not in a ditch." Click.

I dropped the phone back into its cradle with a stifled sigh. Dawn was unpacking her knapsack in her room, and Flavia had stretched out in the overstuffed armchair in my tiny living room and was leafing through back issues of *The Mountain Astrologer.* I picked up the phone again and dialled my parents' number. My mother answered on the first ring.

"*Mamaleh*! Oy, I was so worried! I know, I know, it's silly, you're a grown woman and you can take care of yourself, but when I called so many times and you weren't there ..."

"Mama, I told you I'd be away this weekend," I reminded her. "Everything's fine, okay? So what's up?"

"What? Something should be up?"

"What did you call me for?" I tapped my finger against the phone receiver. "You sounded as though you had something to tell me."

"Yes! I did — and I'm so glad you called now, because she's sitting right here with me. We've been having such a good chat. Almost like having you at home again. She reminds me of you, just a little."

I love my mother dearly, really I do. But sometimes I wonder whether she's deliberately obtuse to drive me crazy. I wouldn't put it past her.

"Who's with you, Mama?"

Flavia looked up at the tone in my voice. I gave a thin smile and she shrugged sympathetically. Were all mothers like this?

"You know, I told you! The *rebbe*—Masha. Remember? From Russia?"

I paused, casting my mind back over my most recent conversations with my mother. It seemed to me she'd mentioned something in passing about Russia, but I couldn't recall the details. Then again, I hadn't known there was going to be a test.

"A Russian rabbi? A woman? Right, I think I remember now," I said. Well, it was only a partial lie.

"Good, so you'll come, then!" my mother pronounced, with an air of satisfied finality.

"Come? Come where? Mama, what are you talking about?" My increasing desperation must have come through in my voice, because Flavia put down her magazine and leaned toward me, looking concerned.

"To supper, of course! To meet Masha! You did say you wanted to meet her, didn't you?" There was a warning in her voice. I'd better want to meet her.

"Of course! Sure, I want to meet her. When?" The last thing I wanted was to have supper with some Russian rabbi—organized religion has never been my strong suit, and I couldn't think what I'd say to this woman, whose whole life was probably a whirl of holy days and blessings and Talmudic arguments. Nevertheless, my mother appeared to believe I'd committed myself to coming over, so I'd have to do it, or suffer the wrath of Rosie.

"Why, tomorrow night! Katy, you don't remember this at all, do you?" The accusation in her voice was sad rather than angry. I'd take angry over sad three to one any day. Lower guilt factor.

"Mama! Come on, I'm just a little frazzled, that's all. Of course I remember. I just don't know the particulars, okay? Like when you want us there, and what we should bring."

"You don't have to come if you don't want to," she said. "I know you have a busy life ..."

I gritted my teeth. "Mama. I want to come. Really. It sounds like ... fun. Meeting Marsha and all — I'm sure she's very interesting. Now, what time would you like us to be there?"

"Masha."

"Pardon?"

"Not Marsha. That's an English name. Masha Streltsov is from Russia. St. Petersburg. Of course, it used to be some other name, back when the Communists were there, but now it's St. Petersburg again. Crazy Communists, always renaming things that had perfectly good names to begin with."

"Oh. Sorry. Mama, please — what time?"

Rosie, having won hands down, was gracious in her victory. "*Mamaleh*, any time. I'm putting the roast on at four, and it's a big one."

I tried to calculate in my head. "Okay, so how about if we get there by six-thirty? Oh, and Mama, we have a guest staying with us. Flavia, my friend from the States. Do you mind if we bring her?"

"Of course, bring your friend! You know your friends are always welcome here! But Flavia — what kind of name is that?"

This was my mother's none-too-subtle way of asking, "Is she Jewish?"

"I really don't know, Mama. Oh!" I suddenly remembered Peter's message. "Mama, Peter called, he's in Montreal. He said to tell you he'd love to come, but he's going to be out of town for the next little while."

"Oh." My mother managed to infuse that little word with a world of disappointment. She adores Peter, and the feeling is mutual. "Well, maybe he can talk to Masha some other time, then. He said he wanted to meet her, too. In fact, maybe it was Peter I talked to, not you. I remember now. He said he'd like to interview her, that's what it was."

"Uh, sure, Mama. I'm sure he'd love to meet her too. She sounds very interesting. Look, I have to go. See you tomorrow, okay?"

I closed my eyes and rubbed my temples after I'd hung up. Some days I could handle my mother's phone calls better than others.

"What's up? You sounded a bit tense there. Your mama giving you a hard time?" A sympathetic smile played at the corners of Flavia's mouth.

"Well, apparently I committed us to having supper tomorrow with my parents and some female rabbi who's visiting from Russia. I don't remember having done it, but that doesn't matter to my mother. It's probably just as well — the food will be better than anything I could make. And you'll love my parents. Everyone else does." Hauling myself to my feet, I headed to the kitchen to make some coffee. The brew I'd downed this morning had worn off, and I was in dire need of a caffeine push just now.

Flavia chuckled. "Katy, you sound like you're announcing the end of the world. How bad can it be?" she called after me. "Besides, I'd like to meet your parents. They sound like fun."

"Really, it's fine," I said over my shoulder. "My mother has an incredible talent for getting under my skin, that's all. And I guess I'm a bit tense after yesterday. I'm starting to feel like dead people are following me wherever I go. Not that I'm paranoid or anything."

Dawn had emerged from her room at the mention

of my mother. “We're going over for supper?” she asked. “What's she making?”

“Roast beef,” I said. “But you can eat the kugel or something, if that bothers you. Listen, would you mind checking out in the hall for the paper? Your dad asked me to collect them for him while he's away, and I forgot to look when we came in.”

I don't subscribe myself, as the pathetic rags that pass for newspapers in this town just annoy me. It's disloyal, I know, since my ex-husband works for the larger of the two local papers, but I just can't bring myself to donate money to the already bulging coffers of the slavering right-wing nutbar who's somehow managed to appropriate much of the news industry in this country. However, that doesn't stop me from sneaking glances at the headlines from time to time, or stealing Peter's papers when he's away. He'll just recycle them anyway, so I might as well read them.

Dawn tossed the thick Saturday paper on the kitchen table, and I rifled through it as I waited for the coffee to finish dripping. On the City page, something caught my eye. As I read the story, the bottom seemed to drop out of my stomach. I put my coffee down and re-read it, just to be sure I wasn't hallucinating.

“Dawn! What's the name of that teacher again? The one who took off with your trip money?”

“Acres.” She pronounced it as though she'd just found something distasteful in her mouth. “Why?”

“Did he use a wheelchair?”

Dawn nodded. “He was in some kind of a car crash, he told us. He's paraplegic — uses an electric wheelchair to get around. Why, Mom, what's going on?”

I showed her the page. “Looks like they've found him.”

The article was short and to the point.

High School Teacher's Body Found
National Capital Commission workers draining the Rideau Canal for the winter made a grisly discovery near the docks at the Dow's Lake Pavillion this morning. The remains of a man's body was found still strapped to an electric wheelchair, NCC spokeswoman Doris Nightingale stated. Police have tentatively identified the victim as Geoffrey Acres, a teacher at Lisgar Collegiate Institute, who was reported missing October 1. Police were unable to estimate how long the body had been in the water, except to say that Acres had probably drowned "at least a few days ago." Acres had been missing since he disappeared with no notice from his teaching position at Lisgar. No one from Acres' family could be reached for comment. Anyone with information regarding Acres' death is urged to contact Cst. Reginald Dufours at 555-0818.

"Oh my God." Dawn sat down heavily, staring at the newspaper. "The trip money. Someone must have killed him for the money. Oh, God, I feel sick!" She cradled her head in her hands, and I massaged her shoulder, in a futile attempt at comfort. The apartment felt cold, suddenly.

"What's going on?" Flavia had wandered into the kitchen. "What's all the commotion?"

"We just found out what happened to Dawn's teacher, the one who took off with the money for the class trip to Paris. It looks like he drowned in the Canal, strapped into his wheelchair," I explained in a low voice.

"Holy toledo! And here I thought Canada was this nice quiet little backwater. I feel like I wandered onto the set of *Homicide*! Is it always this exciting up here?"

"Well, let's not jump to conclusions," I said. "It doesn't say here whether he fell in or was pushed."

"How could he have fallen in, without anyone noticing?" Dawn's voice was full of tears. "That chair of his was big — someone would have at least noticed the splash. Someone would have at least tried to save him."

"I don't know, honey. We don't have all the details, it's hard to say what might have happened. Though I think you're probably right — unless he did it deliberately."

"Mom, we should call the police about this. They might not know about the class trip money, and they need to know. What if someone saw him with the money, grabbed it from him, and then just pushed him into the lake? And I've been sitting here all week, thinking he was a thief, blaming him ..."

"Oh, come on Dawn, I'm sure your principal must have told the police about the money. It does say he was reported missing earlier in the month — wouldn't they have mentioned it then?"

Dawn made a rude noise. "Yeah, right. They weren't even mentioning it to us, Mom. Things like that just don't happen at Lisgar." She pursed her lips and tilted her chin up in a deadly imitation of her school's vice-principal. "Come on, what's the harm? If they already know, that's fine. If they don't, it could have something to do with Mr. Acres' death. We can't keep that to ourselves, not if it might help them find out what happened."

I didn't respond. She was right, I knew she was, but somehow I just didn't have the stomach for yet another round of police questioning. Unreasonable as it sounded, I felt we'd done our share this weekend, and I just didn't want to get involved again.

"Mom? Did you hear me?" Dawn looked directly at me. Her face was tear-stained and pale.

"I heard you. You're right. We should. I just ..."

"What? You don't want to, is that it? What are you scared of, Mom? You might have to get involved again?" Her voice was full of contempt.

"You don't have to get all belligerent about it, Dawn. I just really don't want to get tied up in another murder case. I will call, but maybe I'll check in with Benjamin first, and see what he thinks."

"What the hell for? Can't you do anything without running to him for help? What's he going to do, hold your hand for you? I thought you were so big on your feminist principles! Rah, rah, sisters are doin' it for themselves and all that stuff. How come you have to drag him into everything these days?"

Suddenly I felt desperately tired. "Dawn, please lower your voice. I'm not running to him for help. I just thought he might know a bit more about what's going on, whether our information would be useful to the police. I'd rather not get into another big *tsimmes* unless I really have to. I'm getting way too old and tired for this, Dawn. That's all."

"You never would have been like this before — you *are* scared, aren't you?"

"Dawn, I said let it drop. I meant it." My voice was shaking. "I'll do what I think is best, and that's going to have to be good enough, do you understand?"

Something in my tone must have warned her not to push any further, for she just put her head back down into her hands and sniffed loudly. Flavia kept glancing between the two of us, unsure what to do.

I poured myself another coffee, slopped some milk into it, and carried it out of the kitchen. Was I being a bad mother, leaving my daughter to cry? Well, today I just didn't have the energy to flagellate myself. I flopped down on the couch and dialled Benjamin's home number. After a few rings, his machine picked up. I admit to a certain relief — somehow at that moment, talking to a machine struck me as much easier than trying to interact with a live human being.

"Benjamin? It's me, Katy. We just read in the paper about that teacher, Geoff Acres, who was found in Dow's Lake. He used to be Dawn's teacher, and last week he disappeared with something like fifty thousand bucks that he'd collected from the students for a trip to France. We didn't know if the police already knew this, and I was thinking maybe you could give us some advice, you know? About whether we should phone and tell them, or whatever. Okay, well, call me back if you get a minute. Talk to you soon."

When I'd hung up, Flavia, who'd left Dawn alone in the kitchen, looked at me quizzically. "This guy Benjamin is supposed to be your latest squeeze?"

"More or less. Why?"

"Well, you sounded like you were calling your stockbroker, that's all."

I lifted the coffee mug to my lips and scalded my tongue as I took too much in one gulp. "What, I should come over all romantic on him? He'd probably die of the shock. Benjamin isn't like that, Flavia. Neither am I."

Flavia shrugged. "Hey, I'm not judging you. Just noticing."

"Yeah, well. If I even hinted that I was about to become mushy with Benjamin, Dawn would be down my throat about it. She doesn't even think he and I should be allowed to hold hands in public, let alone whisper sweet nothings at each other. Believe me, you haven't lived till you've had Dawn supervising your dating behaviour. She's worse than my mother."

"I can imagine it." Flavia laughed. "But seriously,

how come you call him by his last name? Isn't that a bit impersonal?"

I shrugged. "I don't know. We started out that way, and now it's what comes most naturally, I guess. What are you getting at?"

"Hey, honeybun, don't get your back up! I just wondered, is all."

I managed a small smile. "Well, I won't pretend this is one of the great romances of the century, but Benjamin and I do okay. I'm getting a little long in the tooth for the moonlight and roses scenario, you know. I don't expect anyone to sweep me off my feet any more. Besides, if they tried, they'd probably get a hernia."

"Honey, no one's ever too old for it. You've just forgotten what it feels like to let yourself love someone, is all."

Unfortunately, I hadn't forgotten at all. In fact, I remembered it all too well. A year and a bit ago, when my old flame Brent had come back into my life, I'd thought we could go back to the heady romance of youth and I'd been terribly mistaken. Thinking of that now felt like a lump of hot lead in my chest, and I concentrated on swallowing my rapidly cooling coffee.

"Katy? You okay? I'm sorry, sometimes I get a bit carried away. I didn't mean to upset the apple cart, darlin'."

I nodded. I really was not interested in continuing this discussion.

"I'm fine. Really. Listen, it's way past lunch time, and I don't know about you, but I'm starving. I thought we'd be at the island all weekend, so I didn't shop for food. How about we go out and forage for something to eat?"

Flavia brightened considerably, and Dawn must have heard me, because she stopped sniffling in the other room, and blew her nose loudly.

"I'm not that hungry," she said at first, but eventually she allowed me to persuade her to join us, even if she could only manage a bowl of soup. There's more of my mother in me than one might think; I still worry if my daughter skips a meal. Hey, maybe this mitigated my earlier neglect. I hoped so.

The vegetarian Chinese food place around the corner from my apartment serves an excellent hot and sour soup, and spring rolls to die for. The restaurant was nearly empty when we got there — we'd missed the lunch crowd by a wide margin, and most people wouldn't be thinking of supper yet. An elderly Asian woman sat in a corner near a huge and immaculate aquarium full of large brownish fish, her feet propped up on a chrome kitchen chair as she read a Chinese newspaper. Two men sat on the other side of the room, with their backs to us, heads bent in discussion. Eventually a young woman, very pregnant, emerged from the direction of the kitchen, and wandered over to take our orders.

"You okay now, Dawn?" I reached across the table and touched her hand. She smiled, and the tension in Flavia's shoulders eased visibly. It was only then that I realized how uncomfortable it must be for her to witness our squabbling.

"Mom, I'm sorry I snapped at you about calling the police," Dawn said, after the server had left our table. "I was just freaked out about Mr. Acres, you know? I didn't mean to put so much pressure on you."

"We've all been under a lot of stress," I said. "Let's just try to remember we're all on the same side, okay?" I gave her hand a squeeze.

"I just don't know what to think about Mr. Acres. What do you think happened?" Dawn put both elbows on the table and leaned toward me conspiratorially. "I'm guessing it must have been murder, aren't you?"

"Dawn, how would I know that? The cops aren't even saying whether they think it's a suspicious death yet, at least not in the paper. It's all just speculation, isn't it? I mean, I guess it makes a certain amount of sense that someone pushed him off that dock to get hold of the money he took, but if the police are asking the public for help, that probably means they don't have any leads. We may never know, but at least we know he's not off in Venezuela, living on the beach off his ill-gotten gains, right?" It was meant to be a joke, but Dawn and Flavia just looked at me. Guess I wasn't quite ready for the stand-up circuit.

"Isn't it just a bit weird, though, having two people we know die on the same weekend?" Dawn said. "It's just so freaky. Like something out of a TV show."

"I'll say," Flavia interjected. "Weird doesn't even begin to describe it! Speaking of which, isn't that the guy we met out at the island yesterday?"

"Where?" Dawn swivelled to look, just as the waitress delivered an order of egg rolls to the men's table. As quickly as she'd turned, Dawn spun back toward us, her eyes like saucers. "Mom! She's right! That's Jimmy!" she hissed.

She was right. He didn't look quite as tall and imposing as he had yesterday, but it was definitely Jimmy. Today, he wore a very spiffy-looking suit, probably from Harry Rosen's. Men's suits aren't my specialty, but I'd have been willing to bet he'd paid more for his clothes than I spent on rent each month. The jacket made his already broad shoulders look even more so, and the grey wool pant cuffs draped gracefully over shoes that had been polished till the leather glowed. All in all, quite the male fashion-plate. Not at all like his companion, who looked as though he'd just wandered in from the Union Mission for Men. Unkempt greying hair fell into his heavily lidded eyes, and even from here I could see he was badly in need of a shave. His shabby, grease-stained suit of indeterminate colour strained over a substantial gut.

"What the heck is Jimmy doing with a lowlife like *that*?" Flavia whispered. "I bet that guy wasn't on Mandy's approved list of people to consort with."

"No kidding. Your buddy sure does keep odd company."

"*My* buddy! Hey, sugar, he's no buddy of mine!"

"Oh, right, I forgot. It's his wife you liked so much."

Flavia giggled and poked me in the arm. "Cut it out — you're going to make me spill my soup."

"Look, I don't like this." I was suddenly sober. "Maybe we should leave ..."

Dawn, meanwhile, had risen partway to her feet.

"Hey! What do you think you're doing?" I grabbed her arm, and she tried to shake me loose. When I didn't let go, she glared at me.

"I'm going to talk to him."

"Like hell you are! Sit down this instant!" I hissed.

"Mum, get real! He's wanted for questioning in a murder case, for God's sake!"

"I don't care. We're not getting involved. Now place your rear end in that chair right now, Dawn. If you know what's good for you." The Voice of Motherly Authority.

She gave me a killer look, but sat down obediently enough. I should have known she was up to something.

"*Hey, Jimmy*!" She shouted across the restaurant, startling me as well as the old lady in the corner, who threw her newspaper to the ground and sat bolt upright, black eyes snapping to attention. Jimmy swivelled abruptly at the sound of his name, upsetting the teacup in front of him.

"Shit!" he said, and backed his chair harshly over the cheap linoleum in an effort to avoid getting tea all over his expensive woollen pants.

His companion's reaction was even more spectacular: he leapt to his feet, nearly upending their small table. He reached the door in a couple of strides, yanked it open, but paused briefly at a gesture from Jimmy. Jimmy said something I couldn't hear, but the other guy wasn't having any. Instead, he hissed something in an undertone, and Jimmy let him go, with obvious reluctance.

Then Jimmy got up, pulled his billfold out of an inner pocket of that extremely elegant jacket, and threw a couple of bills on the table in front of the old lady, who said nothing, but started counting the money. Without even glancing in our direction, Jimmy followed his friend, who by now was probably halfway down the block. Dawn jumped up and ran to the nearby window.

"They're getting into a car together," she reported in a stage whisper. "Oh, now Jimmy's getting out again. The car's taking off ... okay, Jimmy's flagged a taxi. He's gone too." She came back to the table and sat down.

"Well, kid, looks like you pissed in the pickles, but good," Flavia chuckled. "Your mama looks like she's about ready to blow a gasket. And I don't think Jimmy-boy was all that thrilled to see us here, do you?"

Flavia was right. Steam was coming out my ears.

"Dawn, that was completely inappropriate!" I hissed. "You had no business doing anything of the kind! For one thing, what if you were right, and Jimmy did kill Mandy? You just cleverly alerted him to our presence here. If he'd been startled enough, he might have tried to hurt us. You had no way of knowing how he was going to react, did you?"

"Well, no ..." Dawn looked only marginally repentant. "I never thought of that. I just wanted to see if he'd act, you know, guilty. And he sure did, didn't he?"

"Maybe," I said. "Maybe he was just startled that someone would holler at him from across the room while he's trying to have a peaceful lunch with his friend. Or maybe he thinks you're a freaking fruitcake, which he would have every right to think, given how you've acted toward him since you met him."

"Oh, come on, Mom, get real. That guy was no friend. I bet it was one of his underworld connections. Did you see the way he was dressed?"

"'Underworld connections'?" Suddenly I was seized with the urge to laugh. "Dawn, you've got to stop watching cop shows on TV. They're obviously getting to you. Did you ever think that maybe the guy he was with was a friend? We don't know who he was."

"Well, I wonder if Constable Hendricks should know Jimmy's in town? He's probably hiding out from the law, you know. That's probably why he ran away like that. I'll bet you anything. He saw us and panicked." Dawn was on a roll.

"Okay, okay. I hate to admit it, but you could be right," I said. "Do you still have Hendricks' number? Maybe when we get home we could give him a call."

"Oh, sure, Mom, and by then Jimmy'll be in Montreal or someplace, and they'll never be able to find him. Come on, give me some money, and I'll use the pay phone over there."

"Have it your way, Junior Crime Fighter." I scrounged in my purse for some loose change. "If it'll make you feel better, go for it." And if it'll get you off my back, I thought. I was finding Dawn's relentlessness a bit hard to take today.

Flavia and I nursed our bowls of hot and sour soup, and eventually Dawn returned to our table, looking less than delighted.

"Nu?" I asked. "What happened?"

"He just took the information. Didn't sound excited, and when I asked if they were still looking for Jimmy for questioning, he said they'd done all they needed with him. And then he thanked me for being such a good little citizen, and hustled me off the line."

"So you're happy now, right? We've done our civic duty, and we can forget all about Mandy and Jimmy and that lot?" There might have been a trace of sarcasm in my voice, but I was dead serious.

"Yeah, sure, Mom." Dawn was the very picture of innocence. "Unless we see him again, that is."

I laughed; I couldn't help it. "Arch-criminals beware, the Girl Genius is on the case. What are you planning to do, make a citizen's arrest? Hendricks already said he doesn't need him. Are you going to do your own personal interrogation, complete with bright lights and a truncheon?"

Flavia joined in my teasing, and eventually Dawn started to smile, then giggle. Our mood was much lighter leaving the restaurant than it had been going in. As we strolled home in the late afternoon sun, Flavia suggested we rent a movie for the evening.

"I have an even better idea," I said. "Isn't that new movie playing out at the cineplex — the one about the Titanic?"

"*Titanic*?" Dawn looked less than impressed. "Aw, geez — it's supposed to be this big romance thing, isn't it? I just don't think I'm in the mood for that. Plus, I told Sylvie I'd come over tonight. She wants to rent *Revenge of the Toenail Clippers*."

At least I think that's what I heard her say. I didn't bother to ask for clarification.

But Flavia was keen on the idea of an evening out. "Honey, you are so right. A little escapism — that's just the thing we need. Why don't you phone your boyfriend, ask him if he wants to come along?"

"What do you want to see him for?" Dawn kicked at a pebble.

I pretended I hadn't heard her. "Sure, maybe I'll do that. And I can check up on whether the cops know about Acres and the class trip money while I'm at it. See, Dawn? I'm being a good citizen too."

"Hah," Dawn said. "He'll just give you shit for taking an interest. You watch."

As it happened, Benjamin was indeed free that night, and he even acceded to my choice of movies. We hadn't been out together in a couple of weeks, and he claimed to be missing me. I didn't mention anything about Geoffrey Acres on the phone, and neither did he — either he hadn't got the message, or it had been a stupid question, and he didn't want to embarrass me. Either way, I was just as happy to avoid the topic.

"Honey, you got this guy on a string," Flavia confided in a whisper, after I'd hung up from my conversation with Benjamin. "If he'll come with you to chick flicks, it means he's willing to follow you anywhere."

Somehow, the idea of Benjamin following me, puppy-like and adoring, didn't send a thrill up my spine. But, as I'd already told Flavia, perhaps I'd reached a level of maturity where it was no longer necessary to expect thrills from my love relationships.

"That's kind of a frightening thought," I said. "Couldn't he just give me a nice foot rub, instead? Now that's something I could use. That and about three weeks' worth of sleep."

11

Dawn had already taken off to Sylvie's place by the time Benjamin showed up at the door, wearing a shirt which might at one time have been white. It wasn't actively dirty so much as tired-looking, as though he'd slept in it. See, this is the advantage of our kind of relationship. If I were married to someone like Benjamin, God forbid, I'd have to force him to iron his shirts before going out in public. Even worse, I might have to iron them myself. We're really much better off this way.

I introduced him to Flavia, and he didn't even blink when I told him she was another astrologer. I guess he's used to me by now.

"So — what's all this I hear about you withholding evidence in the Acres murder?" The tiniest of smiles played around the corners of Benjamin's mouth. Flavia might be right — the old Benjamin wouldn't have joked about such a thing.

"Oh, that. Well, we saw the newspaper story, and Dawn was wondering whether the police knew the whole story. She's all hot under the collar about it. Seems Acres disappeared from Lisgar a couple of weeks ago, right in the middle of class, and he took along about fifty thousand dollars in cash. It was money for a class trip to Paris and it hasn't been seen since."

"Whoa, bet there are a lot of pissed off kids in that class right now," he said.

"Not to mention the parents. Not all of us can afford to fork over another chunk of cash," I agreed.

Benjamin scratched his chin. "Seems to me I might have heard something about it. It's not my case, but a guy down the hall from me mentioned getting a call from a very tightly-bound lady at Lisgar. She didn't want to come right out and say Acres made a dash with the cash, but that was the upshot of it. So that was Dawn's teacher, huh?"

"Yep. And now she's all distraught — doesn't know whether to be furious with him for wrecking the class trip, or guilty that he's dead. She's not saying so, but I know my kid."

"Poor Dawn. It's rough when you find out that the adults around you are fallible."

"Tell me about it. I think I'm a big disappointment to her these days." The instant the words were out of my mouth, I wanted to pull them back. Benjamin raised an eyebrow.

"You? Why would she be disappointed in you? You're a great mom, Katy."

I shifted uncomfortably. "Oh, I don't know. Just teenage stuff. She thinks I'm getting all stodgy and timid in my old age. Maybe I am, I don't know." I tried to defuse my words with a smile.

But Benjamin was on another track. "Speaking of interesting cases, I also heard something from a buddy of mine who works the OPP detachment down at Smith's Falls. Seems there was a convention of astrologers or something this weekend, and someone died under mysterious circumstances. You wouldn't happen to know anything about that one, would you?"

I felt like a kid who'd suddenly been apprehended while pinching penny candy at the corner store. Heat crept up my neck to my face, and I didn't look at Benjamin.

"Ah, I thought as much," he said. "As soon as I heard about it, I figured you'd be right in there like a dirty shirt. Want to tell me about it?"

"Not really," I said. "There's not that much to tell. We were there, but we only met the victim about half an hour before she died. She wandered off, and next thing we knew, she was dead. She had some kind of allergy to bees and wasps, and she got stung, and that was that. Dawn is convinced her husband snuck over to the island and killed her, but I'm reserving judgement. I still think it could have been an accident. Or something."

"Katy, Katy, Katy," Benjamin chided. "I just don't understand it. How come every time there's a murder anywhere in the vicinity, you pop up? If I didn't know better, I'd think you were some kind of Moriarty character — you know, a criminal mastermind who manages to never get any blood on her hands."

He chuckled at his own joke, but I didn't think it was all that funny. Tears sprang to my eyes, and I ducked my head, not wanting Benjamin or Flavia to see. Okay, this crying at the drop of a hat business was going to have to stop. Get a hold of yourself, I told myself sternly. I blinked back the tears and concentrated hard on forcing that lump back down my throat. It worked, for the moment at least.

Flavia sprang to the rescue. "Hey, it's not Katy's fault! We were all sitting around having lunch, minding our own business, when the dog who lives on the island showed up with a snout full of wasp stings. Next thing you know, the place is crawling with cops, everyone's in an uproar, and the AstroFest is over. Shortest weekend in history. We got out of there as soon as we decently could, I'll tell you that much!"

Benjamin shrugged. "Well, as long as you maintain your neutrality on this one, you should be fine, Katy. I'd hate to see you get messed up again, you know?"

I managed a weak smile. I think he was trying, in his own peculiar Benjaminish way, to be supportive. He'd been the first on the scene last winter, and he'd seen since then how hard that death had hit me. In fact, last winter is when he and I had started seeing one another on more than a professional basis. He'd started coming round to see how I was doing, and I'd found it a comfort, having him there. He's a big, solid guy who listens more than he talks, and that was just what I needed at that point in my life.

"Don't worry, I have no intention of getting any closer to this one than I already am. Now, are we going to see this movie, or what?"

We piled into Benjamin's car, and for the next few hours I allowed myself to be swept into a celluloid dream of young passion and the chillier aspects of the North Atlantic. The popcorn was good, too, if you discounted the alleged butter-like substance the dead-eyed kid behind the counter dumped all over it. On the way back home, Flavia insisted on sitting in the back seat.

"You two just feel free to drop me at Katy's, if you want to go on alone," she said. I couldn't see her winking at me, but she might just as well have flashed a big neon sign. "I can manage by myself, and I'm sure Dawn'll be home by now. You two should go on and have some fun, you know?"

It's a good thing it was dark in the car. I felt a flush creep up my neck and into my cheeks. Benjamin cleared his throat, and I stifled a giggle. The fact of the matter is, he and I were not exactly a wild and crazy couple, and going off for a hot evening of making out in the back seat had never really been in our repertoire. I guess it was my fault, really. He'd made it clear he'd like more of a, well, relationship, but I had distinctly chilly feet. In fact, our last conversation had centred on this very issue.

He'd been hurt that I wouldn't stay the night at his place. "Can't Dawn stay with her father for one night?" he'd asked.

I'd shaken my head. "Her father's out of town again. On assignment. Benjamin, it's not that I don't want to stay, but ..." My voice trailed off.

"Katy, how many times have we had this conversation?" Benjamin, who'd had his arm around my shoulders, moved away from me on the couch. I didn't pull him back.

"I don't know," I sighed. "You know it's not that I don't like you."

"Actually, I'm not sure I know that at all. It's like you've got some kind of invisible wall around you, and you're not letting anyone get close. Not even people who really care about you."

"I'm sorry. I'll try, really. I know it hasn't been easy, these last few months."

We'd left the conversation there, and he'd driven me home in near-silence. As we'd approached my building, I'd turned to him.

"Benjamin, I don't want to keep you on a string, you know? I'm not trying to be difficult, really. If you think you'd be better off with someone else, I'll understand."

Benjamin had turned to me, taken my face in his hands. "Katy, I don't want someone else. I want you. But I guess we'll have to wait until you're ready, huh?"

And that had been that. We'd chatted on the phone a couple of times, but he'd been busy with work, and we hadn't actually seen one another since then. Of course, Flavia couldn't have known that.

"It's okay," I assured Flavia. "We didn't have any plans. Benjamin can just drop us off, right?"

"You bet," he said, but I thought I detected a faint hint of regret in his voice. Or was I projecting? Didn't matter. Tonight was not going to be our night of passion, that's for sure.

He and I exchanged chaste kisses, and I jumped out of the car and was halfway up the steps of my building before Benjamin's car pulled away from the curb. Flavia hurried after me.

"What's he got, some kind of social disease? You took off like you had a rocket up your butt!" she scolded me.

I just made a face and shook my head. "We've got some issues we're trying to work out. Tonight just wasn't the best time for it."

"I know you do," she said impatiently. "That's why I offered to make myself scarce."

I turned to face her. "What the heck do you mean, 'you know we do'? How do you know any such thing?"

She gave a wry smile. "Katy, I told you. I feel things. It's just the way I am; I can't help it."

"Well, you're wrong here." I knew as the words left my mouth that they were lies. "There's nothing wrong between me and Benjamin. We're just fine. It's just that we're both really tired tonight."

She gave me an odd look. "Sure, honey. I'll stop hassling you about it, if that's what you want. But if you ever want to talk, you know I'm here, right?"

"I know." I turned and started up the steps again. "Come on, let's get inside. It's freezing out here."

Dawn had indeed arrived home before us, and she was in a state of high agitation as we came in.

"Mom, you won't believe who called," she said, before I was even through the door. She was practically vibrating with excitement.

"Hey, you know what, kid? You're right! I don't have a clue!" I slipped off my jacket and hung it in the hall closet. "Flavia? You care to hazard any guesses?"

Flavia just shook her head. I hoped I hadn't pissed her off, outside.

Dawn was still quivering in front of me.

"Maybe you should just break the suspense and tell us," I said.

"Ha. Ha. Ha. Well, she called just a couple of minutes ago, and she sounded really scared," Dawn said. "I told her you'd call her back as soon as you got in, but she said you can't — there's someone there who might be monitoring all her calls."

"Dawn, knock it off. Have you been taking lessons from your grandmother, or what? Who called, already?"

"Rowan. You know, Jimmy the Killer's kid sister. Mandy's best friend. She says Jimmy's keeping her prisoner in her own home. Do you believe me now?" Smugness radiated from her like a halo of righteousness.

"Right, Dawn. So if he's keeping her prisoner in her own home, why doesn't she just call the cops? Cut out the middleman, you know? Why involve me?"

"Oh, come on, Mom! You saw how she was around Jimmy at the island. She worships him, hangs on his every word. She wouldn't rat him out to the cops."

"Did she tell you this?"

"Not in so many words, no. But she said there wasn't anyone else she could call."

"So what does she want with me? What am I supposed to do for her?"

Dawn shrugged. "Guess you'll find out when she calls back. I'm sure it's got something to do with Jimmy and Mandy, though. What else could it be?"

"Maybe she wants Katy to look at her horoscope and figure out when she's going to grow a spine," Flavia suggested helpfully. "Or she thinks we all killed Mandy, and she wants to give us our gold medals in person?"

I made a rude noise. "You're both out to lunch. I think she wants to confess to the murder herself. After all, wasn't she the first on the scene, when we were all looking for Mandy? And who had more motivation? Can you imagine having to hang around with Queen Mandy day in and day out? I tell you, if I were Rowan, it would come down to homicide or suicide."

Flavia stiffened. "Hey, watch it. I was with her when we found the body. She nearly jumped out of her skin, and then she started wailing and crying. Not the noises a person would make, if they'd just managed to off their obnoxious sister-in-law. Besides, as we all know, I have a motive, too. Who's to say I didn't do it?" She smiled, but her voice was tense.

"Flavia, cut it out," I said. "If you want to confess, go right ahead, but I won't believe you. For one thing, when would you have found time? You were only in the washroom a few minutes, and whoever killed Mandy needed time to get her down to the shed, push her in, throw in the bottle with the wasps in it, and hold the door shut while they waited for her to die. That's a fairly complicated scenario, even for someone as multi-talented as yourself."

Flavia relaxed slightly, and chuckled. "Yeah, you're right. I think my guilt program has been working overtime today, 'cause I just can't find it in my hard little heart to feel sorry that Mandy died. She was a flaming bitch on wheels, and she never cared who she hurt when she was alive. Why should I feel sorry she's dead?"

Dawn opened her mouth to answer just as the phone

rang. For a moment, I sat staring at it, wondering what to do. I was in no great rush to talk to Rowan. I'd washed my hands of the whole thing, and frankly, I resented her invading my personal time and space like this.

"Come on, Mom, pick it up!" Dawn grabbed the receiver and handed it to me. Decision made. Thanks, kid.

"Fine," I sighed. "Hello?"

"Katy? Is that you?" Rowan's voice was even smaller than usual.

"Rowan? You'll have to speak up, I can hardly hear you. What's up?"

"I really need to talk to you. Could you come over?"

"What, you mean to your house? Can't we talk on the phone?"

"No — it's not safe. I'm really sorry, but could you ..."

"Well, maybe tomorrow." I didn't bother to hide my reluctance.

"Not tomorrow — now. It's kind of an emergency. Please?" Her voice shook on the last word, and she sounded as though she was about to cry. Well, she was probably overwrought, which was no huge surprise, given the weekend's events.

I really, really did not want to go traipsing out into the night to visit Rowan, no matter how little and sad and helpless she sounded.

"Listen, I don't know if I can make it over there tonight."

"Oh, God, I think I'm going to go crazy here," she sniffled. "I don't know what's going on, but I'm so scared, and you're the only person I can talk to ..." She let out a soft sob. I waited. "Please, Katy, I've only got an hour before he comes back, and I don't want him to know ..."

"What? What are you talking about? Until who comes back?"

"Jimmy ..." she moaned. "He said he'd be back by

midnight, and I just don't know what to do."

"Rowan, why don't you call the police? Maybe they can help you, if Jimmy's bothering you in some way. You could go to a shelter for the night, you know. They'd take you in."

"No! It's not like that — he's not beating me or anything. Look, I really don't want to talk about this on the phone. Please, if you could just come over for a few minutes, it would mean so much to me."

No, Katy, no. Bad idea. Do not pass Go. Do not collect $200. And yet, could I really just hang up on Rowan, leave her terrified and alone?

"Okay, I'll be there. But just for a couple of minutes, okay?" I started mentally kicking myself as soon as the words were out of my mouth.

"Oh, thank you!" The relief in her voice was unmistakable.

I hung up, and closed my eyes. "I cannot believe I just allowed myself to get roped into this," I said, to no one in particular. "Could someone please call the men in white coats? I think I'm ready for them now."

"Mom! What did she say? What did she want? Come on, tell us!"

"Dawn, don't badger me. She wants me to come over to see her for a couple of minutes. I don't know why, exactly. She doesn't want Jimmy to know I'm coming, and she sounded upset. That's all I really know."

"Jimmy! Hah!" Dawn spat. "I knew he was a bad actor, didn't I tell you so? I bet he's threatening Rowan, now that he's got Mandy out of the way. I bet she knows too much, and he's decided to bump her off too. His own sister! That bastard!"

"Dawn, stop. Just stop. I'll be back in half an hour or so. You should go to bed, it's late."

"What!" My daughter shrieked. "I'm coming with you, there's no way you're going to see her without me, Mom!"

"I really don't want you ..." I started. But what could it hurt, really? Rowan wasn't exactly a dangerous criminal, and neither was Jimmy, no matter what Dawn thought. "Oh, for God's sake, fine. Get your jacket. But nothing's going to happen. I'm going to talk to her, calm her down, and leave. I'm sure you'll be bored to death."

The three of us piled into the car, and I found my way back to Rowan's condo in New Edinburgh. In any other city, this kind of condominium development would be behind walls and gates, and it would be guarded by sullen-looking guys in cheesy faux-cop uniforms. Ottawa's not big on gated communities yet, though. I suppose this is something small for which to be grateful. I parked the car in the guest area, and found Rowan's place with no trouble. She answered the door almost instantly at my knock, leading me to believe that she'd been standing next to it, awaiting our arrival. When she saw Dawn and Flavia, she looked perplexed for a moment, but her good hostess genes kicked in, and she ushered us inside with a wan smile.

I don't spend a lot of time in the homes of the well-to-do, and I suppose I'm probably easily impressed, but Rowan's home looked to me like something out of a decorating magazine. It was one of those open-concept places, with softly gleaming hardwood floors and potted ceiling lights that threw shadow and light in exactly the right mix. Large leather wing chairs created a living area on the other side of a couple of pillars, and the whole place was lined, floor to ceiling, with built-in wooden bookshelves, in the same lovingly polished hue as the floors. All in all, it made my pathetic attempts at home decorating feel pretty small and useless. For a millisecond, I allowed myself to wonder whether Rowan had employed my friend Carmen to make this space so beautiful, but I managed to suppress that renegade thought before it could do any damage.

"Thank you so much for coming," Rowan whispered. "I wasn't sure if you would."

"You're welcome," I said. "But I don't understand why we're here, exactly."

"I know, I'm sorry. I didn't mean to be all mysterious on you. But I'm really afraid, and I thought you seemed like a strong person. Someone I could talk to."

"Why are you whispering?" Dawn asked.

"I'll explain it all to you. Come in, sit down. I'd offer you tea, but there really isn't time."

Obediently, we trooped into the living area. I sank into one of the leather chairs, absently running my fingers over the soft, supple upholstery. I could learn to live like this.

"When you dropped me off here this afternoon, I was really upset," Rowan began. "I didn't know what to do, or who to call, but about five minutes after I got in, someone was pounding on my door. I was scared, at first. I thought maybe whoever had killed Mandy had come for me, too. So I used the security camera, but it was just my brother. You know, Jimmy. You met him at the island."

"What exactly was he doing on the island, anyway?" Dawn demanded. "I still don't get how he managed to get there so quickly after Mandy died."

Rowan shook her head. "I don't really know. He wanted to talk to her, to try to get us both to come home with him, he said. He didn't tell me why, and there wasn't really time for me to ask. Anyway, that's not what I wanted to talk to you about. The thing is, when he first showed up this afternoon, he just hugged me really hard, and said he'd been worried about me. He didn't hang around."

"Does he often just pop in to make sure you're okay?" Flavia asked.

"Not really. I see him a fair bit, because I'm at their place a lot. Or at least, I was, when Mandy was still there." She gave a sad smile. "Anyway, about an hour after he left this afternoon, Jimmy was back, and he had this friend with him. A great big ugly guy, named Aaron. Jimmy said Aaron would have to stay with me for a while, just until Jimmy could get some stuff arranged. I asked him what he was talking about, but he wouldn't tell me. I started to panic — I couldn't figure out what he was talking about, why he wanted this guy to be here, but he just said he'd always taken care of me before, and I'd just have to trust him."

"Huh?" Flavia made a puzzled face. "I don't get it. Who's this Aaron fellow? What's with that?"

"Well, Jimmy told me he's involved in something that he can't talk about, and he said someone might try to get to him through me. He's ten years older than me, you know, and he always looked out for me when we were kids. So I asked him if the same person who'd killed Mandy was coming for me, but he wouldn't answer me. He said I didn't need to know anything, and the less I knew, the safer I'd be."

"So why do you need me to be here?" I asked. "Do you want us to take you to the police or something?"

"And where's Jimmy's buddy now?" Dawn butted in. "I mean, if he's supposed to be protecting you, he's not doing that great a job, is he?"

"The two of them left together, and Jimmy said they'd be back by midnight. They had some things to arrange, he said. Then he told me I have to go on a trip with Aaron for a few days, just until things settle down. There's this cabin up at Parry Sound or someplace like that. Katy, I'm not the smartest person in the world, I know that. But one thing I know for sure is that I don't want some big surly guy around, watching me all the time. That's what he was doing this afternoon, just watching me. Whatever I did, he was there, pretending to read or whatever, but I knew that he was watching everything. It was creepy. I don't want to go away with him, not even for five minutes."

"Well, you don't have to, do you? Couldn't you just say no?"

"I tried that this afternoon. I told Jimmy point blank that I wasn't going any place with that guy, and I wanted them both out of my house. Jimmy got this really funny look on his face, and told me I was just going to have to trust him, that he knew what was best for me."

"Well, you're right that it all sounds pretty strange," I said. "But I'm afraid I really don't understand where I come into this. What do you want me to do? I can drive you to the police station, if you'd like." I was starting to sound like a broken record.

Rowan shook her head, a small, impatient gesture. "No, that's not it. Okay, this is going to sound stupid. I know I sometimes get too emotional about things, but I'm really scared, Katy. Jimmy seemed so … so different. Not himself. He was grim and kind of mean, the way he was talking. He wouldn't listen to me, he just kept saying I had to trust him. And I do trust him, I do … but I don't trust this Aaron character, not at all. He's scary-looking, and dirty, and … I can't go away with him, I just can't!"

"So — you want us to do what, exactly? You say you don't want the police involved, which kind of limits our options."

"Well, I was hoping … oh, I don't know. I'm worried, you know, that maybe …" She shook her head, then drew a deep breath to calm herself. "Come on, Rowan, spit it out. Okay. Jimmy isn't acting like himself. I'm worried that maybe he did have something to do with Mandy's death, after all. I couldn't believe it at first, but maybe I'm just too blind to see clearly. Jimmy and Mandy fight like cats and dogs, you know, even though I really think they do … that is, they did love each other. I was thinking that maybe, if I gave you Jimmy's birth date and all that, you might, you know, check and see. If he could have been the one to kill Mandy, that is. I just can't stand thinking about it …" Her face crumpled, and she reached for a tissue from a half-empty box on the coffee table.

I frowned. "You called me up in the middle of the night, and made me come all the way over here, so I could do an astrological chart for your brother? Rowan, don't you have more important things to worry about, if you're about to be sent off to the boonies with some evil henchman you don't even know?"

Rowan shook her head, still unable to speak. She reached into her pocket and pulled out a business card, slid it across the table to me. I picked it up. *James P. Healey, MBA. Director, Member Services. Foreign Exchange Bank of Canada, Inc.* On the back, Jimmy's birth date, time and place were scribbled in green ink. I tossed it back on the table, but Dawn picked it up and studied it, while I tried to talk to Rowan.

"Look, this is totally wacko. I don't see what good it will do for me to look at Jimmy's chart," I tried to explain. "It's just not possible to tell whether or not any given person could have committed a murder, from their birth chart. I couldn't tell you anything specific — it wouldn't do you any good at all."

Rowan blew her nose, then looked directly at me. "I just need to know, that's all. I thought you might be able to help me. I'm sorry … Katy, I'm so scared!"

"I understand that," I said, more gently.

"Rowan, there's something else, isn't there? Something you want to ask Katy?" Flavia leaned forward, tapping the edge of the coffee table.

Rowan stared at her for a moment, opening and closing her mouth.

"Yes, there is," she admitted finally. "It's just that ... well, I was thinking that maybe I could come to your place for a while. You know, to hide out. I don't want to go with Jimmy's friend, I don't know him and I don't trust him. And I don't see why I should be the one to leave town, just because Jimmy's all paranoid about people being out to get him. So I thought I could maybe just hang out with you, just for a couple of days, and then I could come back here. I'm sure Jimmy will be back to his usual self by then. I'd pay you for your trouble, of course." She ended with a bright smile, incongruous in her tear-splotched face.

I started to speak, then thought the better of it. The furnace clicked on in the room's silence, and I jumped slightly. Rowan tensed, awaiting my verdict. For a moment, the room spun around me, and then the anger rose through my body like a pillar of flame, forcing me to sit up very straight in my seat.

"No." My voice was glacial. "Absolutely not. Not a way in the world you're bringing this mess into my life. Rowan, I don't know what's going on here, but I'd have to be a complete moron to let you come and stay with me and my daughter, even for a minute. What if Jimmy's right, and someone really is trying to hurt people close to him? Or what if you're right, and he killed his wife? You think I want the people I love placed in danger? You think I'd take that kind of risk, for someone I barely even know? I can't believe you'd even ask me such a thing!"

The force of my words seemed to carry me to my feet. I gestured to Dawn and Flavia.

"Come on, you two. We're going. This is a waste of our time."

"But Mom —"

"Not another word. We're going."

Rowan, who had been flinching away from me like a whipped dog, stood as if to stop me, her arms spread in a gesture of pleading.

"Please, I didn't mean ... I wasn't thinking ... I mean, I didn't think about you. Oh, God, I'm sorry! Really, please, couldn't you just take me to a hotel for the night? I can pay, I promise! I won't be any trouble ..."

"Call a cab," I snapped. "Or take a bus. It's all the same to me. Just leave me out of it."

In the car, no one spoke for quite some time. Well, except for me — I muttered under my breath as I drove, cursing other drivers who had the temerity to get in my way. I hadn't overreacted to Rowan's request — had I? I mean, there was no way in hell I was about to get us involved in anything even remotely shady. Hadn't I already learned my lesson in that department? What kind of idiot did Rowan take me for?

Finally, Dawn broke the heavy silence. "It's not like she's trapped there, is it? I mean, if she can pick up the phone, she can call a taxi, can't she?"

"Of course," said Flavia quietly. "There's nothing at all stopping her, except her own fear. And her loyalty to her brother. She's split right down the middle inside."

"Mom, I know where you were coming from when you said no like that, but I just can't help thinking, what if something does happen? I wonder if maybe we should call a cab for her, you know?" Dawn said.

I sighed. "If she had the gumption to call me over like that, I can't see why she wouldn't just call her own cab, honey. I think she just wanted someone else to take the responsibility for her. She didn't want to be the one to do it. That way, she could tell herself she was still being a good little sister, that it was those other bad people who pushed her to get away from Jimmy and Aaron, or whatever his name is."

"You know what?" Dawn sounded excited suddenly. "I'll bet you anything you like that Aaron is that lowlife we saw in the restaurant with Jimmy. I bet he was making the arrangement to kidnap Rowan, right then and there. That's why the guy got so scared and took off like that!" Dawn rubbed her hands together. "I knew it! I knew it! He was up to no good!"

"I felt such sadness coming from her." Flavia raised her voice to be heard over Dawn's victory chant. "She relies on Jimmy so much that she can't imagine doing anything to get out from under him. You could see it when we were at the island — she hung on his every word. And she let Mandy push her around too. Sad that she thinks so little of herself."

"Here's what I don't get ..." Dawn paused for a moment. "If Big Brother Jimmy was all that concerned about her welfare, why did he dump her on the beach like that, just sitting there waiting for someone to come and bump her off, too? Some big brother he is — makes me glad I never had any siblings!"

"And he might have drugged her, too," Flavia said. "At least, if you believe her about never taking anything stronger than aspirin. She was right out of it. Took her a good twelve hours just to wake up."

"Hang on, hold the phone," I said. "Look, you two, I don't think we're ever going to figure this one out, but it doesn't really matter. What matters is that some thug isn't going to come banging on our door looking for Rowan, and for a change, we're not going to find ourselves staring down the wrong end of a gun at the end of the day. That's a victory, as far as I'm concerned. Come on, let's get inside and get to bed. I'm beat."

I pulled up in front of my building. It wasn't as opulent as Rowan's, but it sure looked good right about now. Within fifteen minutes, I was in my bathrobe, fixing a bed for Flavia on the couch.

"Aren't you forgetting something?" Dawn was in her pyjamas, and she stood in the bathroom door, speaking through a mouthful of toothpaste.

"What?"

"Shouldn't you call Benjamin?"

"What for?" It's not like we called one another every night, or something. Besides, I'd just seen him, not two hours ago.

Dawn retreated to the bathroom, spat, rinsed, and reappeared in the doorway. "Mom, are you losing it, or what? We just got back from Rowan's place, and she saw Jimmy this afternoon. And he could be over there again, by now. Maybe Hendricks thinks he's through with him, but it sounds like he's plotting to kidnap his own sister now. I think the least you can do is let your boyfriend know about it." She said it like having a boyfriend was some kind of nasty condition, right up there with psoriasis. I let it pass.

"You're right." I dialled Benjamin's number, but got his answering machine. I hung up again. "He's asleep."

"Keep trying, Mom! Come on, it's only ten after twelve — if the police hustle it, they can get there before Jimmy leaves! If he's really on the up and up, he can explain himself to them when they get there, right?"

"Why don't you call your cop buddy, the OPP guy?"

"Fine, I will. Give me that." She grabbed the phone.

Given the hour, I don't know why we expected to find

Hendricks at his desk, but after a brief wait, Dawn was talking to him. She explained our visit to Rowan's house, and Rowan's fear that Jimmy planned to hold her against her will. When she hung up, Dawn looked triumphant.

"They're going over as we speak," she said. "It's not OPP jurisdiction, but Hendricks said they'd get the Ottawa police right on it. I bet they catch Jimmy red-handed."

"Doing what? Visiting his sister?"

"Mom, don't be obtuse!" Dawn rolled her eyes. "Weren't you listening before? If they find him at Rowan's place, trying to strong-arm her into his car with some big enforcer named Aaron, they might realize that he's more involved in this than they thought, right?"

"I guess so." To be honest I really didn't care much, one way or the other. "Okay, is it all right if we go to bed now? I really need some sleep."

"I'll second that," Flavia said.

"Oh, Mom? One more thing. Constable Hendricks said someone might be over tomorrow sometime to take statements from us, if things go down the way I think they will over at Rowan's. Okay?"

"Shit, again?" Flavia didn't look pleased. "I really don't think much of all this, you know. Having all those cops around yesterday and this morning was giving me the jitters. I started feeling guilty, even though I hadn't done a thing."

"Don't I know it," I said. "Well, never mind. We'll jump off that bridge when we come to it. I think we'll all feel better if we get some sleep." Queen of Platitudes, that would be me.

However, within a few minutes, the lights were out, and I was, if not sleeping the dreamless sleep of the innocent, at least horizontal. It was a definite improvement.

12

SUNDAY, OCTOBER 16
Sun conjunct Mercury ✦
Venus conjunct Mars, conjunct Pluto ✦

Sunday morning, I slept in. When I woke, it was to the relentless patter of rain on my bedroom window. The apartment was chilly, and I wrapped my bathrobe around me and warmed my feet in the lambskin slippers Peter had bought me for Hannukah years ago, before we ever knew our daughter would become an animal rights maniac. Her rabid vegetarianism and insistence on wearing no animal products only evolved a couple of years ago, and while I admire her ability to stick to her principles, I have to admit I don't necessarily share them. I'm sure this is a moral failing of some kind, but tough.

Dawn was still asleep, but Flavia was already up. She was working her way through my accumulated piles of magazines, some of which dated back three or four years. I'm always thinking I'll get around to reading and/or throwing them out, but they seem to breed when I'm not looking, and all of a sudden, where there were two, there are ten.

"Hey," she said, from behind an old *Vanity Fair*. "Did you know all this stuff about Dr. Laura? Sheesh!"

"Nope, but I suspected it all along," I replied, en route to the kitchen and my one essential household appliance, the coffeemaker. I ground the beans and set the coffee to brew, then slouched back into the living room.

Flavia put the magazine to one side and rubbed her hands together, trying to warm them up. "Listen, I'm thinking I shouldn't impose on your hospitality any longer," she said. "You know, I was supposed to leave tomorrow morning, but I'm wondering now if I should change my ticket and take off this afternoon. It's not like y'all need an extra person hanging around here, now that we're not doing the AstroFest, right? And I'm really kind of wanting to just get home and lay low for a bit."

"Flavia, don't be silly! I know this weekend hasn't exactly been a barrel of laughs, but I really have enjoyed having you here. And my mother's expecting you to join us for supper. You incur the wrath of Rosie at your peril, you know!"

Flavia chuckled, but shook her head. "Honey, it's been a hell of a couple of days. I need to get back home, get my head on straight, you know? You and Dawn are just the sweetest people, but I never expected to get involved in a murder when I came up here, and I really just want to get back to normal."

"Flavia, are you afraid you'll have to talk to the police again?" I don't know where that one came from, but it was out before I could stop it.

She flushed. "No! No, that's not it at all! I didn't do anything wrong, so why should I be afraid?"

"Well, that's just what I was thinking. But you sounded pretty uncomfortable last night when Dawn said Hendricks would be sending someone over, so I wondered ..."

"Look, when we were on the island, I had the distinct feeling that the police thought I had something to do with Mandy's death. I already told you, sometimes I get flashes of what people are feeling. And that Henricks guy was looking at me real funny for a while there. I didn't, I couldn't — I'd never do that to anyone, no matter how I felt about them, and believe me, until Friday, I hadn't thought about Mandy in dog's years. And even at my lowest point, I never would have thought about actually killing anyone."

"Well then, you don't have to worry, right? It's not like you've got a rap sheet as long as your arm, is it?"

She flushed even more intensely. "Don't be ridiculous. I just don't like being involved in all this. It feels like ... like bad karma, or something."

"Well, it's up to you. I can't stop you, that's for sure."

"Katy, I — no, never mind. Pass me the phone, would you?" She dialled the airline, and within ten minutes she'd switched her ticket to a flight that left just before noon. I didn't really want her to leave, but I could see the sense of her argument. If I'd been her, I'd have been longing for my own bed, and some measure of sanity again.

By the time Dawn stumbled out of her room, rubbing her eyes and complaining that there was no tofu in the house, Flavia was nearly packed.

"Hey, you going already?" Dawn flopped into the armchair. "I thought you didn't leave until tomorrow. I was going to take you down to the Market today."

"I'm sorry, honeybunch, I really am. I was hoping I could prevail on your mama to give me a lift to the airport." Flavia didn't look at me.

"Of course," I said. "I just wish you'd reconsider —" I stopped myself. It was her decision to make, and I couldn't stop her, no matter how misguided I thought she might be.

It's not a particularly long drive from Centretown to the airport, but the dismal weather and our restrained spirits made it seem endless. The trees along the airport parkway had begun to lose their leaves, and the ones that remained were no longer brilliant, but faded and sad-looking in the rain.

We hugged Flavia good-bye outside the US departures area, and she left, turning to wave as she sailed past the ticket agents.

"Wow, that was some hasty exit," Dawn commented. "I thought she wasn't supposed to go back till tomorrow?"

I shrugged. "She was a bit worried about the cops coming over again today. I think we were all unnerved when Mandy died, and Flavia has this paranoid idea that the cops are out to get her. She said she has some kind of psychic ability or something, and she could feel that Hendricks suspected her. I think it's her own guilty conscience talking, not some sixth sense."

"So what — is she a serial bank robber, or something? What does she have to feel guilty about?"

"Well, I think she wasn't exactly heartbroken to see Mandy die — but maybe she felt badly about not feeling worse, you know what I mean? Plus, our generation — the ones who grew up in the sixties — tend to have a healthy fear of authority, you know."

"Yeah, all that protesting and smoking illegal substances. Peace, love and eternal grooviness. Well, it's too bad she had to go. She would have liked Sabte's roast beef."

By the time we got back home, the light on the answering machine was blinking furiously. The first message was from Hendricks, saying he and another cop would be by to chat with us at around two. The second was from Benjamin.

"Katy? Did you try to phone me last night? Your number was on my call display. Listen, something's come up.

I need to talk to you about the murder on Sycamore Island. I'll call back, and we can set something up, okay?"

"What the hell is that all about?" Dawn demanded. "Since when does the Exalted Benjamin have anything to do with OPP business? I bet he just wants to stick his nose in, get a piece of the action. He can't stand to see someone else investigating a major crime ..."

"Come on, Dawn, give it a rest, would you? You were the one who told me to call him last night, remember? Besides, Benjamin's a very nice person. You just have to get to know him. He's actually got a pretty good sense of humour, if you'd give him half a chance."

"Huh. Well, I'd like to know what he thinks he's doing, that's all. I bet Hendricks won't be very happy if Benjamin starts tromping all over the OPP case in his size thirteens. Hendricks told me sometimes police get totally territorial about their cases, you know." She was obviously pleased to be privy to this bit of cop talk.

"Whatever. Listen, do you want some lunch? I think there's some leftover curried lentils in the freezer, I could heat it up."

We were eating our lunch at the kitchen table, Dawn absorbed in a sci-fi thriller she'd borrowed from Sylvie, while I glanced through the sales flyers from the local grocery store, searching for deals that might help me save a buck or three, when the doorbell sounded. Dawn jumped up, but I was in no particular hurry. Carefully, I chewed and swallowed my mouthful of lentils, one of Dawn's specialties, and pushed back my chair.

Dawn, Hendricks and another officer I didn't recognize were already ensconced in the living room when I sauntered in and sat down.

"Ms. Klein, nice to see you again." Hendricks' smile didn't quite reach his eyes. "Your daughter here tells us you have some information about Rowan Healey?"

"Yes, we do." Dawn leaned forward eagerly. "She called here last night, while my mother and Flavia were out at the movies. She said she needed to talk to my mom, that it was urgent, and that Mom shouldn't call back, because it would be too dangerous."

Hendricks cocked his head, like a dog on scent. "She said that — that it would be too dangerous? Did she use those exact words?"

Dawn paused for a moment. "Okay, I don't think she used the word 'dangerous'. She said there might be someone monitoring her calls. So then she did call back, after my mom got home, and she said she wanted Mom to come over there, and when we got there —"

"Wait — 'we'? You both went to Ms. Healey's home?"

"Well, yeah. I wouldn't let Mom go alone — I thought she might need my help. And Mom's friend Flavia came with us, too. We couldn't just leave her sitting here. So when we got there, Rowan was all agitated and upset, and she said her brother, Jimmy — the one I told you about, you know, who ran away from the island before you could question him? — well, she said he was practically holding her prisoner, and that he'd hired some thug to watch her every move, and that this Aaron guy was going to take her away somewhere, for her own protection, he claimed. Only Jimmy and Aaron had to go take care of something for a little while last night, and Rowan wanted to come home and stay with us, to get away from them."

The other cop scribbled furiously, trying to keep up with Dawn's barrage of words. Meanwhile, Hendricks turned to me. I more or less repeated Dawn's story, without the editorial commentary, and confirmed Rowan's outrageous request to stay with us. Hendricks narrowed his eyes thoughtfully.

"How would you describe Ms. Healey's emotional state at the time you left her?" he asked.

"Distraught. Upset. I think she was afraid her brother and his friend might come back, but she also didn't want to get him into any trouble. She said he was trying to force her to leave town for a while, but he wouldn't tell her why. She wanted to stay with us, but I told her that would be impossible — the last thing I wanted was to have her brother come pounding on my door. I don't go looking for trouble, especially where my family's safety is concerned."

"Of course not. So Ms. Healey was distressed, but still alive when you left her residence?"

My heart sank. In my experience, the police only ask this kind of question when the person under discussion is no longer presumed to be on the earthly plane, so to speak.

"Is she — is Rowan all right?" I asked. My throat felt too tight, and I choked the words out. "Has something happened?"

The two officers exchanged glances. "We're not really at liberty to discuss the case just now," Hendricks said. "There are reasons of jurisdiction ..."

"What do you mean?" Dawn demanded. She'd obviously caught the hint too.

Hendricks looked like his underwear had suddenly grown several sizes too tight. "I'm afraid I can't really discuss this any further." Then he looked straight at me. "Ms. Klein, I have to ask you and your daughter for a bit of assistance here. I need you, both of you, to keep everything we've discussed here in complete confidence. Do you think you can do that?"

Dawn's eyes grew very wide. "Why? What's going on?"

"Nothing that we can talk about at this point in time,

Dawn," Hendricks said. "But our investigation is at a very delicate point right now. I don't want anything to jeopardize it, if you know what I mean. And that means no discussion of anything we've talked about today. Not with friends, not with loved ones. Okay?"

Dawn nodded. "Sure. I understand."

Hendricks smiled. "We do appreciate your help in the matter." He and the other cop got to their feet in unison, as though on some invisible signal. "If you think of anything else that might be helpful, you have my number."

When they'd gone, Dawn cocked her head at me. "What the ... what do you think that was all about, Mom? Something must have happened to Rowan!"

"It sure sounded like it. I can't figure out what they meant about jurisdiction issues, though, unless —"

"Unless the Ottawa-Carleton police are working on one case, and the OPP are on the other," Dawn finished. "That must be it, Mom. Why don't you call Benjamin? He'd tell you."

"So suddenly it's okay for me to phone him?" I couldn't resist a light dig.

Dawn had the grace to blush.

"Well, I didn't say he was totally useless," she admitted. "He might be able to give us some information."

"Boy, that's so big of you! You're just the soul of charity, you know that?"

"Well? Are you going to phone him, or not?"

"Nah. He said he'd be calling me, that he was busy. There's no rush — whatever happened, there's not a lot we can do about it. Plus, didn't you hear what Hendricks just said about keeping our mouths shut about this?"

"Sure, but that doesn't include other cops, right? I mean, Benjamin's supposed to be this big shot, so it's probably okay to talk to him about it."

"We'll see, Dawn. Maybe we should check with Hendricks first, don't you think?"

I tried to sound nonchalant, as I struggled to override the inner voice that prodded me: *What about Rowan? You left her there, and now she's — well, we don't know what's happened to her, but it doesn't look good. I hope you're good and pleased with yourself! If you'd brought her home, she'd be here now, not lying in a ditch somewhere ...*

Shut up, I argued with myself. It's not your fault. She's probably fine, anyway. She just went out of town with Jimmy, and he'd never hurt his own sister. Would he?

Our curried lentils were stone-cold now, and neither of us felt very hungry. It was already three in the afternoon, and we'd be chowing down at my parents' place in a few hours. I scraped the remains of our lunch into the garbage, and did a cursory tidying of the apartment. I admit it: I was killing time until I heard from Benjamin.

I was trying to cram a stack of papers and assorted junk from the kitchen table into my tiny, already overstuffed writing desk, when a bunch of stuff popped loose from the pile and fell to the floor. Cursing quietly, I knelt to gather it up again. There, amongst the bills and miscellaneous advertisements, was the business card Rowan had tried to give me last night. Jimmy's birth data.

I sat back on my heels, looking at the card more closely. Well, I had nothing constructive to do right now anyway. Might as well take a gander.

Miraculously, Dawn was not hogging the computer, so I called up my astrology program, punched in the data, and voilà! Instant birth chart. Jimmy had the Sun in iconoclastic Aquarius, with proud, me-first Leo rising, and an analytical Virgo Moon. Interesting combination, I thought, grabbing a pencil and starting to make notes on a pad of yellow paper. He had a tight stellium — the Sun, Venus and Mercury — sitting right on the cusp of his seventh house of marriage. He'd look for the unusual, the off-beat in a marriage partner, and he'd have a unique approach to the institution itself. That Leo rising would give him a sense of determination, a need to call the shots; I wondered how this had gone over with Mandy. Not particularly well, I shouldn't imagine. Funny, though — an Aquarius cluster in the seventh house seemed to signify someone who wanted to run away from the constraints of marriage, not someone determined to cling to his partner. Hadn't Rowan said that ending the marriage had been Mandy's idea? And Jimmy had told me his impromptu visit to the island had been spurred by his wish to reconcile with his beloved Mandy. Something wasn't adding up here.

Aries ruled Jimmy's midheaven, so he was no wimp when it came to his career and public image. That figured — he was some kind of high-powered financier, wasn't he? I turned the business card over. Foreign Exchange Bank of Canada. Funny, I'd never heard of that particular financial institution. Probably a financial haven for some of our off-shore millionaires, the ones who want to claim the benefits of Canadian citizenship without actually doing anything so inconvenient as paying taxes, to filter their money out of the country.

Back to the chart. Mars, the ruler of the midheaven, sat in moody, intense Scorpio, from whence it not only squared Pluto, but was inconjunct the Midheaven. Hoo boy. Talk about your basic affliction of Mars — this guy would like nothing better than a good fight to clear the pipes from time to time, and woe betide anyone who got in his way! Strong-willed wouldn't even begin to describe him, I thought, scribbling furiously. He wouldn't be the sort to go off like a firecracker — rather, he'd go into a slow burn whenever he was thwarted, and the intensity of the anger would build, rather than dissipate, over time. In the best-case scenario, I could see him diverting all that Mars/Pluto energy into his work, throwing himself into it and climbing straight to the top. Authority figures could be a problem for him, though, dating back to childhood. This was a person used to acting on his own, who wouldn't take kindly to being told what to do.

I wondered how he'd managed to co-exist with Mandy. She'd had an exceptionally strong Mars influence in her chart, too, hadn't she? I tried to recall what Flavia had said. Hadn't Mandy's Mars opposed Pluto? Putting Jimmy and Mandy in a room together would be roughly the equivalent of adding nitro to glycerine. Good thing they'd never had any children — I wouldn't want to be the one to get caught in their crossfire.

I was so engrossed in Jimmy's chart, I almost didn't hear the rap at the door.

"Mom, aren't you going to get that?" Dawn called, from the direction of the bathroom.

Reluctantly, I closed the screen I'd been working on, and went to peer through the spy-hole on the door. It was Benjamin, and there was someone behind him I didn't recognize. I slipped the latch open.

"Thought for a moment you'd gone out," Benjamin said, without giving me his usual peck on the cheek. "Katy Klein, this is Staff Sergeant Robert Fowler. He's with the Major Crimes unit too, and we're working together right now. Do you have a minute?"

Something must really be up — I hadn't heard Benjamin this formal since I'd thought he wanted to arrest me for killing Adam, lo these many months ago. Clearly, he wasn't eager to display the nuances of our relationship to this Fowler guy, whoever he might be. Well, fine, I could play along with that.

"Of course, gentlemen, do come in." I held the door open and smiled my most saccharine smile. Benjamin gave me an apologetic look as he passed. Robert Fowler was a tall, thin man bordering on gaunt, with a thatch of black hair that he'd slicked back more or less successfully, except for a cowlick that just wouldn't quit. It stuck up on the back of his head like a rooster's comb. He wore wire-rimmed glasses, and looked more like a university professor than a cop, but as he came into my apartment, he took in every detail, the way I've seen Benjamin do countless times before. Something they learn at cop school, Benjamin told me once. Always be aware of your surroundings.

"Ma'am, I understand you have information regarding the whereabouts of Rowan Healey?" Fowler started right in, no preliminaries.

"What's going on? I've already spoken to Constable Hendricks of the OPP, just this afternoon," I said. "My daughter and I told him everything. Can't you just talk to him?"

Fowler shook his head. "He's not investigating this particular case, ma'am. He's looking into the Weatherburn murder. Detective Benjamin and I are investigating another incident."

"What kind of 'incident'?" I persisted. "Why won't anyone tell me what's going on?"

"Rowan Healey has disappeared, Katy," Benjamin said. "There's reason to believe her life might be in danger. And you were her last known contact."

Ah. That explained Hendricks' discomfort when he'd been here earlier. Why is it always so hard to pry information out of cops?

"Oh. Okay. Well, as far as I know, she was worried

that her brother, Jimmy, wanted her to leave town for a while, with some body-guard type he'd hired for the occasion. Aaron, I think she said his name was. That's really all I know."

"Did she tell you why her brother wanted her to leave town?" Fowler thrust his hands into his pants pockets and jingled some coins. His left foot had taken on a life of its own and was tapping away on the hardwood floor.

"She wasn't really clear on that point, no. She didn't say this out loud, but my guess is that she suspected Jimmy might have killed his wife. Rowan seemed really freaked out, and she seemed afraid of her brother, even though she obviously loves him. Actually," I amended, "maybe she was more afraid of this Aaron guy. She said Jimmy had always looked after her, but she was nervous about going off with someone she didn't know."

"Did she say where Jimmy's friend might be about to take her?" Fowler stopped jingling his spare change.

"Um … Owen Sound? I can't remember. Out in the boonies somewhere, I know that for sure. I don't think Rowan was clear about where they were going, either. I think she said Something-or-other Sound — Owen Sound, Parry Sound, something like that." I motioned with my hand, the universal signal for "way the hell out there someplace."

"Katy, Owen Sound and Parry Sound are pretty far away from one another," Benjamin said gently.

"Yeah, well, she didn't show me on a map," I snapped. "I'm just telling you what she told me. If you don't like it, you can always go hunt down some other witness to harass."

"Katy, no one's harassing you …" There was an edge to Benjamin's voice.

Fowler jumped in, changing the subject rapidly.

"And you say this Aaron person was going to take her to wherever they were going?"

"I think so. At least, that's the way it sounded. She said Aaron was going to be watching her, and that Jimmy had told her the less she knew, the safer she'd be. He told her he's involved in something dangerous, and he wants her out of the way. Reading between the lines, it sounds like he's got himself mixed up in something criminal, and that's why his wife was killed. Of course, he could just be saying that to cover himself, who knows? Rowan said Jimmy had looked out for her since they were kids, so she felt like she had to trust him, but she was still scared. She asked ..." My voice trailed off.

Benjamin prompted me. "What did she ask you, Katy?"

"Well, she wanted to come over here, to hide from Jimmy. I told her no. Now I'm not so sure I made the right decision."

Benjamin rubbed my shoulder, the first spontaneous sign of affection since he and Fowler had arrived. "It's okay, Katy. You did the right thing. This isn't something you'd want to get mixed up in."

Dawn had come into the room, and was listening carefully. "I have a question," she said.

Benjamin cocked a bushy eyebrow in her direction. "Go for it."

"Well, when Hendricks and that other guy from the OPP came here a while ago, they told us to keep a lid on what we knew about Rowan and Jimmy and Aaron. Why? What's so delicate about this case?"

Benjamin looked startled for all of a millisecond, before his usual saturnine mask came down. He and Fowler exchanged glances, and then he said, "It's probably just one of those jurisdictional things, Dawn. Nothing for you to worry about." To Fowler he said, "Okay, I think we should get back. They might have some word by now."

Fowler nodded. "Thank you, Ms. Klein. We'll be in touch."

Oh, goody. I could hardly wait. I saw them to the door, closed it behind them.

"Wow, so he actually did it. He kidnapped his own sister! What a creep!" Dawn leaned against the doorway to the bathroom. Her body language fairly screamed, "I told you so!" but she had the maturity not to say it out loud. Or the self-preservation instinct.

"Dawn, I'm not going to argue with you about this. Yeah, I guess it does look like Jimmy's gone and got himself in a whack of trouble. Now, do you mind? All this excitement's worn me down. I'm not as young as I used to be, you know. I'm going to take a nap."

And that is exactly what I did, though I didn't exactly sleep. I lay on the bed, with images of wasps swirling round in my head, and dead, swollen bodies, and cops swarming around the island with notebooks in hand, writing down everything I said ... I returned to wakefulness with a jolt, the phone ringing next to my ear. Eyes half-closed, I groped for the receiver.

"Hello?"

"Katy?" The voice was distant and thready, and for a moment I didn't recognize it. Then I sat up, pressing the receiver to my ear to hear better.

"Rowan? Is that you? Where are you?"

"I'm not sure ... I'm in a washroom, at a gas station. We've been driving for hours, and I told him I had to pee. Katy, please help me!"

"Okay. Okay." Think, Katy. "Um ... do you know which highway you're on? Did you see any signs?"

"Oh, God, I don't know ... maybe, uh, sixty? I've never been this way before."

"Is Jimmy with you?"

"No! Oh, God, I have to go. Someone just came in." Click. The line went dead.

Shit. I closed my eyes, tried to slow my breathing. I dialled Benjamin's work number, got his voice-mail. I relayed the conversation briefly and hung up, rubbing my forehead. Another minute and I'd have known what kind of car they were driving, who she was with, where they were going ...

No. Wrong. This is not your business, Katy. You passed on the information, that's all you need to do. I got up and went to the bathroom, splashed some water on my face. I really should give Greg a call, follow up on my resolution to get some professional help. Not that there was anything wrong with me, but it might be good just to talk to someone once in a while. Unload, get those feelings out there. All the stuff I used to tell my own clients.

"Mom, who was on the phone?" Dawn called from the alcove, where she was ensconced with her computer.

"No one," I lied. "I think it was a wrong number."

"Mom!" She stretched the word into three, possibly four, syllables. "I heard you ask if Jimmy was there. It was Rowan, wasn't it?"

"Yeah, okay, you got me. It was, and I've already passed the message on to Benjamin. And that's the end of it, okay? Now, do you have your shoes on? We have to get over to your grandparents' place in time for supper."

Dawn gave me a look as she passed me on the way to grab her jacket, but she didn't say anything. I appreciated her restraint. Maybe she was gaining wisdom.

13

My parents' house is in the west end of the city, an enclave of expansive post-war bungalows and semi-detached houses set back on huge treed lots with lawns that could double as golf courses. I'd spent my childhood and much of my misspent youth out here, tooling up and down Carling in my best friend Carmen's '65 Mustang, dropping in at the Lady Jane doughnut shop to hobnob with the bikers, who'd seemed exotic and dangerous at the time. Ah, youth.

As we pulled into my parents' driveway, a familiar feeling washed over me — not peaceful, exactly, but lulled. Comforted. Even before we got to the front door, a faint, tantalizing smell of roasting beef reached my nostrils, and I was suddenly ravenous.

My mother opened the door before I'd touched the handle.

"*Mamaleh*! Dawn, sweetheart, come in! How's my little girl? Has your mama been feeding you? You look a little pale, Katy, are you getting enough sleep? And where is your friend?"

"Mama, slow down!" I protested. "Flavia had to go home, something came up."

Mama clucked. "Nothing serious, I hope. Well, never

mind, you're here, and that's enough. Now, don't just stand around like strangers, come in, come in!"

We hung our jackets in the hall closet. Rosie hovered nearby, and ushered us into the kitchen. "Masha and your father are out in the back yard, feeding his little birds. They're like his babies, you know. Pays them more attention than he does me."

"Oh, come on, Ma, you know that's not true," I began, until I caught the twinkle in her eye. Lighten up, Katy, I told myself. "Mama, the roast smells amazing."

I sniffed appreciatively, and was rewarded with one of my mother's beaming smiles.

"You see, I knew you were hungry! We eat in a few minutes, I just want to finish frenching these beans. You're still eating meat, aren't you, Katy? Not like my *meshuggeh* granddaughter here. Eats nothing but vegetables now, and she's practically wasting away." She rumpled Dawn's hair to soften her words.

"Sabte, come on — I don't mind if other people eat meat, I just choose not to, that's all."

"To be fair, Mama, we're both eating a lot more healthy. And she's teaching me how to cook." A slight exaggeration, but I caught Dawn's grateful glance, and smiled back at her.

This satisfied Rosie, who sat at the kitchen table, expertly slicing green beans into a pot. I leaned against the counter, peering out the window for a glimpse of my father. There he was, down among the lilac bushes, pouring bird seed into one of his feeders, and chatting with a young woman I took to be Masha, the Russian rabbi. She hardly looked old enough to be a rabbi — with her long hair, tied back carelessly into a ponytail, and her flushed apple cheeks, I'd have put her closer to Dawn's age than my own.

"Mama, tell me again — who's Masha, and why is she here?" I opened a drawer and began counting out silverware, while Dawn spread a cream-coloured table cloth over the dining room table.

"Oy. Such a story she could tell you," Rosie said. "She's here for a week only, doing a workshop with Rabbi Schiffman. Then she goes back to Montreal."

"But I thought you said she was from Russia? What's she doing in Montreal?"

"She's been there almost a year, since she left St. Petersburg — you should ask her to tell you that whole *megillah*. What a trip! But the *shul* in Montreal hired her right away to work with the new immigrants, the ones from Russia who don't even know what it is to be Jewish, poor things."

"How can you be Jewish and not know it?" Dawn asked.

"*Feh*!" Rosie mimicked spitting. "The Communists — nearly as bad as the Nazis." She scowled at the beans as she sliced them with extra vigour. "They suppressed all religion, but especially the Jews. Tore down the *shuls*, threw people in prison, kept Jews from leaving the country. Jews, families who'd lived there for centuries, started saying they were Russians or Ukrainians, just so their children could go to university or get a job. So, over the years, they forgot. They didn't light the *shabbos* candles, they didn't say the prayers, they didn't celebrate the holidays. Stalin didn't have to kill them — he just erased their memories. And the leaders after him were just as bad." She clucked in disapproval.

"That's awful!" Dawn said.

My mother shrugged. "It's Russia." She put down her paring knife and wiped her hands on her apron.

"But aren't things different now?" I asked.

"Different, yes. But still there are thousands, maybe hundreds of thousands of Jews in Russia who still don't know a *mezuzzah* from a *tuches*. And some of them have come to Canada. That's what Masha has been doing — teaching them."

As if on cue, the kitchen door opened, and Masha stepped in, followed by my father. His face was wreathed in smiles as he hugged first Dawn, then me.

"Masha, this is my daughter, Katy," he said. "And her daughter, Dawn."

Up close, Masha looked older than I'd thought at first. The first hints of crow's feet were forming at the edges of her twinkling dark blue eyes, and her thick chestnut hair was streaked with grey. But she spoke in rapid-fire, deeply-accented English, and her voice was girlish and high.

"Is a wonderful garden your father builds," she told me. "We see the birds, they eat from our hands! I think they are ..." She paused, searching for the word. "Trains? No, trained. Trained to come to him. Quite wonderful." She pronounced it "voun-derful", just like Mama did sometimes, when she was tired.

"Tch!" My mother shook her head. "Bernard, you know you shouldn't let those filthy birds come so close — didn't Dr. Morgenstern tell us they could carry disease?"

My father nodded. "We'll wash." One side of his face crinkled into an affectionate smile at Rosie, but the other remained mask-like. Since his stroke a couple of years ago, my father had become even more economical with his words. He was more mobile now, but a few traces remained of his "cerebro-vascular accident."

"Yes, yes, wash, and use lots of soap. Not too long for supper now, and maybe you could ask Masha to say a little blessing? After all, we don't have a rabbi to visit every day, do we? We'll put you to work, Masha!" My mother bustled around the kitchen, nattering more to herself than any of us. "Katy, it's too bad your friend had to go back home, there's more than enough beef. I told the butcher we'd need enough to feed six, and he gives me a roast that could feed an army. Where did you say she was from, again, your friend?"

"Michigan, Mama. She lives in Ann Arbor. She's from Texas originally, though."

Rosie nodded, as though this explained everything.

I opened the door to the breakfront in the dining room, and pulled out a platter for the meat. Masha peered past me, curious about the array of antique plates, silver *kiddish* cups, *menorim*, and bric-a-brac.

"Ah, look at this fish! We see nothing like this in my country. This looks very old." She put out her hand, and I gave her the hammered silver, hollow fish, whose joints allowed it to twist and flex back and forth.

"It's a *havdalah* fish," I explained. "It belonged to my father's family. You put the spices in the mouth, like this. Then you pass it around the table, and everyone is supposed to smell it, to make a sweet week."

"Is to make the fragrance of *shabbos* last all week long," Masha corrected me, with a smile. "And the braided candle is to make shadow and light. We say thank you for making darkness and light, *shabbos* and the rest of the week. Then we put the candle out in the wine, and —" She snapped her fingers. "*Shabbos* ends. Rest of the week starts."

I forgot — I was trying to teach a rabbi about *shabbos* traditions. But Masha looked so little like any rabbi I'd ever encountered, I could perhaps be forgiven my lapse. We trailed back into the kitchen, where I asked my mother to assign me another task.

"Katy, sit!" she commanded. "There's nothing left to do, and you make me feel old, fussing around like this. Why don't you just sit for a while, while I finish up here?"

"Sure, Mama." I pulled up a chair at the kitchen table, and Masha went off to wash her hands for supper.

Mama looked around, satisfied herself that we were alone. "Katy, I have to ask you something."

"Mm-hmm? What, Mama?"

"I saw on the news this morning, something about a teacher who got killed. Drowned in Dow's Lake. They mentioned Dawn's school, and I was afraid "

I was silent for a moment. "Mama, I wasn't going to tell you. I didn't want you to worry."

"I thought so." She carried the pot of green beans to the sink and drained the water from them. "How is she taking it? She looked a little pale when you came in, and she's been so quiet tonight."

"Not very well. He went missing a while ago, with the money for a class trip. Now this."

"I had to turn off the television. Masha couldn't watch it — she begged me to turn off the news, but she didn't have to ask me twice. We were shocked." My mother shook her head sadly, and sighed. It always surprised me, her being staggered by the brutality of modern life. A survivor of Hitler's death camps, she'd lived through unimaginable horrors, and somehow I always felt that this ought to have inured her to the news of the day. But it hadn't. My mother's gift was her capacity for moral outrage, for renewed grief at each new act of inhumanity.

I had only told her the sketchiest of truths about the events of last winter, and now I was glad I'd kept most of it to myself. If one of us had to carry around the memory, better it should be me. Blinking ferociously, I opened a plastic bag full of toasted slivered almonds, and sprinkled a few on the platter of beans, for garnish. Then I carried the roast out to the table.

The others filed into the dining room, while my mother and I brought dishes full of green beans, rolls, horseradish to accompany the roast, and a potato kugel my mother had just whipped up for the occasion. No one could accuse Rosie Klein of underfeeding her family.

Masha said a brief blessing, and we all sat down, tucking in enthusiastically. For a while, all that could be heard was the clinking of silverware on china, and subdued sounds of appreciation.

"Masha, Mama says you're here to teach new immigrants about Judaism." It felt a little lame, after talking to Rosie about the grisly remains of Dawn's teacher, but I've never been great at the art of small talk.

Masha didn't answer me at once. She seemed to be searching for words. "Yes ... immigrants, that's right. New Jews, I call them. They are not, of course, but they feel new, to themselves and to me. I'm going to be working with Rabbi ... er, Rabbi ..."

"Schiffman," my mother supplied. "The new *rebbe* — he's only been here about, what, Bernard? Fifteen years?"

Dad nodded. "He's not new any more, Rosie." He grinned his off-centre grin, taking the edge out of his words.

"Maybe not, but he's so young! Of course, young rabbis bring new ideas, new energy," she amended, realizing that her guest was even younger than Schiffman, whom I estimated to be in his mid-fifties at least.

Between mouthfuls, we chatted in a desultory manner about synagogue politics, a subject on which my mother has an almost endless supply of both gossip and opinions. I glanced at Dawn a few times, trying to gauge her mood, but her face was set in the blandly polite mask she wears when the conversation around her doesn't hinge on her favourite topics: her computer, the environment, vegetarian cooking, or, lately, the assumed guilt of Jimmy in the murder of his soon-to-be-ex-wife. Not to accuse my daughter of having a one-track mind, or anything.

We had finished dessert, and were sipping decaf as we were treated to an exposition on the foolhardiness of the president of the congregation, who apparently saw no need for outreach to Russian Jews, when the first yawn crept up on me. My mother, of course, pounced.

"Oh, I knew you must be tired. I can always tell — you get such dark circles under your eyes," she said. "You should go on home, get some sleep, *mamaleh*."

She and my father exchanged glances. He nodded, as if something had been settled between them.

"But before you go, there's something your father and I want to show you." Mama stood up, gesturing to us to follow.

I must have shown my alarm. Dad chuckled. "Don't worry. It's nothing bad. Come."

Masha, Dawn and I followed my parents through the kitchen, down the stairs to the garage. Dad opened the door to the garage, and ushered us through with a small flourish.

We stood, uncertain what to expect. Their car, a lumbering Crown Victoria that looked nearly new despite being more than a decade old, gleamed softly under the solitary bulb in the ceiling. Had they had it painted? What was I supposed to be noticing, here? I looked at my mother questioningly.

"*Mamaleh*, we've been thinking," she said. "Your father hasn't been able to drive since his stroke, and you know I've always hated this car. I can hardly see over the dash, and I feel like I'm driving a bus. I decided last week, it's time for us to get a smaller car, one I can drive myself. But this one is a good car, lots of life in it, and we thought, your father and I ..."

"We wanted to give it to you," he finished. "For your birthday."

Gulp. Okay, fine, my birthday had come and gone a short time ago, and my parents had already given me a gift — a book on astrology and Judaism. It was lovely, and I'd appreciated it, but this? I had to admit, a car would be a nice luxury — I sorely missed my beloved Karmann Ghia, which I'd had to relinquish when I'd left my good salary at the Royal Ottawa Hospital for the meagre earnings astrology now brought me. But this ... this land-yacht was not exactly what I'd have chosen. If I'd had the choice. The gas bills alone would put a huge dent in my careful budget.

Dawn was stifling a giggle — she could read the look on my face. Maybe I just wouldn't drive it very often. I could keep it in a garage somewhere downtown. Somewhere where no one could see it. The thing practically screamed, "Little old lady driver at the helm!"

"I don't know what to say," I said, at last. "It's too generous — really, you shouldn't ..."

"We can't have our granddaughter riding around in that rattletrap tin can Peter calls a car," Mama said, in a tone that dared me to contradict her. "And you're a grown woman. You should have a car of your own, Katy."

I stood there blinking, trying to think of the gracious response. What would Carmen have said? My stomach clenched at the unwanted reminder of my oldest friend, but I forced my mouth into a semblance of a smile.

"Well, thank you. This is ... really not what I expected! Mama, Dad, thank you both so much." I enfolded my parents in a hug, and kissed each of them in turn.

"Happy birthday, sweetheart," my father said. There were tears in his eyes. Truth be told, there were tears in mine, too.

14

Dawn and I drove the rental car home, telling my parents we'd come back the next day to collect The Behemoth, as Dawn had quickly dubbed my parents' too-generous gift.

"I thought you were going to fall over in a faint when they said it was your car now," Dawn giggled.

"Yeah, well, I couldn't very well tell them I wouldn't be caught dead in that great honking thing, could I? And they were so pleased to be able to give me something really special. God, I feel terrible for not appreciating it more."

"Well, you keep telling me you're getting old, Mom. Maybe this is really the car for you?" I could hear the grin in her voice, and I slapped her leg gently.

"Shut up, kid. Old is one thing. That car is quite another. That car says 'elderly, bordering on senile'. Or 'cop'. Take your pick."

"Well then, it'll come in handy, when you and Benjamin go hand in hand off into the sunset, won't it? Him being a cop and all."

"We're not going hand in hand anywhere, Dawn. You just wait till you get your own boyfriend. I'm planning to be merciless."

"Why do you think I haven't told you about him yet?"

I laughed, and reached out to give her hand a squeeze.

At home, the light was flashing on my answering machine, but I took my time getting to it — as usual when I return from a visit to my parents, I felt bloated and overfed, and I just wanted to sit down and digest my supper. Besides, I suspected my caller would be from one police department or another. Why spoil a perfectly good mood by getting into a discussion about who killed or kidnapped whom? They'd wait.

Dawn noticed the light, though, and stood over me, machine in hand. "Aren't you going to check this?"

"Kid, you are getting to be a major pain in the butt," I sighed, but I took the answering machine from her, set it down on the coffee table, and pushed the button. As I'd predicted, Benjamin was first up, and he was all business.

"Katy, got your message about Rowan. Thanks. Listen, I'd like to get in touch with your friend Flavia, okay? Could you have her call me back, as soon as you get this? There's a little confusion I want to clear up."

"Confusion? What kind of confusion? He doesn't think Flavia had anything to do with Mandy's death, does he? What an idiot!"

"Dawn, you're worse than I am — stop jumping to conclusions. He's not saying Flavia killed anyone. He's just saying there's some confusion, okay? Now, if you don't mind, I'm going to listen to the rest of my messages. Is that okay by you?"

"Yeah, sure," Dawn mumbled. "He's still an idiot."

That tore it. The tattered remains of my good mood vanished.

"Dawn, stop that this instant!" I commanded. "You know perfectly well that you're just saying that because you have a petty little grudge against Benjamin, and you don't want me going out with him. Well, he and I are seeing one another, and you're just going to have to get used to it, whether you like it or not! Like it or lump it, kid."

"Fine!" Dawn flushed with anger, turned on her heel and left the room, slamming the door to her bedroom as she went. There was a brief silence, followed by the sound of muffled sobbing.

I slumped into the couch, let my head rest against the back pillows. What was wrong with me? I knew Dawn was sensitive about my relationship with Benjamin, but I'd rubbed her nose in it all the same. I just couldn't say anything right to her these days, and frankly, she was getting on my nerves. All that raw, bounding energy, and she could be so damn stubborn and opinionated ... all right, all right, she was just like me. I admit it. But we'd always managed to accommodate one another before — what was different now? Was it some weird adolescent thing? Nah, she'd sailed through puberty with barely a nod to rampaging hormones. I'd thought she was above all that temper tantrum nonsense. I'd thought we had it made, the perfect mother and daughter duo. Well, maybe I'd just become too smug, and now my hubris was coming back to bite me.

It was early yet, but suddenly I was bone tired. I called Benjamin back, but he wasn't there — typical, to leave me a message telling me to call right away, and then not pick up the phone when I did. I left him a message anyway: "Benjamin, it's me, Katy. I don't know what confusion you want to clear up, but Flavia's already gone home. I have her e-mail address and phone number if you want them, though. Call in the morning, okay? I'm beat, and I'm going to bed."

I began my nightly routine: double-locking the front

door, checking the locks on all the windows, peering out each one to ensure that no evil-doers were hiding in the shrubbery outside. I only started doing this last winter, and sometimes I caught myself checking the same window twice, three times, just to be on the safe side. I knew I was venturing into obsessive-compulsive territory, but I couldn't seem to stop myself. Mark that down — something else to tell the shrink, when I got around to scheduling an appointment. Tomorrow. I'd call tomorrow.

I was brushing my teeth when I heard a small, tentative rap on the front door. I spat, rinsed and wiped my mouth. There it was again, only a bit louder. I got to the door and peered through the fish-eye lens. Benjamin. Alone this time.

It took me a few seconds to undo the locks and security chain, but finally I opened the door.

"Katy, I'm sorry," he said. "I didn't realize how late it was."

"It's only 10:30. Reasonable to expect me to be up, but didn't you get my message? Is this a social call, or what?"

He looked embarrassed. "Yeah. No. Sort of. I wanted to talk to you, but there are some business things I wanted to sort out, too. Do you mind?"

"Not really. Come on in. I got your message about Flavia — what's going on?" I crossed the room and settled on the couch, tucking my legs up under me, smoothing my bathrobe over my knees. Benjamin remained standing, fiddling with a button on his cuff.

"Well, some things have come up. I hate to spring this on you, especially after that thing with your friend last winter."

I took a deep breath, expelled it slowly. "Benjamin, do me a favour. Don't treat me like an idiot. What's going on? Is Flavia in trouble? Come on, just tell me. Whatever it is, I can take it."

He looked around the room. "Where is she? Has she gone to bed already?"

I shook my head. "No — if you ever listened to your telephone messages, you'd know. She's gone home."

"Home? What do you mean, 'home'? You mean, she's left the country?"

"Yeah, sure. She was tired, the island retreat had pretty much gone down the toilet, and she didn't feel like hanging around. What's wrong with that?"

Benjamin gave me a look. "A lot, but never mind. I'll deal with that in a second."

"Benjamin, what's going on? Why are you acting like the guy in *Dragnet* all of a sudden?"

"There's a lot you don't know about your friend Flavia, Katy. To start with, that's not her name." The button, which had been holding on by a couple of frayed threads, came off altogether. Benjamin sighed, tucked it into his pants pocket, and eased his bulky frame into the armchair across from me. I waited for him to speak.

"I thought you'd jump all over me when I said that," he said. "You don't look surprised."

"Well, I'm not. Come on, Benjamin — with a name like Flavia, you've got to think either her parents were both cruel and unusual, or she made it up. It's not exactly yer basic All-American name, right? But it's not a crime to take on a new name. At least I don't think it is. Am I wrong?"

"No. Not unless you use it to escape conviction for a felony. And I'm not saying she's doing that!" he added hastily, as though reading my mind. "It's just that she's got some ... well, some problem areas in her background. Stuff that's making our friends at the OPP a little antsy. And I have to tell you, her taking off like this doesn't make her look any better. I talked to Hendricks this afternoon about this Rowan Healey thing, and he filled me in. When I heard, I thought I'd better talk to you about it first."

I felt as though I'd swallowed a large rock, and it had just settled in the pit of my stomach.

"What do you mean?" I asked, knowing full well that I wouldn't like the answer, whatever it was.

"Well, it turns out that your friend, whose real name is Margaret Elliott, by the way, knew Mandy Weatherburn a little better than she was letting on. She told Hendricks and his crew that she'd met her briefly, but it goes further than that. They were classmates in college, and at least one of their old school chums recalls hearing Flavia ... that is, Margaret, saying she'd love to see Mandy dead."

"Oh, come on, Benjamin — how long ago was this? Weren't you ever young? People that age say all sorts of stupid things they don't really mean."

"Don't get all defensive, Katy. I'm not saying I think she offed Mandy, but we have to check up every lead we get."

"Okay, fine, but don't you think this is just a bit on the obscure side? I mean, Mandy's got a disgruntled soon-to-be-ex-husband running around on the loose, evading questioning by the police. Doesn't he look like a bit of a better prospect than someone who was pissed off with Mandy twenty-five or thirty years ago, over a stolen boyfriend?"

"You know about the stolen boyfriend?" Benjamin's voice was sharp.

I flushed. "Well, she did mention something about it, but I didn't think —"

"Dammit, Katy, you keep doing this!" Red in the face, Benjamin pounded a fist into his open palm. "You can never just tell me the whole story, can you? What is it with you? You think you know better than me, what's relevant to a case? What's wrong with you?"

My own face felt hot. "Nothing! There's nothing wrong with me! I just didn't want to see my friend get in trouble for something she couldn't have done, that's all! But I guess in your universe, that's some kind of major character flaw, right?"

"She is. Not. In. Trouble." Benjamin was making an obvious effort to control his temper. "Not yet, anyway. There's a difference between being a suspect and being wanted for questioning, as you should know by this time. And so far, she's in the latter category, by the skin of her teeth. So — is there anything else you conveniently forgot to mention to me? Maybe the killer confessed to you, but you thought I wouldn't really be that interested? Anything I should know?"

"No." I realized that I sounded like a sulky four-year-old. "Not a thing. Anyway, if Flavia's not in trouble, what's the big deal? Why are we having this fight?"

"Katy, you have this habit of shooting the messenger, do you know that?" Benjamin crossed his arms across his chest and cocked his head, looking at me impassively.

"Well, yeah, if the messenger is saying something patently silly, I do," I said.

"And you know for a fact that your *friend*," he spat the word out, "your dear friend whom you've never even met in person until this very weekend, had nothing to do with Ms. Weatherburn's death? You can tell me categorically that she couldn't have nursed a grudge over the years, then seen her chance and taken it?"

"No, I can't tell you that." My voice began to rise. "All I can tell you is that I know she didn't do it. She told me all about the baby ..." I stopped myself. Good one, Katy.

"She did, huh? And did she tell you about spending six years in the state mental hospital? And about sending death threats to Ms. Weatherburn on a regular basis for the next three years, until she was arrested and made a guest of the state for another year? We're not talking about a little college tiff here, Katy. Margaret Elliott had a major hate on for Mandy Weatherburn, and you said yourself, she knew Mandy was deathly allergic to wasp stings."

Shit. This is not what I wanted to hear. I threw my head back, breathed in through my nose, out through my mouth. Calm, Katy. Calm.

"Okay, Benjamin. You're right, I didn't know about that other stuff. But I was with Flavia for all but about ten minutes before Mandy died. I still don't see how she could get all the way from the lodge to the shed, push Mandy in, toss in a jar full of wasps, hold the door shut until Mandy was dead, and then make her way back up to the lodge without a hair out of place. Riddle me this, copper."

"You checked your watch? You know for certain she was only gone ten minutes? I thought you said you kind of dozed off, and then you got into a conversation with Rowan? Couldn't you have got a bit mixed up about the time?"

"I don't know. I suppose so," I said slowly. "I don't like where this is leading, Benjamin. And why are you doing this? I thought Hendricks was in charge of this case."

"He is. But there are a number of reasons to hook the two cases together, and we're working in close cooperation with the OPP now. Sharing resources, the whole bit. So I elected myself to come and talk to you — I figured I'd be cutting you a bit of a break. Shows what I know, huh?"

Reluctantly, I smiled. "Yeah, and I snap your head

off for your trouble. Sorry about that."

Benjamin shook his head. "Never mind. I'm used to it. Listen, when exactly did Flavia leave?"

"Noon. She told me she just wanted to get home, but to be really honest, I had to wonder whether she was avoiding talking to the OPP again. She said she thought they suspected her, and she didn't like it. Benjamin, what do you think you're doing?"

He hopped up from his chair quite nimbly, considering his size, and picked up my phone. Punched in a few numbers and spoke tersely. "She's gone. Yeah, back to the States. I don't know, check that with Customs and Immigration. Yeah. Go for it. Tell him I authorized it. Okay. Yeah. I will." He hung up, put the phone back on the side table, and remained standing.

"This doesn't look good at all, Katy, I have to tell you."

"Benjamin, stop acting like she's some kind of fugitive! We had a hell of a weekend, and Flavia wanted to get home. That's all there was to it."

"So she didn't tell you?"

"Tell me what?"

"That the OPP investigator told her not to leave the country, that's what. Hendricks had a gut hunch about your friend, and from the looks of things, he wasn't too far off."

I sat back, shaking my head foolishly. I felt dazed. So that's why Flavia had said the police suspected her. She hadn't been paranoid; they really had. Shit. Meet Katy Klein, world's worst judge of character.

"Are you okay? You look like you just saw a ghost. Do you want some water?"

"I'm fine," I managed. "No, I didn't know Hendricks told her to stay here. She didn't tell me that, exactly. Just that she thought Hendricks suspected her. That's when she told Dawn and me about the pregnancy and all. And … oh, shit, Benjamin, I might as well tell you. It can't get any worse. When we first saw Rufus, the dog, and realized that if he'd been stung then Mandy might have been too, we were all really panicked. Everyone except Flavia. She told me we might as well not bother rushing off to find Mandy. She said she was already dead."

Benjamin nodded. "Did she say how she knew this?"

"Just that she had a feeling. I thought she meant, you know, a psychic feeling, or an intuition or something. After all, we were at an astrologers' retreat. It sort of made sense at the time. And she does seem to have some kind of talent for picking up other people's feelings. Like, over at Rowan's place last night, she knew that Rowan wanted to ask me if she could stay here, before she said anything about it."

"Well, that's as may be. I have to tell you, when I was on the phone just now, I authorized one of my colleagues to put out a warrant for the arrest of Flavia Jerome. It's going to be tricky, we'll have to go through the feds to get her back here to stand trial, but we're going to do it. Just so you know."

I nodded miserably. "But why? I thought you said she was just wanted for questioning? What made you change your mind?"

Benjamin stared at a point somewhere above my head. "Gut hunch. Katy, she lied to you — she knew damn well she wasn't supposed to leave the country, but she went ahead and did it. What does that say to you?"

"I don't know." I sighed. "It all seems so … so wrong, somehow. But what the hell do I know? Just do whatever you have to do."

Benjamin reached for my hand. "Katy, I can't tell you how sorry I am. I know this is the last thing you wanted.

Listen, I have to get home and try to catch some sleep, but I'll call you tomorrow, okay?"

"I don't know, Benjamin. I'm feeling like warmed-over shit right now. Can we take a raincheck? I need some time to think things through."

He looked pained, but all he said was, "You do what you need to do. When you're ready, you know where to reach me."

We left it at that.

After he'd gone, I wandered through the apartment, trying to clear my head. Flavia couldn't have killed Mandy — could she? Was I really that stupid, or self-delusional, that I couldn't see what was right in front of my nose? Don't answer that.

I reached for the phone and dialled Flavia's number. Come on, come on, pick up, I begged silently, as the phone rang over and over at the other end of the line. Nothing. Not even an answering machine.

I sat down at the computer, booted up, and headed for my e-mail program. I didn't bother checking my new mail, but went straight to the "compose" function.

> Dear Flavia:
>
> I was sorry to see you rush off this morning, but I understand your feelings — this was not exactly the weekend either of us bargained for, was it? Now, though, something's come up, and I really, really need you to either e-mail or call me as soon as you get this. I'm not sure what's going on, but I have to talk to you, ASAP.

I hit "send" and sat back in the chair. She'd reply; she always did.

Before I finally turned in for the night, I slid open the door to Dawn's room. She lay fully clothed on her bed, staring at the ceiling. When she saw me peeking in at her, she snapped her eyes shut.

"Honey?" I whispered. "Dawn?"

No answer.

"Dawn, I just wanted to say I'm really sorry for barking at you like that. We've all been under a lot of stress, but I shouldn't have done that."

She rolled away from me, and something about the set of her shoulders told me I should leave her alone. I blew her a kiss and closed the door gently.

15

I lay in bed, duvet pulled up around my chin, contem-plating the cracks in my own bedroom ceiling. My brain was in overdrive, thoughts and images whirling around like a frog in a blender. Sleep was now far beyond my grasp, and I had a full day planned at the office tomorrow. Unfortunately, knowing that I needed to sleep was making it harder and harder to relax; I sat up in bed, turned on the light, and grabbed a paperback off my bedside table.

When the phone rang, it was almost a relief. I reached over and grabbed it before it could wake Dawn. The bedside alarm clock read one-fifteen a.m.

"Katy?" The voice on the other end was a low whisper.

"Who is this?"

"Katy, it's me, Rowan. I'm sorry to call so late, but I didn't know what else to do."

"Rowan? Is that you? You'll have to speak up, I can hardly hear you." I wriggled into a semi-sitting position. "Where are you?"

There was a faint click on the line, followed by a humming sound, and suddenly Rowan's voice came through much more clearly.

"I wouldn't have called you, but I didn't know where else to turn, now that ... now that Mandy's gone."

"Rowan, where are you?" I repeated. "You're not still at the gas station, are you?"

"No, of course not. We're in ... hang on, I forget the name of the lake. Skeleton Lake, I think it's called. I was surprised this cell phone even worked, we're so far out in the wilderness. But that doesn't matter. I have to tell you something."

"Rowan, just tell me what you need from me, okay? I can't help you unless I know exactly what's going on." I felt terrible, speaking so sharply to someone apparently being held hostage, but the woman's circuitous conversational style was really starting to get to me.

"I don't want to even say it. It's too awful, and I don't know if it's true ..."

"Rowan, *please*. Stop talking in circles."

"Okay. I think ... well, I don't think it exactly, but it might be true. I think Jimmy might know who killed Geoffrey. Or .... .oh, God, I can't even think this! Or maybe he did it himself." She ended on a whisper, and I wasn't even certain I'd heard her right.

I clutched the bedclothes to me as though for protection. "What? Who the hell is Geoffrey? What are you talking about, Rowan?"

"Did you read the paper yesterday? There was an article — they found Geoffrey's body. In the Canal. I saw it in a restaurant on the way here."

"Geoffrey — do you mean the high school teacher? Mr. Acres? Rowan, please — try to talk sense. What makes you think Jimmy had anything to do with that?"

"I *told* you." She sounded peeved. "I heard Jimmy and Aaron talking about it. At least, I think that's what they were talking about. I couldn't believe it; I don't want to believe it. I just don't know! I wasn't going to say anything, but I've been crying about it all day, and I just had to, you know, speak to someone."

"And so you picked me." Wow. What an honour.

"I can't do it myself," she said. "I just can't. I've picked up the phone fifty times today, and started to dial, but each time, I have to put it back down. He's my brother! I can't believe he'd do such a thing, and I can't just call the police on him — it would be … too cold-blooded. Don't you see?"

"Well, I hope he appreciates your loyalty. What exactly did he say about Geoffrey, to make you suspect he'd killed him?"

"I wasn't supposed to hear them. Actually, I didn't hear Jimmy, just Aaron, but that was enough for me. They were on the phone. Jimmy keeps phoning to check on me, to make sure Aaron hasn't slit my throat yet, probably — the guy's a real lowlife, Katy. You wouldn't believe …"

My patience, such as it was, was getting a wee bit frayed around the edges. Lord knows I wanted to help get Rowan home safely, but that seemed to be the least of her worries just now; she seemed far more concerned about her precious Jimmy.

"What did they say, Rowan?" I enunciated each word carefully. "Just tell me what you heard, okay?"

"Okay. Right." She inhaled deeply. "Aaron said, 'Did you read the paper this morning?' and Jimmy said something. Then Aaron said, 'Yeah, it's him. They got a positive ID on the body. It's right here in the paper.' Jimmy said something else, and Aaron said, 'Yeah, it was Victor, all right. He does it all for you.' And then he laughed, but in a kind of mean way, and said a whole bunch of other stuff that I didn't understand. It's like he was speaking in code — it just didn't make sense to me. But at the end, he said, 'Look, let's not kid around here. Geoff's gone, and you're going down for it, unless you move fast.' And that's all I heard."

"So you think Jimmy had this Victor guy kill Geoffrey? Why would he do that?"

"I don't know. I've been worried for a long time that Jimmy was up to something illegal — he gets these weird phone calls, he has to take them where no one can hear, and he's been really tense and distracted for the last, oh, six months or so. Not himself. Ever since he started this new business, things have been so strange."

I swallowed my impatience. "Rowan, where is Aaron now?"

"He's asleep, in the back room. I'm out on the porch. Katy, it's really creepy here. There's no noise at all, and it's dark as pitch outside. I'm afraid to even go to the washroom, it's that dark. We have to use this outhouse —"

"And where is Jimmy, do you know that?"

"I'm not sure. In Ottawa, I think. At least that's what he said before we left. He said he'd stay back and monitor the situation."

There was something else I wanted to ask her, but the thought was eluding me just now, playing hide and seek in my over-tired brain. There was a high-pitched beep on the line.

"Oh, the cell's running low," Rowan said. "And I don't know if I can recharge it out here. We don't have electricity. Katy, please — I can't bear to do this myself, but could you please call the police for me?"

"I will," I promised. "Oh! I just remembered what I wanted to ask you. You sounded as though you knew Geoffrey Acres — do you?"

"He's our little brother." Rowan's phone beeped again, and the line went dead.

Well. If I'd been wide awake before, now I was sitting bolt upright, on full alert. I picked up the phone to call Benjamin. I wasn't about to have him accuse me of withholding information again — and it certainly did sound as though Jimmy and his good buddy Aaron were up to no good.

Benjamin picked up after several rings, sounding like a hibernating bear awakened from his long winter's snooze.

"'Llo?" He grunted.

"Benjamin, it's me, Katy. Wake up, I have to talk to you."

"Katy? Is that you? Is everything okay?"

"Fine, I'm fine. Listen, are you awake?"

"Getting there. What's up?"

I told him about Rowan's call. "She was quite clear about what she heard, Benjamin. She thinks Jimmy killed Geoffrey Acres, or at least that he had some guy called Victor do it for him. And she says Acres is their little brother, which I don't quite get. For one thing, how come their names are different?"

"You never heard of people marrying twice? They could be step-siblings. I'll look into it. Where did you say Rowan was calling from?"

"Some place called Skeleton Lake. She says she's out in the wilderness somewhere, but she was a bit vague about exactly where. Her phone cut out before I had a chance to narrow it down."

"Okay, I'm on it." Benjamin was all business, as though he'd never been asleep. "This is good information, Katy. Thanks for calling."

"You're welcome," I said. "Do I get my apology now, or later?"

"Apology? Oh, right. For not believing you about Mar

—I mean, Flavia. Well, how about I see how this tip pans out, and then I'll make it up to you? You like roses?"

"Not really. But I'm very fond of freesia. And chocolate would be good. Dark, not milk. Actually, chocolate covered coffee beans would be even better. Espresso, if they've got 'em."

"You got it, hon. Talk to you soon."

Sleep never came that night. I lay on my side and watched the red numbers on my bedside clock change, minute by minute, until the sky grew almost imperceptibly lighter, and finally the first tentative rays of sunlight crept through the curtains. I'm getting way too old for this, was all I could think, as I heard Dawn's alarm go off, followed by her padding into the bathroom. Even the strongest coffee couldn't help me now.

MONDAY, OCTOBER 17
Sun conjunct Mercury ✦
Moon square Jupiter ✦
Venus conjunct Mars ✦

While Dawn, who was still giving me the silent treatment, buzzed her trademark breakfast concoction in the blender, I splashed cold water on my burning eyes and puffy skin. I looked at myself in the bathroom mirror—a mistake. Some careworn old hag with bleary eyes and more wrinkles than Mother Teresa peered back at me. Lovely. I'd scare any clients away, looking like this.

As I prepared my morning infusion of caffeine, I tried to check out the Dawn situation. She looked calm enough, sipping her breakfast mix du jour. I decided to tempt her with a morsel of information.

"Had an interesting call last night after you went to bed," I said nonchalantly. Her ears perked up, but I let the sentence hang between us.

I could see she was interested, but her voice was still sullen. "Oh yeah? Who was it?" She stuck a teaspoon in the revolting-looking mixture she was drinking, and gave it a quick stir.

"Rowan. She was on her cell phone, from some lake out in the middle of nowhere." I told her about Rowan's suspicions, and slowly, my daughter seemed to come to life. By the time I got to the part where Jimmy might have killed Geoffrey, Dawn's eyes glittered with excitement.

"See? Didn't I tell you? I knew he was up to something. What else did she say, Mom? This Aaron guy is holding her prisoner, isn't he? So let's see, they'll be able to nab Jimmy on two counts of murder, plus one forcible confinement ..." She held up her fingers. "He's going away for a long time, Mom. Did you tell all this to the cops? What did they say?"

"Dawn, you watch too much television," I laughed. "I did call Benjamin, and he said he'd take care of it."

Dawn made a moue of dissatisfaction. "Why didn't you call Hendricks? He's the one who's actually handling the case. Don't you think he'd want to know?"

"They're working on it together now — the OPP and the Ottawa police. I'm sure Benjamin will pass along the word," I said.

Dawn thought about this for a while, and apparently decided to concede the point. Then, "So, what's the deal with Mr. Acres, anyway? Do you think he's really Jimmy and Rowan's brother? I mean, his name's not the same as theirs, or anything."

"Yeah, that's what I said. But Benjamin pointed out that people can get divorced — they're probably half-siblings or something. Anyway, what puzzles me is why Jimmy would suddenly start trying to kill off his family. Is he some kind of psychopath, or what?"

"Well, he could have offed Mr. Acres for the class trip money," Dawn suggested helpfully. "Fifty thousand is a lot of money, you know. And as for Mandy, I can think of a million reasons. No, a million and one. Her personality, and her bank account. She was going to divorce him, wasn't she? And I bet that would leave him with a lot less money than if she just croaked on him."

"True enough. Maybe his new business isn't going as well as he might like, and he needs some cash. Though I can't imagine fifty thousand bucks being enough, and if he's after Mandy's money, he's going to have to wait a while — it can take ages to get wills read and all the money distributed."

"Yeah, but if she'd divorced him like she wanted to, he'd have nothing. That's what they said at breakfast the other day, don't you remember? There was some big prenuptial agreement or something, and he was going to lose a whack of cash if she left him. So he kills her, trying to make it look like an accident. Some accident."

"You could be right. I guess we'll find out when the cops catch up with ol' Jimmy." I drained my coffee mug and rinsed it out. "Listen, I have to go over to Zayde and Sabte's this afternoon to pick up that damned hearse of a car. I'll be a bit late getting back, okay?"

"Sure. I'd come with you, but Sylvie and I are working on a project for French class together. We're writing a play. Her mom's out of town, so I said I'd stay and help her cook supper. I'll eat at her house, okay?"

I kissed my daughter good-bye, and headed off to work.

16

I had only been gone the weekend, but it felt like several weeks since I'd last pushed open the heavy oak door of my office on Second Avenue, in the Glebe. For nearly five years, I'd complained bitterly about my little hovel of an office above Fruits of the Earth, a bakery along Bank Street. It was a sweatbox in summer, frigid in winter, and the scummy excuse for a landlord could be counted upon to forget to change burned out bulbs or broken steps in the dark, steep stairway, and to abuse me verbally when I had the gall to complain. Finally, the events of last winter had forced my hand, and now here I was in my ideal office: a ground-floor front room in one of the stately old houses that line streets in this part of the city. The floors were solid oak, the walls freshly painted, and the windows high and elegant.

And my new landlady was as unlike John Keon as it is possible to be. For one thing, I believe she belongs to the species *homo sapiens*. Samantha, or Sam as she prefers to be called, is a tall, lanky woman of indeterminate age, somewhere between fifty and seventy by my reckoning, with grey hair clipped short, and a propensity for purple: violet, deep indigo, mauve, plum, burgundy — her wardrobe runs the gamut. She greeted me today wearing mauve tie-dyed leggings, over which she'd thrown a dark purple velveteen duster, embroidered and sequined to within an inch of its life. I guessed, correctly, that she was heading out to Bank Street for a spot of shopping.

"Morning!" She grinned and held the door for me. "Great day. Off to get some groceries. Having people over for supper tonight. Good weekend?"

How to answer that question? I fudged. "Not too bad. And you?"

"Went canoeing. Shitty weather, so I came back. Nice while I was out there, though."

"Great!" I forced enthusiasm into my voice. "Well, guess I'd better get to work. Have fun with your shopping, Sam."

Nodding, she let the door slam behind her, and I fumbled in my purse for the key to my office. The phone had already started to ring by the time I got the door open, and I grabbed it quickly, before the answering machine could.

"Mom!" Dawn was out of breath. "Mom, you're not going to believe this!"

My heart started thudding. "Dawn? What is it? What's happened?"

"Nothing's wrong, don't worry! You'll never believe who I just saw!"

"Who? Dawn, what the hell are you up to? Where are you calling from? Aren't you supposed to be in school?"

"Mom!" She stretched the word into three or four syllables. "Just listen, okay? I'm fine, okay? I was walking to school, when this black car pulled out in front of me, just as I was going to cross Elgin. I happened to look inside, and you'll never believe who was driving—it was Jimmy! I couldn't believe it. I just froze."

I expelled my breath loudly. "Oh, for heaven's sake, Dawn — if you're going to start seeing this guy around every corner ..."

"It was *him*, Mom, I swear. And the weirdest thing about it was, there was someone else in the car. And I recognized her, too."

"Oh, let me guess. It was ... let's see — Clyde Barrow? Oh, no, you said it was a woman. Bonnie Parker? And the two of them were off to hatch bank robbing plots together, right?"

There was silence on the other end of the line, and I realized I'd gone too far. Plus, my child of the nineties probably didn't even recognize my antiquated references.

I sighed. "Okay, Dawn, I'm sorry. Who else was in the car?"

"Well, if you're not interested ..." She suddenly sounded very formal.

"Come on, I said I was sorry. Who was it?"

"Mom, it was Masha! You know, the little Russian *rebbe*."

Now it was my turn to stay silent.

"What's the matter, you don't believe me? Look, I got a good look at her, and it was definitely her. In fact, when she saw me looking, she turned her face away and said something, and the car sped up and took off. Would she have done that if she hadn't known I saw her?"

"Dawn, where are you now?"

"At the Second Cup on Elgin. I just called Hendricks, and then I thought I should let you know why I was late for school. I mean, it was for a good cause, right?"

Suddenly, my lack of sleep caught up with me in a rush. My head throbbed, my throat felt scratchy, and my eyes were gritty with fatigue. "Sure, honey. I'll write you a note tonight, when I get home. Good sleuthing. Now get to school, okay?"

"I'm on my way." I could hear the smile in her voice, and I smiled back.

After I'd hung up, I pressed the replay button on my answering machine, and jotted down the messages. Nothing too startling — the usual mishmash of clients wanting appointments, my regular phone clients who rely on me to start their weeks off right, and new referrals, sounding shy and hesitant at contacting an actual astrologer. The last message made me sit up and take notice, though. It was Flavia. Her voice sounded dry and distant.

"Katy, I got your e-mail. I'm not at home now, so don't try to call back. This weekend really shook me up, and I'm feeling like I need to recharge my batteries a bit, so I'm going to a yoga retreat for a few days. I hope you're okay, my friend. Give my love to Dawn, too. I'll talk to you when I get back."

A yoga retreat. Was she being deliberately obtuse, or did she really not know what was going on? I didn't want to think that Flavia could have had anything to do with Mandy's death — she couldn't have, could she? Didn't Rowan's phone call prove it? And yet, would an innocent person panic and run the way she had? I thought back: she'd decided to take off right after she'd heard the cops were coming over again, hadn't she? Which would seem to indicate, if not guilt, at least a guilty conscience. Then again, I know just how she felt about seeing the cops once more. It's always a nerve-wracking experience, even if you haven't really done anything. I just didn't know any more.

Suddenly, my throat clogged with tears. I cradled my head in my arms, sniffling slightly, until a sob built up in my chest and burst out of me in a long, low moan. I sat there, dripping tears onto my green blotter for a good ten minutes. Afterward, I sat up and fished around for a box of tissues. I blew my nose and scrubbed the last of the tears away, grateful that I hadn't bothered with mascara this morning. I sat back in my chair and closed my eyes, waiting for the burning to subside, and cursing my own weakness. I was starting to feel like some kind of perpetual fountain, tearing up at the least provocation.

My first instinct was to call Benjamin about Flavia's message, but I didn't want to speak to him when I was feeling this fragile. Greg. I'd call Greg. He'd understand. Monday was his admin day, so I wouldn't be interrupting a session with one of his patients. I picked up the phone and dialled his number.

"Katy? You don't sound good. Are you all right?"

I nearly lost it again at the sound of his voice. "I had the shittiest weekend, you wouldn't believe it. Do you have time for lunch today?"

"Of course," said my friend. "You're okay, though? You sound pretty rough. You want me to come now?"

"I'm feeling my age, that's all. Bring tissues," I said. "Maybe we can just pick up a hot dog and go to the park or something. I don't think I'm fit to be seen in a restaurant just now."

Greg agreed to drop by and pick me up at noon, and I hung up, feeling a tiny bit better. I still didn't much feel like calling Benjamin, but I figured I'd better face the music sooner rather than later. Fortunately for me, he wasn't in his office, so I left a message on his voice-mail.

"Benjamin, I just heard from Flavia. She called and left a message on my machine here at the office. Didn't say anything about Mandy, or being on Canada's Most Wanted List. Just said she was off to a yoga retreat, and that she'd be in touch. I'll let you know if I hear anything else. Over and out."

There — I'd done my civic duty. Benjamin would be so pleased. Now, time to get down to earning a living.

The hours didn't exactly fly by, but I was able to immerse myself in constructing and delineating a chart for a new client, a job I normally love. This time, I was just going through the motions, but I didn't really care. I'd get the job done, collect my fee, and that would be that. This would be my new approach to life: one foot in front of the other, slogging through it, getting the necessities done, and trying not to notice the rest. Anything had to be better than feeling like I was about to cry every two seconds.

When the knock came at the door just before noon, I expected Greg. Instead, it was Peter.

"Hey, what are you doing here? I thought you were in Montreal, skulking around digging up dirt on some poor unsuspecting evil-doer." I hugged him, pulling him into the office. He looked behind him, and shut the door carefully.

He hugged me back, but perfunctorily, and gave the office a thorough once over. His face, normally boyish, was a strange shade of grey, creased and tense with worry. I wondered when he'd slept last. Then again, who was I to talk?

"Looking for listening devices? I'm pretty sure the place is clean." I smiled at my own feeble attempt at a joke.

"It's not funny, Katy. That's why I'm here. I didn't want to talk about this at home, and since you and I have different last names, I figure there's less of a chance that anyone'll know where you work. Or that I'd come here."

"Peter, what's up? You look like your best friend just died."

He flinched, as if I'd hit him. "Not my best friend, no."

My heart lurched. "Who? Peter, is Dawn okay? I just talked to her this morning! She promised she'd go right back to school! Peter, what ...?"

"No, no, Katy, nothing like that! I'm sorry. Dawn's fine," he said. "Listen, I just came from Montreal. You know Mike?"

"Sure, the guy you've been working with on this big top secret investigative deal. Tall, grey hair, looks like he could use a good meal. Even more paranoid than you. What about him?"

"He's dead, Katy."

I didn't say anything, but my eyes widened. "Maybe we should sit down, and you should tell me what's going on." I kept my voice slow and steady.

Peter deposited himself on the brand new futon couch I'd bought last winter to replace the other brand new futon couch that had been destroyed by fire, which replaced the old futon couch that had been damaged by vandals. I think I am personally responsible for keeping the world's futon couch tycoons in business. I hope they're appropriately grateful.

"Katy, it's very complex, and I still can't tell you everything, but you know I've been on this story for the past couple of months, right? Ben figured I could handle it, after the Christian Soldiers story broke last winter, and he paired me up with Mike, one of the top investigative guys in the business. It was a big step up for me."

I nodded. "He's the one who did the story on the Hell's Angels last year, right?"

"Yes. He's been covering the motorcycle gang warfare thing for a number of years, but he's also done stuff on other forms of organized crime — the cocaine cartels, the black market in illegal immigrants, cigarette smuggling, money laundering, you name it."

"And now he's dead. What happened?"

"He was walking from his apartment building to the dépanneur, to get his morning coffee. He'd just come out of the store when a car pulled up, and a guy wearing a hockey mask and carrying a gun jumped out. He shot Mike five times in the chest, jumped back into the car and drove away. The cops said Mike was dead before he hit the ground."

"Who do they think it was?"

"Well, it could either be someone from one of the gangs who's held a grudge — and he's pissed a lot of people off, over the years — or it could be the people we're investigating now. I'm leaning toward the latter, because we've been doing a lot of digging, and I think we're getting close to something."

"In which case —" I spoke slowly, but he interrupted.

"Yeah, in which case, I'm next up on the dance card."

"Shit." My mind had gone blank. I stared at Peter, and he fidgeted in his seat.

"You said it, kid. My only hope at this point is that they haven't figured out much about me yet, but Mike and I were in this together. Chances are, if they knew his routines well enough to know when to kill him, they've got a fix on me too. These people are incredibly efficient, once they get the wind up. Katy, I can't even begin to tell you how dangerous they are. They don't just kill the person who pisses them off — they take whole families down, just to show they can. Mike wasn't married, but the cops are guarding his parents twenty-four-seven. I'd be a lot happier if I knew you and Dawn were someplace safe, where no one can find you. Like, say, your parents' place. I'm pretty sure no one could find you there, especially if you got someone like Greg to take you. The Flaming Deathtrap is a bit too recognizable."

"Oh, right, and put my parents in danger too! Brilliant." I shook my head. "Peter, if you want us to have some kind of police protection, go ahead and do it. But there's no way in hell I'm bringing my parents into this. Besides, there's no room for us there. Masha's using the spare room right now. And Dawn's annoyed with me these days, as it is."

"What for? And who's Masha?" Peter looked puzzled for a moment. Then his face cleared. "Oh! Your mother told me about her. The little Russian *rebbe*. I wanted to see if I could talk to her ..." He stopped himself.

"Why would you want to talk to her?" I know Peter. When he's on the trail of a story, he doesn't believe in idle chit-chat. If he'd wanted to talk to Masha, he'd had a reason for it.

"Katy, I already told you. I can't talk about this."

"Ah, so she does have something to do with your story." I didn't bother to hide my triumph.

Peter flushed, but said nothing.

"Let me guess." I tilted my head and gazed at the ceiling, pondering. "Hmm ... Masha's from the former Soviet Union, right? And you've just been in Montreal, tracking down some kind of big underworld deal that you can't talk about. And the very latest in organized crime these days seems to be the new, improved Russian maffiya ... am I getting close?"

"Katy, *shut up*!" Peter hissed, leaning close to me. "Just shut up, okay? You don't know what kind of trouble you could be getting yourself into here. If anyone heard you, and thought you knew something, our whole family would be gone, do you understand? Just like that!" He snapped his fingers in front of my face, and I recoiled.

"Sorry, Peter, I'll stop now," I said, chastened. "Look, is there anything I can do?"

He shook his head, and hauled himself upright. "Nope. I'm going to go talk to the cops now, and see if I can't get you guys some kind of protection. Just keep your eyes and ears open, okay? You can call me on the cell if you need me — I won't be going home for a while. One of the things the Montreal cops told me was to keep varying my routines, never use the same route twice, so that's what I'm going to do. And I'm ditching the Flaming Deathtrap, too. Getting myself a rental car. Keep safe, Katy."

"I'll try," I said.

I helped Peter find his way down the hall and through Sam's very well-equipped kitchen, and let him out the back door, feeling vaguely foolish. It's not that I didn't find his story credible — it's just that I couldn't imagine some gang of Russian mobsters targeting us, for real or imagined infractions. And even if they were after Peter, God forbid, why would they pick on me or Dawn? On the other hand, if Mike had really been murdered in broad daylight by some thug who felt confident enough to just drive up, plug him, and drive away, did I really want to take chances?

I was mulling over these questions when Greg tapped lightly on the open door of my office. I jumped.

"Hard at work, I see," he said. "Ready for a break?"

"Readier than you can imagine, my friend. Choose your hot dog vendor. Lunch is on me today. To make up for our gourmet experience in the bowels of the Royal Ottawa Hospital."

As we sat on a verge of grass under a tree whose leaves were only now in the process of turning a brilliant yellow, I chewed my bratwurst in silence, wondering whether to tell Greg about Peter's visit. I decided against.

After all, I had promised Peter my silence; I owed him that. And it wouldn't help Greg to know.

"So ... tell me about your weekend," Greg prompted.

Weekend? Oh, right, the weekend. The reason I'd been on the edge of a nervous breakdown when I'd called him this morning. In the face of Mike's murder, it all seemed very old news now. Some domestic spat, not quite on a par with Russian mobsters.

However, I gave Greg the abbreviated version — Mandy's death, Jimmy's sudden appearance on the scene, Rowan's phone calls and her suspicion that Jimmy had killed their brother, my worries about Flavia. Not to mention the fact that Dawn and I couldn't seem to exchange two civil sentences in a row. He listened carefully, nodding now and then, and prompting me when I paused.

"So you think Flavia might have had something to do with it after all?" he asked, taking off his glasses and cleaning them slowly on his shirt.

I sighed. "I don't know. Sure, why not? She said it herself, she had a motive. More of a motive than we knew, as it turns out. And yet ... I just can't see it, Greg. I can see her getting mad, but whoever killed Mandy had to have planned it out ahead of time. You know, they'd have to know she was allergic to wasps, they'd have to collect a bunch in a bottle, get her to the shed, throw the wasps in, lock the door, and keep her there until she was dead. Don't you think that if Flavia had been carting around a bottle full of wasps in her luggage, I'd have noticed? And I don't care what Benjamin says, she really was only gone for a few minutes. There was no time for her to kill anyone. No, she couldn't have done it."

"But you're worried."

"Well, yeah!" I exploded. "I mean, where the hell is she? And why did she take off so quickly, when the cops had specifically told her to stay put? Why the hell is she acting so guilty, when she's not?" Tears filled my eyes again. Angrily, I scrubbed at them with my sleeve.

Without a word, Greg passed me a tissue. I snorted into it, and balled it up, along with my bratwurst's paper wrapper. From where we sat, I tossed the wad into a nearby garbage can, disturbing the wasps that had congregated, attracted by bits of food and the dregs of other people's juice cans. They spread upward, annoyed but undeterred, and then settled back into their appointed task: collecting food for the winter.

Mandy's face, swollen and purple, her tongue protruding grotesquely between heavily glossed lips, a lone wasp crawling along her cheek ... I shivered, and Greg took my hand.

"You've been through a lot lately," he said softly. "Please, let me help."

"Don't." I shook my head, trying to shut him up, shut his voice out of my head. Didn't he see, if he kept talking I was going to lose it right here and now, run screaming down the streets, tormented past the point of endurance, and then it would be all over for me. I would dissolve into a puddle of grief and rage, no good to anybody, and then what? Who would look after Dawn? Who would take care of my parents?

"Please," I whispered again. "Don't."

Greg seemed to understand. He lapsed into a gentle silence, and we finished our drinks sitting there on the verge, watching the traffic rumble by along Bank Street.

17

By late afternoon, I was more than ready to close up shop and head out to the west end to pick up The Behemoth from my parents' place. It wasn't that my work that day had been particularly onerous, but just that my mind wasn't co-operating. I kept allowing myself to become distracted. I caught myself more than once just staring at the walls, my brain completely blank and numb. Each time, I'd give myself a mental shake and get back to work, but by five, my fatigue had caught up with me. A nice long bus ride was just the ticket for me. Maybe I could catch a little nap on the way.

I caught a northbound bus on Bank Street, and squished in amongst a chattering mob of university students, some of whom politely moved aside for me. Every year when the new crop of students shows up at Carleton, they seem younger and younger. I think they must be letting Grade 7 students in there by now.

When I got off to transfer to the 95 along Albert Street, a large, unkempt man stumbled up against me and muttered an apology. I turned, and my stomach clenched — I'd seen this guy before. In a Chinese restaurant, with Jimmy, on Saturday. I recognized the suit, such as it was. Aaron. But wasn't he supposed to be out in the boonies somewhere, guarding Rowan? What the heck was he doing in downtown Ottawa?

"Hey!" I called, but he was already halfway down the street. He was moving at quite a clip, and I didn't see much point in running after him, so I let it go. I did make a mental note to let Benjamin know I'd seen the guy, though.

The 95 bus barreled along the Transitway, Ottawa's grudging answer to a subway system. It's a series of roads that cut through the city, enabling buses to travel unimpeded by regular traffic, stopping at grim concrete and glass stations to allow passengers to transfer to local routes. I got off at Westboro, and decided that the three-kilometre walk to my parents' house wouldn't do me any harm. A sharp breeze had come up, and I thrust my hands into my sweater pockets.

As I walked the gracious, tree-lined streets, I mulled. Should I have made more of an effort to call Benjamin right away and let him know I'd literally bumped into the guy we'd seen with Jimmy at the restaurant? It was a moot point, really, because I didn't have a cell phone, and by the time I reached my parents' house the guy would be long gone. But how coincidental had our meeting been? Had he been following me, or was he just some random guy, a low-life friend of a probable murderer? And what was with Dawn's report that she'd seen Masha in Jimmy's car? Granted, she was just a tiny bit fixated on pinning Mandy's murder on Jimmy, but why would she have imagined Masha with him? I'd be seeing the rabbi in a few minutes — maybe I'd just come right out and ask her.

My mother came to the door, wiping her hands on a tea towel.

"Katy! *Mamaleh*, it's good to see you!" She embraced me as though we had not just seen one another the night before. “Where’s Dawn? Have you eaten yet? We were just going to sit down — why don’t you join us?”

“Mama, Mama, slow down,” I laughed. “Dawn stayed home, and no, I haven’t eaten. Whatever you’re having smells good, though.”

“Leftovers, that’s all. Beef from last night, and I made some knishes to go with. Masha just called and said she’d be late, so we’ve got extra. Come in, come in! Bernard, Katy’s here!”

I shrugged out of my sweater, hung it up, and kicked off my shoes. “Masha’s not here?” I asked.

“No.” My mother frowned. “She’s been gone all day. It’s very strange.”

“What’s the matter? I thought she was supposed to be working — maybe she just got held up at the *shul*.”

Mama shook her head vehemently. “She’s not there. She hasn’t been there all day. I went over this afternoon to pick up the list for my *yahrtzeit* calls. That new secretary, she wants to do everything now on the computer, it drives me crazy, but what can you do? I told her, the old list has worked for the past ten years, but no, she wants to do it her way. I don’t like to complain, but ...”

“Mama,” I interrupted gently. “Masha ... ?”

“Yes, yes, I’m getting to that.” She hoisted a platter of puffed, golden potato knishes and bore it to the dining room table. “I thought I’d drop in and say hello while I was there, maybe bring her a little lunch, but she wasn’t in the rabbi’s office. ‘Where’s the *russischa rebbe*?’ I asked, but no one could tell me. She wasn’t there today, and they haven’t seen her since last Monday. That’s a whole week, Katy, and yet she goes out our door first thing every morning, chirping like a little bird, and comes back every night. Until tonight.” Rosie shook her head mournfully. “I just don’t know what to think.”

"Well, did you ask the rabbi where she was? I thought she was apprenticing under him, or something?"

"He said he didn't know, either. But I think he does." She scowled. Rosie is a very tolerant person, but she does not like being lied to. "When he told me he didn't know, he couldn't meet my eyes. And when I said I thought it was strange, Masha being gone for so long, he just waved it off, as though he hadn't begged me last month to give the little *rebbe* a place to stay while she was here. 'Oh, it will be such a help to the poor ignorant Russian Jews,' he said. And now — this!"

My guess is that the rabbi hadn't had to twist my mother's arm too hard — providing hospitality to others is her stock in trade. Still, I could see why she was worried.

"Mama, did she say where she was calling from, when she phoned to tell you not to wait for dinner?"

Rosie shook her head. "I asked her where she was, and she just changed the subject. But I thought I heard voices. Men's voices," she added darkly.

"That could mean anything," I said, as much to myself as to my mother. "Well, I guess it's her business, and it sounds like she's got Rabbi Schiffman's approval, so it's really not our problem, is it?"

"I still don't like it," said my mother, just as my father came into the kitchen.

"What don't you like?" he asked.

Rosie clamped her mouth shut, and looked at me meaningfully.

"Nothing, Dad," I said. "It's okay. Just that Masha won't be joining us for supper. So ... is there anything I need to know about the car before I take it?" Clever subject-change, Katy.

My father the retired engineer launched into a long explanation of the car's quirks and features, while we sated ourselves on cold roast beef, knishes, and my mother's special coleslaw, complete with half sour pickles. When we were done, my father led the way to the garage, and handed me the car keys.

"Don't forget, the knob on the cigarette lighter is missing. Also, the dome light needs to be replaced, and you might have to ride the brake a bit," he cautioned me. "And this engine will be bigger than what you're used to. It's a V-8, and you're used to the little four cylinders, so it might seem kind of jumpy at first. Be careful, Katy. It's a good car, but it needs handling."

I opened the front door and eased behind the wheel. Well, I certainly wouldn't have any difficulty with leg room in this baby. In fact, I had to reach underneath and pull the seat up a notch to enable my feet to reach the pedals comfortably. I peered around into the back seat, where I could easily have entertained four or five guests, had I the mind to do it.

The car was more than a decade old, but everything in it gleamed as though it had just been driven off the lot. Well, a few weeks with Dawn and me should take care of that. Somehow, every car we drove seemed to become a crumb and litter magnet. I liked to think of it as a lived-in look, but I could imagine my parents' horror, should I allow muffin crumbs and spilled coffee to disturb the pristine shininess of this immaculate front seat. I was going to have to invest in one of those little car vacuums you see on late night TV. I could see my future as a car owner stretching out before me. It was not necessarily a pretty sight.

However, I hadn't the heart to hand the keys back to my father, who stood beside the still-open door, grinning like a little kid at having given me such a fabulous gift.

"It's great, Dad!" Well, it would be nice picking up groceries all at once, instead of trekking home trailing a bundle buggy through the snow and slush this winter. And now maybe Dawn and I could take a few short trips, perhaps up to the Gatineaus, which would be ablaze with colour this time of year.

Dad closed the door gently, and I rolled down the window. My mother had joined us, and they leaned over in turn to kiss me good-bye. Then Dad flipped the switch on the automatic garage door thingy, and I backed The Behemoth slowly into the driveway. To be fair, the beast handled pretty well, considering that it was the size of a small freighter. I found the turn signal, and still moving cautiously, backed into the street. There, I waved at my parents, who stood with their arms around one another, waving back.

I had no desire to put The Behemoth through its paces on the Queensway, although it was now past rush hour. I'd just drive it around the west end for a while, then head back along the Ottawa River Parkway. I slid the gearshift into drive, and my new car and I purred off down the street. At the first stop sign, I tapped on the brake, but didn't notice any discernible slowing of forward trajectory. I dug my foot into the floor, and felt the car come to a reluctant halt beneath me. Maybe I could get Greg's car mechanic to have a look. I started a mental list. Brakes, dome light, and the electric windows made a funny squealing noise when I tried to roll them down ...

Dawn wasn't home when I got there, so I gave her a call at Sylvie's, just to make sure everything was okay. I hate to think that I may be turning into one of those neurotic mothers who can't let go of the apron strings. On the other hand, the past couple of years had taught me not to take anyone's safety for granted. Dawn was fine. She and Sylvie had finished writing their French play, eaten supper and done the dishes, and were now engaged in the endlessly fascinating task of trying and convicting Jimmy for the murder of his wife and half-brother.

"He's the only one who could have done it, Mom," Dawn explained earnestly. "The more Sylvie and I talk about it, the more obvious it is. The only thing I can't figure out is, what was he doing this morning with that Russian rabbi? She seemed so nice, she didn't look the type, you know?"

"'The type'? What type is that?" I asked.

"Oh, you know. The floozie. The other woman. The murderer's girlfriend. Although I guess if I were Jimmy and I had to choose between Mandy and Masha, I'd probably choose Masha too."

"Hey, hold on a sec! That's quite the leap, from thinking you might have seen them together to making them out to be lovers. And we still don't know for sure ..."

"Oh, come on, Mom! Don't be so dense!" Dawn's voice rose, and I held the phone receiver away from my head.

"Dawn, lower your voice. I don't think it's up to us to decide who killed Mandy and Mr. Acres." I sounded prim even to my own ears. "I'm sure that when the police catch up with Jimmy, the truth will come out. Now, what time do you think you'll be home?"

"Another half-hour," Dawn said. "Bye." She hung up before I could say anything.

The thing is, maybe she was right about Jimmy. But each time she raised it, a wall came down in my mind: I didn't want to think about it. I didn't want to think about who'd locked Mandy in a shed full of wasps, or who'd pushed Geoffrey Acres into Dow's Lake, strapped into a wheelchair. I didn't want to think about the thug who'd filled Peter's colleague full of bullets outside his local dépanneur. It's not that I didn't care — I couldn't care. If I cared, I would have to think about it, and thinking about it made my stomach churn, made my head throb, took me right back to that empty December field, full of blood and snow.

I most emphatically did not want to go there.

18

Dawn arrived home half an hour later, as promised, but she was sullen and uncommunicative. I assumed she was unhappy that I'd tried to throw cold water on her theories about Jimmy and Masha.

We watched television for an hour or so, and then she excused herself and went to bed. I had folded up my needlepoint, turned off the television and was just brushing my teeth when I heard a soft rap on my front door.

I spat, rinsed, and listened. There it was again.

I padded into the living room in my slippers and nightgown, and peered through the peephole. Peter. I expelled my breath, although I had not realized until that moment that I'd been holding it.

"Hi, come in," I whispered, ushering him into the apartment and closing the door quietly, so as not to wake Dawn. "You look terrible — don't they let you shave when you're a fugitive journalist? And you look like you've been sleeping in your clothing."

"I have. I can't stay. I just wanted to touch base for a bit. And pick up some fresh clothes," he added, fingering his rumpled shirt ruefully. "I'm not cut out for this hole and corner stuff, Katy."

"Can't you ask Ben to take you off the story? Surely

he must realize that you're in danger now — doesn't having your partner bumped off by gangsters count as some kind of extreme circumstance?"

"No, you don't get it. I hate to sound like a bad movie here, but I already know way too much. This is big, Katy, really big, and once I break it, and the cops move in, things will calm down. Till then ..." He shrugged.

"Well, how long will that be?"

"I don't know. Days. A week, max. But that's not why I'm here. Remember this morning, I said I'd get the cops to keep an eye on you and Dawn?"

I nodded.

"Well, they're saying now that they don't have the resources for it. I quote, 'Hey, what do we look like? A daycare? We don't have the manpower to babysit every family in town.' And that was the edited version."

"Shit. So ... what do we do? I'm not moving in with my parents — that would just make them sitting ducks too. Maybe I could move Dawn over there, and stay here myself. You and I have different last names, so it's not likely they'd think of looking for her there, is it? The spare room's taken, but ..." I trailed off.

"But what?"

"Nothing. I'm just being paranoid. It's just that I was over there this evening, picking up that humongous car you saw parked outside, and my mother told me their little Russian rabbi wasn't where she was supposed to be. It just made me wonder, that's all."

"What do you mean?"

I started to explain Dawn's suspicions about Jimmy and Masha, but Peter stopped me again. "Wait a sec. Who's Jimmy, and what's he got to do with all this?"

So I had to tell him the whole *megillah* — about the island, and Mandy's death, and Flavia, and Jimmy, and Geoffrey Acres. By the time I'd finished, some colour had returned to Peter's cheeks, and he was pacing around the apartment. He turned to look at me.

"Katy, this is just too weird. So now what? You think Masha might be in league with this Jimmy guy somehow?"

"Dawn thinks that. I'm trying to keep an open mind."

Peter made a rude noise. "You? An open mind? But Katy, that would imply having no opinion!" He grabbed me by the shoulders and stared into my eyes. "All right, whoever's in there, I want you to come out, and bring back the real Katy Klein!" He gave me a shake and let go with a flourish.

I staggered backward, laughing. "Okay, I know it's a bit out of character, but I'm serious. I can't get involved in another mess like last winter, I just can't." Then, to my everlasting shame, I began to cry.

Peter pulled me back toward him and held me until the sobs stopped shuddering through me. He didn't ask what was wrong, but when I was done, he found a box of tissues on the kitchen counter and brought it to me.

"Thanks." I sopped up the mess, feeling like an idiot. "I'm sorry. Things have been getting to me lately."

"Have you thought about ..."

"Yes," I said. "I've thought about seeing someone. But I had lunch with Greg today, and I just couldn't ask him, even though he's offered about sixty times to refer me. Stupid, huh?"

"Hey, you're you. Stubborn as an army mule, and twice as hard-headed."

"Thanks. I needed that. Okay, here's my resolution: I'll call tomorrow, and see if Greg can set me up with someone. This business of crying every two seconds is starting to wear a little thin."

"Good girl. Listen, can I change the subject? I can't

stay here long, and I actually came to bring you this." He reached into his jacket pocket.

"Oh, darling, I can't tell you what this means to me! You really care!" I took the black cardboard box from him and tore it open. "Oh, dang, it's not a diamond tennis bracelet. Peter, what do I want with a cell phone?"

"Just a precaution. Since the police aren't willing to stand guard over you guys, I wanted you to have an emergency contact. I've programmed it to call 911 automatically when you hit this button here." He pointed, and I squinted, then took off my glasses to see which one he meant. One of these days I'm going to have to break down and get bifocals. "And if you hit this one, it dials me directly. I don't really think anything's going to happen, but you know my motto ..."

"'Better safe than sorry,'" I sang. "Yeah, I do. But Peter, let's say I'm on my way to the corner store for a carton of Ben & Jerry's, and some goon with a sub-machine gun decides I'm toast. I don't think a cell phone is going to do me a hell of a lot of good, do you?"

"Look, it's not funny. I just want you to have this, that's all. It'll make me feel better."

Shoot, now I'd hurt his feelings. "Sure, Peter. I appreciate it. And I'll see if I can get Dawn out of here tomorrow, okay?"

"I'd be happier if you would. I wish we could find some place out of town for her, but she should be okay at your parents' place."

"She probably won't mind missing a few days of school, either. But only a few," I said. "Remember, she's in high school now. She can't afford to stay out for too long."

"Are you hinting that you'd like me to wrap this up quickly?" Peter laughed. "Right you are, boss." He saluted sharply and turned toward the door.

On his way out, he looked back at me. "Do me a favour. Keep the phone on you, okay? If you put it in your purse, you'll never find it again, and it's a rental."

I saluted. "Roger. Over and out."

19

TUESDAY, OCTOBER 18
Sun conjunct Mercury ✦
Moon opposition Pluto ✦
Venus conjunct Mars ✦

Dawn was not keen on our plan to protect her from rampaging Russian mobsters. She didn't know the details of why I suddenly wanted her to pack up her toothbrush and move in with Zayde and Sabte, and Dawn is not known for taking adult authority on faith.

"Mom, this is stupid! If there's something going on, at least tell me what it is, so I can make up my own mind."

"Dawn, listen. I'm not just being capricious — your father and I talked last night, and we decided that for your own safety, you should be out of this apartment. And the less you know, the better."

"But why? What's happening? And how come I have to go, and you get to stay?"

"I don't know for sure that I'm going to stay here. I might go spend a couple of nights at Greg's place or something. And I promised your father that I wouldn't talk about what's going on, because it could compromise him if it leaked out."

"Oh, so you don't trust me to keep my big mouth shut, is that it?" Dawn looked daggers at me.

"No, no, that's not it at all. Look, I don't even know exactly what's happening. All I know is that your father is involved in some investigative journalism thing that turned ugly. A guy got killed, and Peter is worried that whoever killed him might turn on us, if they can figure out where to find us. I don't really think we're in actual danger, but I do think it's worth taking precautions, okay?"

"Yeah, I guess." She sighed. "But why couldn't I just go and stay with Sylvie? That way, I wouldn't miss too much school."

"Didn't you tell me Sylvie's mom is out of town? I can't say I like the idea of two fifteen-year-olds staying alone. Not to mention Sylvie's little brother — how old is he, twelve?"

"He's thirteen. And we're nearly sixteen, Mom. We could take care of ourselves, really."

"I don't think so. Come on, get your stuff together. I'll drive you over to your grandparents' place this morning. Hey, think of it as a little vacation — your dad says he'll be finished the story sometime this week, so it shouldn't hurt your grades, and you can just hang around and reprogram Zayde's computer, or something."

"Yeah, maybe I could persuade him to upgrade from a 386. I've been on his case about that one for a while now." For the first time that morning, a smile flitted across her face. "Have you told them I'm coming?"

"I called before you were up. They're looking forward to it. I told them I had to go out of town for a couple of days on work, and I needed someone to look after you. So that's our story, okay?"

"Right. Let's synchronize watches," Dawn said. "Oh, and let me call Sylvie, okay?"

We loaded Dawn's backpack and several tons of school books into The Behemoth, which I'd parked on the street outside my building. Another of the joys of car ownership — I was going to have to rent a parking space for the thing. Oh bliss, oh joy.

Never mind, at least I had wheels, and if I could get Dawn settled with my parents in the next hour, I could be back at my office earning what passes for my living by ten. Rush hour was nearly over by the time I eased The Behemoth up the ramp onto the Queensway and merged seamlessly into the fast lane. Dad had been right — all you had to do was touch the gas on this thing, and you could pretend you were doing qualifying laps for the Grand Prix. We sped along, the car smooth and silent, and Dawn laughed suddenly.

"What?"

"Well, it's just such a change from the Flaming Deathtrap," she said. "I never knew you could drive this fast without your car vibrating itself to death. And Zayde always drove this thing like it was a hearse!"

"It has that funereal look, that's for sure. But we got horsepower under this here hood, baby!" To illustrate, I gave The Behemoth a bit more gas, and we surged forward.

"Mom!" Dawn laughed. "Come on, you'll get us arrested for speeding!"

Obligingly, I slowed down to only twenty kilometres above the posted limit.

"That's funny ..." I glanced in the rearview mirror.

"What?"

"Probably nothing. But there's this blue Pontiac in the next lane. When we sped up just now, it raced to catch up with us. Now it's pulled back into the middle lane."

"Where?" Dawn turned to see.

"Turn around!" I said sharply. "If they really are following us, I don't want them to know that we know."

I checked the rearview mirror again. The car was still there, keeping pace with us. Not so unusual on the Queensway, but Peter's visits yesterday had me spooked. I sailed past the exit for my parents' house, and pulled into the middle lane. The blue Pontiac stayed put. At the next exit, I swerved onto the off-ramp at the very last minute, but the Pontiac managed to stay with us. It was right behind us now, and I caught a glimpse of a man, grey hair, sunglasses.

"Dawn, check your side mirror, okay? See if that guy looks familiar to you."

Dawn obliged. "Um, I don't know ... maybe. Who does it look like to you?"

"Well, call me crazy, but he looks an awful lot like that guy Jimmy was having lunch with, back at the Chinese restaurant."

I heard Dawn's sharp intake of breath. "Shit, Mom, I think you're right! The hat threw me off, but yeah, I can see it now. So what's he want with us?"

"I don't know, but I'm not about to stick around and find out."

I turned north onto Woodroffe, sauntering along as though my daughter and I were just out for a Tuesday morning spin in our ridiculously large car. The Pontiac moved back a couple of cars, but I glimpsed it when we pulled up at a red light.

"What do we do now?" asked Dawn.

"I'm not sure. Honey, get my purse off the floor, would you? There's a cell phone in the front pocket."

Dawn rummaged industriously for a couple of minutes, and came up with the phone. "Hey, I never knew you had one of these! Where'd you get it?"

"Your dad gave it to me." I glanced back as we turned onto Carling. Still there. Which button had Peter programmed to reach him? "Hit that little green button there, that turns it on. Okay, now hit the pound key."

"It's ringing. Dad? Is that you? You sound really far away.... Yeah, we're on our way to Zayde and Sabte's place. But there's this car that's been following us.... I don't know. Yeah, here she is." She passed the phone to me.

Without preamble, Peter said, "Did you get a look at the plates?"

"No, I couldn't see them. Actually, I don't think he has front plates. It's a blue Pontiac, fairly new, and the driver has grey hair. I think we saw him having lunch with Jimmy Healey the other day. Peter, what should I do?"

"Nothing. Just drive around slowly, like you know where you're going, and head toward the nearest police station. Your guy isn't likely to follow you there. Call me back when you get there, okay? I want to know you're safe."

My heart thumping, I drove down Carling right at the speed limit. My buddy in the blue Pontiac did the same, from a distance of three or four cars back. By the time we reached Bronson Avenue, I had absolutely no doubt that we were being tailed; why else would someone follow us west along the Queensway, then back east down Carling?

Dawn, who'd been silent for some time, suddenly piped up. "Hey, Mom? I'm sorry I didn't believe you before. About me having to go to Zayde and Sabte's, I mean. I thought you were just being paranoid."

"Yeah, well, it's not paranoia when they're really out to get you." The joke fell flat, but I didn't care. All I wanted was to get to the police station. Preferably in one piece. "Dawn, take out the phone again. Dial 555-1004."

Benjamin's work number. Dawn dialled, and handed the phone to me.

"Benjamin? Hi, it's Katy. I'm on Bronson about to turn into Gladstone right now, heading east, and I should be at the police station in about five minutes, if this light ever changes. Can you meet us at the door downstairs?"

"Sure." He sounded bemused. "What's up? You planning to sweep in and take me away from all this?"

"You wish. I'll explain when I get there. Oh, and Benjamin? Bring your gun." I hung up, feeling slightly nervous and slightly giggly. I could imagine his face right now, his right eyebrow shooting up nearly to his hairline, the way it does when he thinks I'm being completely outrageous. Well, wait till he heard this one — he'd have a stroke.

I turned from Gladstone onto Elgin, the blue Pontiac right behind me. I could see the driver now, his mouth set in a grim line. It was our friend from the restaurant, all right. There was no mistaking that frizz of grey hair, the unshaven chin. He must have figured out by now where I was heading, and he did not look at all pleased. Tough bananas, buddy, I thought. As I pulled into the small circular drive outside the police station, the guy floored it and flew past me, taking the right at Catherine with a screeching of tires. I flopped back against my seat, still clutching the steering wheel as though it might escape from my white knuckled grip. My heart was racing.

There was Benjamin, ambling out the glass front doors, looking just as quizzical as I'd imagined.

"I never thought I'd be glad to see him," Dawn whispered.

I shushed her as Benjamin leaned his elbows against the car, bending down to talk through my window.

"You want to tell me what's going on, Katy Klein?" He smelled strongly of breath mints.

"Did you see that guy in the blue Pontiac who took off around the corner? He's been tailing us for about twenty minutes now. I first noticed him along the westbound Queensway, so I got off and doubled back along Carling. He stayed right with me, all the way here. Then I guess he figured the jig was up, so he took off in a snit. That's what."

"Ah. And just why would this person be following you? I know you attract criminals like bees to nectar, but this seems a little extreme, even for you."

"Ha ha ha. Most amusing, Benjamin. I should have known you wouldn't take this seriously. Well, as it happens, there is a reason. If you'd like to hear it, you can come and join us for coffee. There's a place down the street that makes a decent brew, right?"

Without a word, Benjamin went around to the rear passenger side door and let himself in. "Hey, nice car, by the way. Lots of leg room. Where'd you get it?"

"I killed a cop for it. Don't worry, he died nobly." Benjamin gave me a look. "Oh, all right. My parents gave it to me. Birthday present," I said.

Though it would have been just as easy to walk to the café, I drove back along Elgin, and found a parking space near the community centre. There is absolutely nothing like the smell of a really good cup of coffee after you've just had the wits scared out of you. I had not known this before, but as we entered the café, I inhaled the rich air deeply, and suddenly felt giddy with relief.

We sat down, Dawn with her chamomile tea, Benjamin and I with our enormous cups of Kenyan dark roast.

"The thing is, I don't know exactly who the guy was, but my ex-husband just told me yesterday that he's been doing some big investigative piece on ... well, he wasn't specific, but my guess is he's been looking into the Russian maffiya. Whoever it is, they shot his partner in

Montreal the other day. Peter's scared, and he thinks we might be next." Dawn looked startled at all this, but said nothing. Benjamin just nodded.

"So last night, he showed up at my place, gave me this cell phone, and told me he's going underground for a few days, until the story breaks. Apparently he came down and asked the police to guard Dawn and me, but they said no. So I was just on my way to take Dawn to her grandparents' house, when I realized I was being followed."

"Good thinking, calling me," Benjamin said.

"I can't take credit for it," I admitted. "I called Peter, and he suggested it."

"So — have you guys caught up with the guy who killed Mandy Weatherburn yet?" Dawn leaned across the table, a challenging glint in her eye. "I saw him driving around yesterday, you know. With this Russian rabbi who's been staying with my grandparents."

"Who did you see?" Benjamin raised an eyebrow at Dawn.

"Jimmy, of course! Isn't he your prime suspect, these days? And he was with Masha, the rabbi."

Shit. I made an involuntary noise, and Dawn and Benjamin both looked at me.

I swallowed my coffee. "Sorry. It's just that ... well, it's way too coincidental to be true, but what if Masha is involved in this organized crime thing somehow? I mean, just because she's Russian doesn't mean she's a gangster, but still ... .If I take Dawn over to her grandparents, we'll be walking right into it, won't we? How stupid can I be?"

Benjamin coughed. "Okay, who the hell is Masha?"

"Masha is a rabbi who's visiting my parents' congregation from Montreal, trying to do some kind of outreach to new Russian Jewish immigrants here," I said. "Except that when my mother went over to the *shul* to check up on her yesterday, she wasn't there. And Dawn did report seeing Jimmy, by the way. Right, Dawn?"

"Well, I called Hendricks, anyway." She avoided Benjamin's eyes. "He told me they'd take care of it."

"It's the first I've heard of it." Benjamin frowned. "I didn't know he was still around town."

"But I thought you said you and the OPP were working on the two cases together," I said.

"We are, but it's not a perfect system yet. And old rivalries die hard," Benjamin said. "Dawn, in future, if you think you've spotted anything, anything that might be relevant to this case, you come directly to me, you understand? You can let your buddies at the OPP know about it too, but if you leave me out of the loop, I'm going to be extremely pissed with you, and I don't care how much I care about your mother ..." He stopped himself, suddenly red in the face.

"Sorry," Dawn muttered.

"Okay, apology accepted. Now, where exactly did you see Jimmy?"

Dawn told him what she'd already told me, and Benjamin wrote it down. "Did you get a license number on the car? Make? Model?"

My daughter the junior detective had indeed noticed these details, and she and Benjamin hunched over his notebook, making sure he got it exactly right. He thanked her, and she sat back, looking pleased.

"Katy, have you heard from your friend Flavia yet?"

I shook my head. "Just what I told you on your voicemail yesterday. Nothing new to report. Listen, getting back to this thing about Masha — how do I know she's not involved in some kind of gang activity too? My mother says she hasn't shown up at the *shul* for the past week, and no one will say where she is. I don't like it."

Benjamin scratched his chin. "Okay, here's what we do. You two come back to the station with me, and I'll make a few phone calls, see if we can figure out who this Masha person is. Katy, I agree with Peter, the two of you should be out of sight for the next little while. One way or another, we'll find you a place to stay."

"See?" Dawn was triumphant. "I told you you should be laying low too, Mom."

"She's right, Katy. Can you call in sick at your office until this blows over?"

"Only if we don't mind starving to death," I retorted. "Look, I'll be fine. I've got clients lined up at work — in fact, one of them should be getting there in about an hour. All I want is to find a safe place for Dawn, and get her to it. I told Peter the same thing last night — we self-employed people don't have the luxury of calling in sick. And if I travel back and forth from my office to my parents' house, I might as well stick a great big neon sign on the place: 'Peter Fischer's daughter is right here, guys, fire at will.' I'm not doing that."

Benjamin gave me an exasperated look, but didn't bother trying to argue with me. We walked back to the police station, and he made us wait in a little white room with a video camera pointing down at us, while he went to make some phone calls. I called Peter and reassured him we were okay, then sat leafing through three-year-old issues of *People* magazine with half the pages torn out, while Dawn jiggled one leg and drummed her fingers on the arm of her chair. Benjamin returned forty-five long minutes later.

"It's okay." He came into the room and closed the door behind him. "She's in the clear. I ran Masha Streltsov's name through one of our contacts with the Russian embassy, as well as with the police in Montreal.

She checks out clean as a whistle. She is exactly who she says she is, a rabbi from Russia. I don't think Dawn should have any problem staying with your parents, Katy."

Dawn's mouth fell open. "But—what about Jimmy? I *saw* the two of them yesterday, driving right past me! It was her, I'm absolutely sure of it!"

Benjamin shrugged. "I don't know, Dawn. Can you be absolutely certain? This woman's credentials are pretty impressive—and she is a rabbi, by the way. I thought I'd check that out, too. Can't be too careful, you know."

God, had Benjamin and Peter somehow been separated at birth? Never mind—at least I had a safe place to put Dawn now. I thanked Benjamin, who offered to have a uniformed cop drive Dawn to my parents' place.

"My dad has already had one stroke," I said. "I think seeing their granddaughter delivered by a cop could easily push both of them over the top. I'll take her. But thanks!" I've learned the hard way that Benjamin tends to take offense when I don't accept his generosity. He seemed okay this time, and let us go with a caution to keep out of sight and let him know if anything happened. I assured him we would.

Dawn groused and grumbled all the way back to the car. "If Masha's such a paragon, working for the embassy and all, what's she doing riding around with that murderer? I know it was her, I just know it! Damn Benjamin. He's just the same as he ever was—discounts my opinions just because I'm younger than he is. We should report him for age discrimination, that's what we should do ..." And so on, for several long blocks. I resisted the urge to tell her to put a sock in it. No point making an unpleasant situation worse. At least she was talking to me, for the moment.

We made it back to the Queensway without further

incident, and as far as I could tell, no one followed or otherwise molested us on the drive back to my parents'. However, I did remember that I had a client waiting for me, so I got Dawn to dial Sam's number, then pass me the cell phone.

"Hey, Sam," I said. "How was the dinner last night?"

"Not bad. Brought a wine I hadn't tried before. Chicken was a bit overdone, though. Good sauce. You're late today — client rang the bell ten minutes ago. Let her in; she's waiting for you."

"Damn. Okay, would you mind telling her I'll be another twenty minutes or so? If she doesn't want to wait, I'll call her back to reschedule."

"Got it. Think she'll want to stay, though. Seemed upset."

"Well, okay. I'll get back as soon as I can."

That would be Miranda, a relatively new client, who probably needed a shrink more than an astrologer. I don't do therapy any more, but some people are happy just to come and tell me their problems, hoping the stars will tell them there's an end in sight. Miranda was one of those. I wondered what she was upset about this time.

It didn't take long to drop Dawn off. I waved cheerily at my parents from the car, and refused all attempts to entice me inside, including my mother's announcement that she'd just pulled a fresh batch of *mandelbrot* out of the oven. It would have to wait. Dawn and I exchanged hugs, and she lugged her stuff into the house as I pulled away and aimed The Behemoth back toward the Glebe.

20

I pulled up along Second Avenue, still on the alert for a late-model blue Pontiac. Everything looked as it should: the huge oaks and maples arched over the street, their brilliant autumn colours filtering the sun, fallen leaves creating a glorious carpet along the sidewalk. A Philipina nanny hustled her charges along, one in a stroller, the other on a tiny bicycle. A golden retriever followed them at a more sedate pace, checking out tree trunks as he passed, paying no attention to the nanny's exhortations to hurry up.

The front door to Sam's house was locked, as was my office. Miranda must have taken Sam's advice and gone home. My office was quiet and dim, the sun having moved past the huge front window already. I dumped my knapsack on the floor, hung my sweater up, and breathed in the smell of the wax Sam used to keep the floors gleaming in this house. The light on my answering machine was flashing, as usual. I crossed the room, and my finger had nearly reached the play-back button when someone sniffed.

I froze, and I believe my heart stopped for several seconds, before it began a galloping beat, presumably making up for lost time. I whirled around. A small, rumpled person sat on my futon, knees drawn up to her chin. This was not Miranda, who tends toward the large and blowsy.

"Rowan! What are you doing here?" I'm sure I didn't sound particularly welcoming, for she cringed, as though I'd raised my fist.

"I'm sorry," she whispered. "The landlady let me in. She said I could wait for you in here — she said you called."

"And you locked the door from the inside," I said. "Don't tell me, let me guess. You're afraid your brother's henchman will find you here. So — how'd you escape the clutches of the evil Aaron, anyway? Last time I heard from you, you were lost in the wilds of Northern Ontario somewhere."

"I got out right after I talked to you. Aaron was asleep, and I realized that if I wanted to get out of there, I couldn't wait for anyone to help me. So I hid in the toolbox on the back of his pickup truck. I took all the tools out and hid them in the woods. He thought I'd left, and he didn't think of looking there, and when he drove into town to look for me, I jumped out when he went to make a phone call in the diner. The cell phone was dead, you see, from when I was talking to you. I waited until he was gone, and then I got a ride with a nice truck driver who felt sorry for me. It wasn't as hard as I thought it would be."

There was a trace of pride in her voice, and I had to admit, I was impressed. I never would have credited this little mouse of a person with the resourcefulness to carry out such a scheme.

"Wow," I said. "But that doesn't explain what you're doing here. Why come to see me? Why not the police?"

She hung her head. "Mandy was my only friend. Well, except for Geoff and Jimmy, but ... well, anyway, I couldn't face talking to the police. I just can't believe Jimmy could have ... well, you know, taken Geoff's life. They didn't always get along, but Jimmy wouldn't do that, not in a million years. So I couldn't go to the police, I couldn't go to Mandy's, I couldn't go home ..."

"Rowan, I don't want to be mean about this, but I'm not exactly your friend," I said. "Not that I dislike you or anything, but we've only just met. And I'm not really sure I want you coming here, when your homicidal maniac of a brother and his big ugly buddy are out looking for you. In fact, I think Aaron already suspects I'm harbouring you — he followed me this morning."

"Followed you?" Rowan's eyes were huge.

"Yes, in his car. I had Dawn with me, too. I really can't expose her to whatever problems you're having. It kind of puts me in an awkward position, do you see that?"

"Yes, but where else can I go? I can't go home, they'll find me there! And with Mandy gone ..." She raised her face, and I saw she'd been crying. I should have felt more sympathetic, given my own recent propensity for bursting into tears, but all I felt was annoyance. She was trying to drag me into a very messy situation, and I was not at all happy about it. However, I didn't want to just turf her out; maybe I could help without putting myself or my family in danger.

I dropped into my desk chair, which creaked alarmingly. "Well, you can't exactly live here. We'll have to find you a place to stay the night. Wait, I think I know." I fished around on the bookshelf next to my desk for my directory of community services, a remnant from my days as a practicing psychologist. "Here it is. I'm going to call one of the women's shelters. You'll be safe there — they don't publicize their addresses, and they help women on the run from violent men. Just because you don't happen to be married to Jimmy shouldn't make any difference. You're still afraid of him, and these places specialize in scared women."

"Oh, thank you!" Rowan's voice broke, and I correctly anticipated another flood of tears. I passed her the box of tissues — between me and Rowan, it was getting a real workout this week.

"Don't worry, this is as much for me as it is for you," I said. The first shelter I called was full, but the second said they could hold a space for a couple of hours. I relayed the news to Rowan, who looked pathetically grateful.

"I'm surprised you didn't think of it," I said. "I mean, you managed to find your way back from — where was it? Goblin Lake? That was pretty clever of you."

"Skeleton Lake. You know, it's silly, really — people like me never expect to have to go someplace like a women's shelter. It's just not part of the equation. We go to the golf club, or the yacht club, or the health spa. Or shopping. At least, that's what I did with Mandy."

"You were friends for a long time?"

"Years. She married my brother right after she moved here from the States. He thought she was the most beautiful thing he'd ever seen, and she could be very charming. When she wanted to be."

"You know, for her best friend, you're sounding a little on the jaded side."

"She wasn't my best friend — I was hers. After a while, I was her only friend, and she basically pushed everyone else out of my life. If I liked someone, she'd make sure they didn't hang around long. She was very possessive, and she liked having me around — you know, the plain girl who makes the pretty one feel even better about herself. She'd have liked me even better if I'd been fat."

"Rowan, you're not exactly Quasimodo, you know. You could be quite attractive, if you stood up straight and looked people in the eye."

"Uh, thanks. I think," she said, with a small smile.

"Geez, I probably sounded just like Mandy there, didn't I?"

"A little. But she was a pro — she could throw out a sentence that cut to the quick, so fast you wouldn't even know what hit you. I've always been a little shy, and she took advantage of that. After a few years, I started to believe everything she said about me — I even let people call me Ronnie. I *hate* that name." She shuddered. "And I started to depend on her to tell me what we'd be doing that day, that week. I never wanted to go to the AstroFest. I know enough about astrology to know that we'd have been way out of our depth there. But she insisted, and what Mandy wanted, Mandy got. Without exception."

"So if you felt this way about her, how come you stayed with her?"

Rowan flushed and looked down. "I don't know. Loyalty, I guess. Or stupidity. Take your pick."

"You don't seem very stupid to me. Stupid people don't figure out ways to get their kidnappers to drop them off in town so they can hitchhike home, do they?"

She gave me a grateful smile, tinged with embarrassment. "I guess not."

"So, is it true she was the one who wanted a divorce from your brother?"

"Sort of. She had dozens of affairs, but mostly she managed to keep them to herself. He found out about one of them about a month ago. He came down on her hard — told her to choose between them. She told him she was leaving, and taking all her money with her, but the stupid thing is, Jimmy had more money than she ever would. Our parents died when I was fifteen, and they left us substantial trust funds. Jimmy never needed Mandy's money, but she always made this big thing of it, like she'd married him out of a sense of charity or something. As if

Jimmy couldn't have had any woman he wanted — he was gorgeous, still is, and he's so sweet-natured."

"Which explains why he had your brother killed and you kidnapped? I still don't see the point of that," I said. "It's not like you were about to turn him in for killing Mandy, was it?"

"I don't know! I still can't really bring myself to believe he killed Geoff. It's just that — well, what I heard sounded bad. Really bad. And he's been so brusque and short with me since Mandy died. It's not like him, not at all."

"Sometimes people snap, for one reason or another. Do you think maybe he got into some kind of jealous rage about Mandy's affair, and did her in?" I was starting to sound like Dawn.

Rowan was shaking her head. "I know he wouldn't have killed Mandy. And he wasn't even there — he didn't show up till after she was already dead!"

"Well, the police will figure it all out. I guess you haven't seen Jimmy since you got back to town, huh?"

"No. Katy, this is just so completely out of character for him. You know, he's always been so protective of me, I've always trusted him completely. Until the other night when he came over and told me he had to have me moved out of town, for my own safety. I told him I didn't need protection, but he wouldn't listen. He just told me Aaron would be by to pick me up and take me someplace safe, and I should trust him. That's when I called you."

Something about this conversation rang a dull thud for me. "For your own protection? Huh. Interesting. You know, someone just said something like that to me, not that long ago," I said. "What does Jimmy do for a living, again?"

"He's an international financier. I don't exactly know what he does, but it has to do with foreign exchange rates and stuff. It's very complex. He and a bunch of other high-powered guys started this business down on the Market a few months ago, and it's really taken off. Not that he needed the money, but I think he likes the challenge of it."

"Foreign exchange?" I shook my head. "I wouldn't know the first thing about it. So ... why would someone in that line of work have the kind of enemies who might be a danger to his family?"

"He wouldn't tell me a thing about it. He said the less I knew, the better."

"So do you know where he's hiding now? The last I heard, the cops didn't know he was back in town, and I think they want to talk to him about Mandy's death.."

"I've heard. He and Aaron talked about it the night they took me up to that horrible little shack in the woods. He told me it would all work out, that eventually I'd see that he'd acted in Mandy's best interests, that he hadn't wanted her dead at all. I believed him, you know? But then I heard Aaron talking to him about Geoff, and I started to wonder, and then I just couldn't stop shaking. Our baby brother ..."

"I meant to ask you about that — how come you guys had different last names?"

"We all had the same mother, but after our father died, she remarried. I was seven, Jimmy was seventeen. Geoff was born when I was in Grade 3, and I was so proud! My very own baby brother. He was such a little butterball ... all my friends were so jealous. In fact, I think Mandy originally had her eye on him, before the car crash. It was when he was in teacher's college. He'd been drinking, wrapped our mother's car around a telephone pole, and broke his neck. After that, he was in a wheelchair, and Mandy lost interest. That's when she went after Jimmy."

"You make her sound like a bird of prey."

"Do I? Funny. While she was alive, I could tell myself that she was just naive, that she didn't know what impact she had on other people. In the last few days, though, I've started to realize how free I feel without her."

"Well, yeah, if you discount the fact that one of your brother's thugs is after you ..."

"Yes, there's that, all right." Rowan giggled nervously.

"Speaking of which, we'd better get you over to that shelter. Do you have everything you need with you?"

She giggled again, high-pitched and fluttery. "I don't have a thing with me. I got out of that place with the clothes on my back. I haven't brushed my teeth in two days. I can feel them growing fuzz, as we speak."

"Yuck. They should be able to fix you up at the shelter," I said. "We can't just walk out of here together — I'll show you how to get out to the back yard. I'll back the car in, you hop into the back seat and crouch. There's plenty of room back there, no one will see."

I was right. Rowan huddled on the floor in the back seat, my sweater thrown over her for extra camouflage. We drove without incident to the shelter, where I parked in the back laneway, and we smuggled Rowan inside, my sweater still draped over her head, as though she were a movie star escaping the paparazzi.

Gen, the staff person who greeted us at the door, took Rowan by the elbow and guided her into the office, where they sat down to fill out the necessary paperwork. I bowed out, and headed back to the office, where I actually hoped I might accomplish a bit of work. My second client of the day was due any time now, and I still had to call the first and reschedule our appointment.

The rest of my clients showed up on time, and I spent the latter part of the afternoon calculating and delineating a progressed chart for Miranda, who had not, in fact, remembered her appointment with me that morning. She was apologetic, which spared me the necessity of apologizing for my own tardiness, so it all worked out neatly in the end.

By the time the phone rang at four-thirty, I was engrossed enough in my work to let the answering machine pick up for me. This was, in fact, a good decision.

"Ms. Klein? It's James Healey here. We met briefly over the weekend, when my wife died. You might remember me. Ms. Klein, I have reason to believe that my sister, Rowan, has been in contact with you. She's a very disturbed individual, and it's important that I find her as soon as possible. She's been known to try to hurt herself, and she's very upset right now because of my wife's death. I'd very much appreciate it if you could call me back as soon as you get this — my number is 555-4532. Thank you." Click.

I rewound the message and listened to it again, jotting down the number out of habit. This guy was smooth — his voice had an edge of concern to it, and if I hadn't just talked to Rowan that morning, I'd have been inclined to believe him. As it was, I dialled Benjamin's number.

"Listen to this." I played him the message.

"I'll be right over. Sit tight." He hung up.

Within fifteen minutes, he was at my door. He pocketed the answering machine tape and then stood patiently while I told him the story of Rowan's visit.

"We'd like to talk to her, too," he said. "Where is she?"

"At Artemis House. I figured it was the safest place for her. Benjamin, can you clue me in on something? What kind of enemies would be most likely to come after someone who was in the foreign exchange business?"

"Well, a lot of those foreign exchange places are just thinly disguised money laundering operations. They don't call Canada the Maytag of the North for nothing, you know. We're a haven for every criminal in the world who wants his money looking clean and pretty."

"So if James Healey was laundering money, he could find himself with a lot of very unsavoury friends." Then another thought occurred to me. "So ... is it just possible that Jimmy could have been for real — that he knew his whole family was being targetted, so he sent Rowan away before anyone could hurt her?"

Benjamin shifted his weight. "It's a possibility." Then he cleared his throat. "Uh, Katy, I know I don't have to tell you this again, but none of this goes any further, right?"

"You mean the tape? Sure, no problem."

"Not just the tape. Rowan's whereabouts, and all that stuff about Jimmy Healey's work. Would you mind keeping that under your hat?"

I sighed. "Who would I tell? I swear, Benjamin, this is starting to sound like one of those cheesy spy movies. People being spirited away for their own safety, everything on a need to know basis ..."

Benjamin interrupted. "By the way, you haven't heard from Flavia, have you?"

"Not a word," I admitted. "But I'm sure there's a good reason."

"Well, when you find out what it is, let me know, would you? Now, I'm going to have to send some guys in here to diddle around with your phone, just in case you get any more interesting calls. Just a little box to record incoming calls — we don't need anything fancy. The crew should get here in the next few hours. Do you mind staying here a while?"

"Not really. Dawn's at her grandparents' place, and I'm not in any rush to get home. This whole thing has me creeped out, Benjamin."

"As well it might," he said. "But you should be just fine, as long as you don't do anything stupid. Or say anything. To anyone." With a brief hug and a peck on the cheek, he left.

21

The sun was setting earlier and earlier these days, a prelude to the dark days of winter that lay ahead. I walked around the office, turning on lights and drawing the blinds, before I got back to work. Despite my brave words to Benjamin and Dawn earlier that day, I wasn't altogether certain I wanted to spend the night alone at my apartment, jumping at my old house's every creak and rustle, waiting for some crazed Russian mobster to burst in and air-condition my insides. On the other hand, I didn't really want to stay here in the office, either. I'd parked The Behemoth in the side driveway, but if my friend in the blue Pontiac really wanted to find me, that big black car was just sitting there, advertising my presence.

I decided to wait until the police had come and wired my phone, and then ask Greg if I could crash at his place. Despite the presence of his twin Siamese cats, Gemini and Ezekiel (aka the Evil Shredders of Doom), who professed a deep kitty love for me despite my ambivalence toward them, at least I'd get a few hours' sleep there. Plus, I could at last follow through on my resolution to ask Greg for a referral to a good shrink. I called, but he wasn't in his office. His secretary assured me, though, that he'd be back early in the evening, and that he'd be certain to call.

Idly, I opened and closed files on my laptop, played a couple of rounds of Minesweeper. I lost both. It's not that I didn't have enough to do, but I was feeling edgy and distracted, not concentrating well. James Healey. I clicked on the file, opened it, and stared blankly at his birthchart, as though I'd never seen it before.

There was that powerful Mars, ruler of the Midheaven, sitting in the fourth house of family, home, beginnings. So he'd chosen a career that would enable him to feel he was defending what was dear to him, in the best way he knew how. And yet, with Neptune opposing the Midheaven, it seemed as though his vision of his mission in life was clouded somehow, occluded by his need to remember childhood as though it were a wonderful, idealized dream. And he'd be obsessed with saving others, rescuing people and situations: here, it seemed was a true romantic. So how did this tie in with the deaths of his wife and brother? I rubbed the side of my nose, pondering. What if Dawn was right, and he really was in the process of bumping off his family? Then again … what if he'd just got himself involved in some kind of shady underworld deal — like, for instance, with the goon Dawn had scared away from the Chinese restaurant — and it wasn't Jimmy, but some organized crime syndicate that was killing off his loved ones?

Suddenly, I was seized with a very bad idea. I knew it was a poor plan from the outset, and I knew that if Benjamin were to find out about it, he'd kill me — if I didn't manage to get myself killed first. But I wanted to know: who was Jimmy, and what was he up to? I picked up the phone, found the number I'd scribbled as I listened to his phone message, and dialled it.

The phone rang and rang, but no one picked up. I let it ring twelve, thirteen, fourteen times, before I finally gave up and dropped the receiver back into its cradle. So much for my really stupid ideas. I went back to staring at Jimmy's chart, as though it could give me the answers I needed. Mars seemed to be the key here. Mars is the planet that describes our energy, our vigour, our ability to act effectively, to have other people sit up and take notice. Jimmy and Mandy both seemed to have a surfeit of Mars energy in their charts.

Unlike me. Where had my Mars gone? In the past, I'd been accused of being too in-your-face, too likely to leap before thinking, but those days seemed long gone now. My Mars seemed to have gone into hiding. I wondered whether it would ever come back.

The phone shrilled by my elbow, startling me. I grabbed it.

"Ms. Klein, this is James Healey. Your number came up on my call display. Thank you for calling back."

Of course — he'd been screening his calls. "You're welcome. But I'm afraid I can't help you find your sister, Mr. Healey."

There was a long silence on the other end. "Can't or won't? I have reason to believe she's been in contact with you recently. I really need to find her, Ms. Klein. It's a matter of life and death."

"So you said. But what makes you think she'd come to me? I hardly know her."

"Please. Let's drop this bullshit, okay?" Suddenly, the smoothness dropped away, and there was raw urgency in his voice. "I know she's been calling you because your number came up on the cell phone where I'd sent her. I need to find her, I can't let anything happen to her."

I paused for a long moment. I didn't really want to admit anything to Jimmy, but I couldn't deny the obvious.

"Okay, fine. I admit she did call me, but it was because she was terrified. You hire some thug to kidnap her and whisk her away to the back of beyond somewhere, you won't tell her what's going on — what did you expect her to do, Mr. Healey? She's scared, and I can't say I blame her."

"Look. I can't explain this to you right now, any more than I could to her. Especially over the phone. I told Rowan the other night she was just going to have to trust that I knew what was best. She's always trusted me before."

"Yes, but that was before she practically heard you admit you killed your half-brother, wasn't it? And we won't even get into what might have happened to your wife. I think that might kind of put a damper on her trust, don't you?"

There was an explosive noise on the other end of the line. I held the phone away from my ear.

"Look, I told Rowan this, and I'm telling you now. I didn't kill my wife, and I didn't kill Geoff. I can't tell you right now exactly what happened to them, but I swear to you, I had nothing to do with their deaths. Ms. Klein, you should know that I am an officer of the law. I can't tell you any more than that at the moment, but you have my word of honour. All I want is to keep my sister safe — she's my last remaining relative, and I love her. I would never, ever let any harm come to her. Can't you understand that?" There was a slight catch in his voice.

A cop? Jimmy Healey was a cop? Wouldn't *that* just rot Dawn's socks? It was my turn to pause and catch my breath.

"Mr. Healey, either you're a terrific actor, or you're telling me the truth. I honestly can't tell which. But can you trust me when I tell you your sister is in a very safe place right now?"

"What do you mean? Where is she?"

"I can't tell you that. But she's okay, I promise. And if that's really what you're worried about, that should be enough for you, right?"

He sighed. "It should. But you don't understand who we're dealing with here. These people are nuts, Ms. Klein. They kill whole families, not just the person they're pissed off with. They don't care who they hurt, and they will kill my sister if they find her, make no mistake."

They don't just kill the person who pisses them off; they take whole families down, just to show they can. Peter's words hummed through my head.

"Listen, Mr. Healey, I have to ask you a question. These people you're talking about, they're organized criminals, right? Like the mafia or something?"

He coughed, cleared his throat. "Something like that."

"And you're a cop, right? So you're trying to hunt them down, bring them to justice or whatever?"

"That's right."

"So ... can I ask what you were doing in a car with Masha Streltsov yesterday morning?"

There was a sharp intake of breath, and then Jimmy hung up with a clatter.

Well. Some people just have no telephone manners. I held down the little hang-up thingy on the phone for a couple of seconds, then released it and dialled Benjamin's number.

"Jimmy just called me again." I conveniently neglected to let him know that I'd precipitated the call myself. No point borrowing trouble.

To my surprise, though, Benjamin was remarkably sanguine about this piece of news."Oh yeah? What did he say? Did you write it down?"

Dang. I'd make a terrible cop. "No, I didn't think of

writing it down. But basically, he tried to reassure me that he's a nice guy. But Benjamin, why didn't you just tell me he was a cop?"

"He told you that?" Benjamin sounded shocked.

"Well, yeah. Is it true?"

Benjamin cleared his throat. "Katy, I can't really confirm ..."

"Oh, for heaven's sake, Benjamin, get off the pot. He told me himself, he's an 'officer of the law'. So I have to assume that you know this, right?"

I might as well have saved my breath. Benjamin has this irritating way of glossing over questions he just doesn't want to answer. "That's not something I can confirm or deny, Katy. Now, what else did Mr. Healey say?"

"Well, he swore up and down that he didn't kill his wife or Geoffrey Acres. He said the same people who killed those two are now after Rowan, too, which is why he hid her away like that. Um ... I don't think I'm forgetting anything. Oh! He got all huffy when I asked him about being in the car with Masha. That's when he hung up on me."

"You asked him about her?" Benjamin drew a deep breath, and I knew I was in for one of his lectures. Sure enough, he launched in. "Katy, let me explain something to you. I am a police officer. It's my job to ask questions, collect information, and possibly even arrest suspects. Are you with me so far?"

"Yes, boss," I sighed. No point trying to argue when he was in Cop Mode.

"Okay, good. So when you announce over the phone that your daughter saw this guy driving around town with this woman, you make things very difficult for me. You make it a lot harder for me, and a lot of other cops like me, to do our jobs. Do you remember me telling you not to talk to anyone about what we discussed earlier this afternoon?"

I admitted that I did. "But Benjamin, how does it hurt if I tell Jimmy he was seen with Masha? It's not like he didn't know it already, is it?"

Benjamin said nothing for a few seconds. I could see him in my mind's eye, squinting as he massaged his forehead. Finally, he spoke. "Katy, I try to be patient, really I do. You don't know the can of worms you're opening here, and I can't explain it over the phone. I don't know how many times I should have to say this to you — leave the cop business to me! "

Now I was starting to get annoyed. "Benjamin, look. I did my best, okay? He called me, I tried to find out as much as I could. I called you and passed it along. As you so frequently and delicately point out, I am but a lowly civilian. How am I supposed to know the correct procedure for interviewing potential criminals over the phone? There's no instruction manual for this, and frankly, I'd think you could be at least a little more gracious about it!"

Deep sigh. "Okay, you're right. I'm sorry. I guess if you didn't have a history of sticking your nose ..."

"... Into cop business," I finished for him. "Yeah, yeah, I know. Just call me Nancy Drew. Except I don't have titian hair, or a roadster. Or friends named George and Bess. But I don't know if you've noticed this or not, Benjamin — this time I've been going a long way out of my way to keep out of this whole thing. It just keeps finding me. Believe me, I'd like nothing better than to avoid the whole stinking, putrid mess."

"I know you would. I said I was sorry. Aw, geez, now I'm going to have to double that order of chocolate-covered coffee beans, aren't I?"

"At least." We hung up on somewhat friendlier terms.

It was not long afterward that two very pleasant young men in street clothing arrived, showed me their police identifications, and set about re-wiring my telephone. I couldn't tell you exactly what they did, but when they left, there was a small metal box attached to the phone, which would apparently capture any and all conversations. I signed a piece of paper one of the nice young men offered me, and they departed, leaving me to contemplate the small metal box.

I called Greg again, this time using the cell phone — I didn't really want my private phone conversations monitored by the Ottawa police, no matter how noble the cause. This time my friend was in his office. Of course I could stay the night at his place; he'd be right over to pick me up.

"No need, I've got this great hulking car now. I just wanted to make sure it wouldn't be, you know, inconvenient."

Greg laughed. "Oh, yeah, I live such a wild and crazy life, all right. Don't worry, you won't be interrupting a thing, except possibly my cuddling with the cats."

"Greg, we need to get you a girlfriend," I said. "It's not natural, your relationship with those beasts. And they don't appreciate you — every time your back is turned, they demolish another piece of your furniture. At least a girlfriend wouldn't claw your apartment to death."

"No, just my bank account, after we get married and she leaves me for her personal trainer." Greg spat the last words out. Personal trainers weren't high on his popularity list, as his wife had left him some time ago for hers, taking with her a large chunk of Greg's net worth. "Trust me, Katy, cats are better. They're loud, but at least they're predictable. And compared to ex-wives, they're quite affordable."

"Suit yourself, friend. Listen, I'll just finish up here,

and I should be at your place within the hour. Does that work for you?"

"Perfectly. Have you eaten yet? I'll order us a pizza."

Food? It suddenly occurred to me that I'd skipped lunch. Well, in all this excitement, perhaps I'd lose a pound or two. Zippedy-doo-dah. Now that he'd reminded me, though, my stomach began to growl, so I hurriedly closed up my laptop, gathered a few files together and shoved them in my knapsack, turned out all the lights, and locked my office door.

Just as I was turning to leave, I heard the phone ringing inside the locked office. Drat. I fished my keys out, and raced for the phone.

"Katy? Is that you? You sound out of breath, darlin'."

"Flavia? Where the hell have you been? I've been worried sick!" Then I realized: our conversation was being recorded. Well, nothing for it now. If she incriminated herself on the phone, so be it.

"I told you, I had to go for some intensive de-stressing," she said. "A yoga retreat I know about. There's this guy who works there, he's helped me out before. I knew I could count on him. He helps me centre myself, you know?"

"Uh, right. Well, did you know the cops up here have their underwear all in a twist these days, because you took off like that? Flavia, Benjamin told me you weren't supposed to leave the country. What's up with that?"

Silence.

"Flavia, you know you sort of left me holding the bag, here. I had to explain to the police that no, I didn't know you'd been asked to stick around until they'd done questioning you, and no, I didn't know that you'd been charged with issuing death threats to Mandy Weatherburn way back in the stone ages. It wasn't a nice feeling, you know what I mean?"

"Honey, I'm so sorry," Flavia said softly. "I didn't know that old stuff would come up again. I'm truly, truly sorry."

"Okay. Okay, I guess. I mean, I accept your apology and all that, but this is a really gargantuan mess, Flavia. What are you going to do now?"

"Do? Nothing, that's what. I never killed Mandy, and you know what? When we saw her on the dock that day, I realized I was finally free of her. I looked her right in the eye, and I didn't feel a thing. You know how many years it's taken me to get there?"

"No, but I can guess. I'm glad for you, but they still haven't caught her killer, and until they do, you're on the hit list. Don't you think it would be a good idea to come back, just to clear your own name?"

"Not on your life, sugar. If they want to talk to me, they can track me down. Now, listen, I have to run. I'm on the air in fifteen minutes. Don't know what my faithful listeners would do without La Divine Flavia to solve their astrological problems." She laughed. I tried to, but it wouldn't come. Instead, I just said good-bye, and hung up the phone.

So. She wasn't coming back. And you know, I believed her — I really didn't think she'd killed Mandy. Thinking back over Jimmy's last phone call, I wasn't sure I wanted to pin Mandy's death on him any more, either. Which left ... well, the other people on the island at the time had been Cara, Jane, Dawn, me, and Rowan. Rowan.

I rolled the facts around in my brain, trying to get them to fit into some kind of pattern. She had accompanied Mandy everywhere but to the bathroom, but she'd admitted that she hadn't exactly been the devoted friend and acolyte she appeared to be. In fact, she'd hated the nickname Mandy had bestowed on her — and perhaps she'd secretly hated her sister-in-law, as well. She came across all mealy-mouthed and soft, but she'd had the guts, and the smarts, to climb into a toolbox on the back of a pick-up truck, then hitchhike all the way back to Ottawa from Parry Sound. She had been out of our sight at Sycamore Island, the same as Flavia had — but she had the advantage of knowing ahead of time that Mandy was deathly allergic to bees and wasps. Maybe when she'd packed their suitcase, she'd conveniently tucked in a jar full of the deadly little critters?

It certainly wasn't outside the realm of possibility. And it was the perfect way to kill off a too-pushy friend. I pictured it: Mandy and Rowan, walking side by side through the woods, Rufus gallumphing along at their sides. Rowan steers them close to the little shed, shoves her friend inside, tosses in the jar of wasps, and bars the door. She was smaller than Mandy, that was true, but she was wiry, and who knew how strong she might be? And rage can sometimes give people an unexpected burst of strength.

As I turned this hypothesis over in my mind, I couldn't really see any major flaws in it. Maybe Jimmy had somehow known ahead of time that his sister was close to cracking. He'd followed them to the island, hoping to save his wife, but it was too late. Loyal to Rowan, he'd taken off, diverting suspicion to himself rather than letting his little sister risk arrest for the murder. Maybe Rowan hadn't been drugged at all, back there on the beach; maybe she'd been faking it, hoping to evade questioning for a while, to give herself time to think up a plausible story. But by the time she "came to," Jimmy was gone, the cops had pegged either him or Flavia for Mandy's death, and she was in the clear.

Oh, the more I thought about this, the better I liked it. Well, okay. I didn't like it, exactly — it is never pleasant, realizing that someone you know is a murderer — but for the first time in days, something was actually making sense to me. Motive, means, opportunity. I'd covered all the bases.

I picked up the phone, dialled Benjamin's number, and got his voice-mail.

"Benjamin, it's me, Katy. I don't want to throw a monkey wrench into your case against Jimmy, but I think I've come up with a plausible scenario about Mandy Weatherburn's death. I'd like to talk it over with you, as soon as you get back from the doughnut shop or wherever the heck you are. And you can double that order of chocolate-covered coffee beans. You're welcome."

Sam caught me on the way out the door.

"Leaving late," she observed. "Dawn not home?"

"No, at a friend's," I lied. "Figured I'd get a bit of extra work done." Oh, great. Now I was starting to talk like my eccentric landlady. I really was in need of some human companionship. A nice relaxing evening with Greg and a pizza seemed like just the ticket for me, right now.

22

Outside, darkness had fallen completely. The street-lamps glowed through the leaves and branches, shedding a dim light on the front of Sam's house. The side alleyway, where I'd parked The Behemoth, was completely shrouded. I picked my way between the car and the side of the next house, reflecting on the architects who'd stuck these huge houses so damn close together seventy-five years ago. Granted, The Behemoth was a wide car, but getting in here in the winter time was going to be a bitch.

As my father had warned, the dome light didn't light up when I opened the door, but I slid into the driver's seat, then felt around inside my purse for the keys. This whole car ownership thing was going to take some getting used to, I reflected, as I stabbed my finger on the tip of a pair of nail scissors. There was the cell phone, but where the hell were my keys? Huffing with frustration, I held up the purse and shook it. There was the tell-tale jingle. They were in there somewhere. I thrust my hand in again, determined to find the damn things ... ah, there they were, under my glasses case. In the dark, I felt for the plastic bulge that signified the car key, as opposed to the house or office keys ... et voilà! Victorious, I fit the key into the ignition, and the car purred to life.

Greg lives in Alta Vista, in one of those apartment buildings with doormen and security systems and pools and such. Briefly, I contemplated dropping by my place to pick up my bathing suit — a nice long swim, followed by a soak in the hot tub, would have done me a world of good, after the last few days. But if Peter was right, it wouldn't be safe to head for home, no matter how short the visit. Never mind, I'd go over the weekend, once this whole mess with the Russians or whoever they were was resolved. And it would be resolved by the weekend, wouldn't it? I massaged the back of my neck with one hand while I drove.

"*Dobri vyechyer*. Good evening, Ms. Klein. Just keep driving, please."

I froze. The soft, husky voice had come from the back seat.

The bottom dropped out of my stomach. Glancing in the rear view mirror, I saw a man, heavy-set, with hair clipped so short his skull was visible through it. He was not smiling. My mouth went very dry, and I began to shake.

"W-who are you?" I managed. "What do you want?"

"We are friends of your husband," the man said, in perfect, if slightly accented, English. "Please continue to drive. No one will get hurt."

We? I checked the mirror again. He was right — there was a second person back there. Same muscular neck. Same haircut. Same lipless mouth.

"What do you want?" I asked again. My voice did not sound like my own. It was muffled, far away. "Where's Pe — my husband?"

"That is not our concern. Not yet, at least. Right now, we wish to ask for your help. Please do not be alarmed." The man's voice was smooth as an anaconda. "You know the whereabouts of a friend of ours. Please to take us there."

"Friend? I don't know what you're talking about."

"From our homeland. Masha Streltsov, a Jew. We wish to speak with her."

"I don't know who you're talking about," I repeated, but the quaver in my voice gave me away.

"Please," the man said softly. "I think you do. You talk about her on the telephone. Do not try to be fooling with me."

For emphasis, he reached between the front seats and prodded me in the ribs with something hard and cold. I glanced down. It was the muzzle of a rather large gun.

A small whimpering noise escaped my throat. Fear coursed up and down my spine.

I couldn't take them to Masha. If I took them to her, I would also be taking them to Dawn and my mother and father. Sweat broke out on my face, dribbled down my back. I forced my lips to move, my tongue to form words, forced air through my teeth.

"What if I say no?" I asked. "What if I don't know where she is?"

"Then I would be upset," the man said evenly. "And I might have to hurt you. Of course, I don't like to hurt people, so it could take rather a long time. I don't think you would be very happy."

I had no doubt that he was right. But I'd be even less happy if my two unwanted guests were to meet my family. I shot a sidelong look at my purse, with the cell phone inside it, on the seat next to me. Would these two notice if I were to reach into it, turn on the phone, hit the 911 button Peter had programmed? I slid my right hand off the steering wheel and let it rest in my lap for a second. I got another prod in the ribs for my pains.

"Please, put both hands on the wheel. I like to know that you are a safe driver. Now, I repeat — where is the little Jew?"

I couldn't speak. A very large lump of something unpleasant had lodged itself in my throat, and my mouth was too dry to open. I shook my head.

"I will not ask you again. You will take us to her. Now."

The lights of Bank Street flashed by, twinkling gaily as though I was not being held in my own car at gunpoint. I brought the car to a standstill at the Fifth Avenue traffic light, and tried to rally my thoughts. I could drive these men in circles around the city, pretending to take them to Masha, but that would get stale pretty quickly, I was sure. The man with the gun did not seem unintelligent, and he was quite likely to notice that we were going nowhere fast. I didn't want to imagine the outcome.

Or I could give in, take them to my parents' house, and try to warn Dawn and my parents to get out of the way … but these two men did not seem as though they would be easily distracted, once they'd set their minds to their work. Even if we all got away, which was unlikely, they'd hunt us down afterward. I couldn't risk it.

What about Peter's trick — I could take them to the police station. But this time, there would be no Detective Benjamin standing reassuringly by the front door, waiting to see me to safety. I'd be on my own, and I probably wouldn't make it out of the car, let alone into the station. And taking them to the cop shop would likely just annoy these guys. I didn't want to annoy them.

There was nothing for it. I made a right turn on Sunnyside, and drove down the hill toward Bronson. The houses on either side of me were lit from the inside, families and students sitting down to late dinners, reading their newspapers, watching television, chatting with friends. It all seemed so intensely commonplace, so familiar, yet completely out of my grasp now. I had had a life at one time — had joked with Dawn, sat down with plates in our laps to shout out the answers to *Jeopardy!*, shared a coffee with Benjamin. That had been my life, but now it had all boiled down to this tiny pinprick of reality: me and two thugs and a gun, in a large car. I sped along Bronson Avenue toward the eastbound Queensway, with a gun stuck in my ribs and no hope of getting out alive.

"Slow down," the man with the gun commanded. "I don't want police to stop us."

Obediently, I touched the brake. Nothing much happened. I pushed harder. Still nothing. The gun seemed to bore into my ribs. I pushed the brake almost to the floor, and we fishtailed slightly, then began to slow.

"Where you are taking us? No tricks," warned the second man. This was the first time I'd heard him speak. His English was not as good as his partner's.

"To the east end," I said, around the cotton that was gluing my tongue to the roof of my mouth. "That's where she is. Masha."

Thug Number Two nodded and sat back, as I turned onto Chamberlain, and headed toward the Queensway on-ramp. Thug Number One eased up the pressure a little, and my ribs thanked him for it.

The Queensway was not crowded at this time on a Tuesday evening, but there was some traffic. I checked around, but didn't see any police cars. Where the hell were they? Any other time I drive along the Queensway, I see at least three OPP cars, cruising for speeders. If I could find one, and perhaps start driving just a little erratically, and they were to pull us over ... but there was nary a one in sight. I cursed silently. I could always try driving erratically anyway, hoping some alert citizen would see me and tattle on me. But what were the odds of that happening?

We sailed eastward along the Queensway, right at the speed limit, me glancing furtively in the rearview mirror every few seconds for any sign of a police car. Please. Please. Just one, one little cop in a car, that's all I need.

My two visitors sat side by side, grim and unrelenting.

"Go faster," the man with the gun said. "Keep up with traffic."

I touched the gas, and the car surged forward with a low rumble. Dad had been right: you didn't have to convince this car to go. Now, stopping, that was another thing. Stopping. Stopping dead.

I had an idea, my second of the day. It was not a particularly good idea, but under the circumstances, I was willing to consider anything, from really fundamentally stupid through not all that terrible. This was probably way down on the list, but it was the only idea I had, and beggars can't be choosers.

We sped past the 17/417 split in the left hand lane, toward the outlying suburbs of Orleans. I strained my eyes, scanning the horizon for the bridge that held up the Jeanne d'Arc Boulevard overpass. It was along here somewhere, I knew it was. It had probably been two years since I'd driven out this way, but I had a mental image of the bridge, with its huge concrete pillars on a wide stretch of grass. It would be perfect for what I had in mind.

My two passengers sat silently, twin statues in the back seat. The one with the gun was in the middle, where he could keep an eye on me; the other was next to the passenger side door. I breathed deeply several times, trying desperately to regain the calm I needed. This was going to take all the concentration I could muster. There would be no room for panic, or second thoughts.

There was the bridge, its lights visible from a kilometre away. I slid effortlessly into the far left lane. There was no traffic behind me, and none ahead that I could see. A perfect, clear road. When we were about five hundred metres from the bridge, I eased my foot downward on the gas pedal, accelerating slowly enough that my captors wouldn't notice right away. I felt the man with the gun shift slightly, but he didn't say anything.

A hundred metres away from the bridge, I floored it. The car shot forward with a roar, rising slightly off its front tires. The man with the gun was thrown backward by the sudden velocity; he shouted something in Russian, struggled to regain his position. I heard the gun fire, felt something searing in my ribs, but it was too late to care now.

"You're not getting them, you bastards!" I cried. And for a brief, singing moment, exhilaration surged through me. They'd never get Dawn and my parents and Peter — I wouldn't let them. I would kill all of us first.

"*Da sveedanya*!" I screamed, my one and only Russian phrase. The car leapt off the highway, headed straight for the concrete pillars. We were flying, airborne for a couple of long seconds, before we hit the ground with a bone-shattering thud. I fought to hold onto the steering wheel, yanking it as far left as it would go, straining against my screaming shoulder muscles, the pain that shot up my side. As the pillar loomed in front of me, I slammed on the brake, jammed it into the floor. The car fishtailed, its heavy rear end flipping back and forth, as we smashed sideways into the pillar. I closed my eyes. Something exploded in my head, there was a flash of light, and then nothing.

23

CRASH INVESTIGATION UNDER WAY

Two burn to death in devastating collision

Onlookers watched in horror last night as a 1987 black Crown Victoria left Highway 17 eastbound, sped across the grass median, and smashed into the concrete supports holding up the Jeanne d'Arc overpass, bursting into flames. One survivor, whose name is being withheld pending notification of family, staggered out of the car and ran several metres down the median before collapsing.

Emergency vehicles arrived within minutes, but it was too late for two of the car's inhabitants. Their charred remains were recovered from the wreckage after the flames had died down. David Corcoran, a paramedic on the scene, said, "We couldn't even get near it. And once we got them out, we couldn't even tell whether they were male or female, they were that badly burned." OPP officer Brendan White confirmed that charges were pending against the survivor for leaving the scene of the accident, but said charges have not yet been laid.

"We don't have enough information yet," he said. "And there is some question as to the suspect's medical prospects. An impact like that can do a lot of damage." White did confirm that alcohol did not seem to have played a role in the crash.

Police say they have tentative identifications for the victims of the crash, but they declined to release them at this time. The investigation will continue.

24

FRIDAY, OCTOBER 21
Sun square Neptune ✦
Moon square Saturn ✦
Venus conjunct Mars ✦

The room was very bright. Too bright. Overhead lights, so white they burned into my closed eyelids. And when I tried to open my eyes, everything started to swim in slow, lazy circles around me. I shut them again. But that was no good, either. With nothing to distract me, my body was a huge pulsing mass of pain. I tried to move my head, but something stopped me. I tried to put a hand up to find out what was holding my head in place, but my arm didn't work, and attempting to move it caused a jolt of electricity to shoot from my wrist to my shoulder. I tried the other arm. It moved, but as I lifted it, pain seared across my abdomen. I gasped, and let my hand fall to the bed.

"Mom?" Someone whispered next to my head. I wanted to open my eyes to figure out who it was, but fear of the room starting to whirl again stopped me. Carefully, I edged one eye open, just a little.

A young woman, a girl really, leaned over me, clutching the steel rail of the bed. She had long hair that hung like a honey-coloured curtain, blue eyes in a heart-shaped face with a very determined-looking chin. She was pretty, but she looked tired, strained.

"Mom, can you hear me?"

Her voice was too loud, too close to my ear. I grimaced and tried to turn my head away, but again I found it impossible to move.

"Mom, don't try to move. You're in a head brace. You were in an accident. Do you remember?"

Car crash. That might explain a few things. I tried to open my mouth to speak, but found that nothing came out.

"Mom, please. You can't talk, you've got a tube down your throat to help you breathe," the girl said. "If you can hear me, just blink your eyes a little, okay?"

I wanted to please this girl — she seemed so gentle and caring. I blinked, then squeezed my eyes shut to block out the light.

"Dad? I think she's awake." The girl called to someone outside the room. There was a soft shuffling noise, and I felt someone move next to the bed.

A man said, "Katy? Katy, can you hear me?"

I blinked again.

"See? I think she can hear us! She can't talk yet, but the doctor was wrong! I knew she'd come out of it."

"It's too early to tell anything yet, honey. We'll just have to wait and see. Why don't you go down the hall and get your grandparents? They'll want to know she's waking up."

The man stood next to me. I could feel him, hear his breathing, but I didn't want to open my eyes again. Everything hurt.

The girl came back, and she'd apparently brought more people with her. I heard whispered voices at the foot of my bed. I wasn't really that interested in what they were saying, unless they were here to take away the pain that seared through my entire body.

The man said, “Dawn, why don’t you go on home, try to get some sleep? I can stay with her.”

“I’m not leaving.” I’d been right about the determination in that chin. This was a girl who knew her own mind. Somehow, knowing that I’d guessed right about the girl made me want to smile.

The man and the girl stayed near me a long time, I think. I drifted in and out of sleep, and once I remember someone coming to jab a needle into my arm, and then the pain moved away from me, into a part of my body I could no longer feel, and I slept.

When I awoke, I was alone, though I could hear people talking in low voices somewhere nearby. My throat felt raw and burned, but I no longer had the feeling that something was blocking it. I tried to open my eyes again, and this time it worked a little better. The light still hurt my eyes, but at least the room was not whirling around me.

There was a curtain pulled around the bed in which I lay, and presently it stirred, and the girl I’d seen earlier came through. There was something familiar about her, but I couldn’t quite place it. She saw that my eyes were open, and broke into a wide smile.

“Mom! You’re awake! Dad, she’s got her eyes open!”

The curtains parted again, and the man came to the head of the bed. He put a light hand on my shoulder, and I winced as the pain shot through me. He jumped back as though he’d been scalded.

“Sorry, Katy. Are you in much pain?”

“Yes,” I whispered, but it came out as a croak.

Strangely, the girl burst into tears. I wondered what I’d said to distress her.

“Katy, do you know where you are?” the man asked.

"No," I said. Was this a guessing game?

"You're in the hospital. You've been here three days now. They brought you here after the car crash — do you remember the car crash?"

"No. Are you a doctor?" He had the look of a doctor — warm, caring. He had fine, long-boned hands that looked as though they might be good at mending broken people.

"Katy, it's me! Peter!" the man said. "And this is Dawn. Don't you know us?" His face crumpled, and tears filled his eyes. He looked bereft, and I wished I could have told him I knew him. I didn't like to distress him. The girl turned her head away. I had the feeling I'd said the wrong thing.

The man and the girl went away after a while, and then various doctors and nurses padded in and out of range for a long time, poking and lifting and checking various parts of me, all of which hurt. No one said very much to me. I suppose I wasn't being much of a conversationalist. Mostly, I just stared at the ceiling, wishing I'd been able to make the man and the girl happier. Wishing I'd been able to tell them I knew them.

25

In time, I discovered the extent of my injuries. I had a fractured skull, which explained the vise-like apparatus that held my head immobile. My left arm was also fractured in three places, my right ankle was broken, and my knees were not at all happy. On the internal front, I was now missing my spleen and one kidney. A bullet had been removed from my abdomen, but fortunately it had not managed to pierce anything absolutely essential. Apparently one of my lungs had ruptured while I was being moved into the ambulance, pierced by the three ribs which had broken when I was thrown forward against the steering wheel. I had several burns — on my scalp, my cheek, my shoulder — but evidently I'd leapt from the car before it actually burst into flames, which made me luckier than two other people, who had perished quite horribly. I felt vaguely sorry for them, but as I didn't know who they were, I couldn't really feel much more than a generalized sense of sadness at lives wasted.

The police had been round to visit several times, but I hadn't much to tell them. They wanted to know who the two men were, and why they'd been carrying guns, and all sorts of other things. I was no help at all.

At first, I didn't really mind having no memory; I had

a feeling that if I'd been able to recall much, I wouldn't have liked it. Two elderly people, my parents, visited me often, taking turns with the man and girl I'd met earlier. They, too, seemed stricken that I had no idea who they were, but the woman cocked her head at one point, and said, "Tch. It will come, Katy, it will come. I saw plenty of people like you during the war. They always came back. You will too."

I wasn't certain what she meant by this, but somehow I felt comforted.

I was examined several times by a neurologist, who told me there was not much he could do. Head injuries, he said, were always tricky, and one could never really predict the final outcome. He used some long phrase — post-traumatic encephalo-something, I think. He told me that my loss of memory was probably both organic and psychiatric, whatever that meant. I didn't really care — I felt I would probably get bored at some point with this very white bed and this small room filled with flowers and cards and stuffed animals, but the moment had not yet arrived, and for now I was content to float.

Dawn and Peter no longer kept vigil by my bed, but one evening, during their nightly visit, Dawn sat nibbling on a doughnut her father had brought.

"Tofu," I said.

"Pardon?" Her head shot up, eyes wide.

"I ... I don't know," I said. "When I saw you eating that, I just thought, 'tofu.'"

Dawn began to giggle. "Mom," she said, "I think there's more in there than anyone's giving you credit for."

"Thanks," I said, though I hadn't the faintest idea what she was talking about.

But gradually, words and phrases began to come back to me. I'd turn my head a certain way, and hear a woman screaming something in a foreign language. Or I'd look out the window at the night sky, and think, "Oh, there's Jupiter. It should be conjoining the Moon sometime soon."

I knew now that Dawn was my daughter, and Peter my ex-husband, though I could not have told you details of giving birth, or when or how Peter and I had married or split. Fragments of the past kept drifting into my consciousness, like stray pieces of a very large jigsaw puzzle. Sometimes I could fit them into the larger picture, but sometimes they just hung there, taunting me. I cried often, from the sheer frustration of knowing that I no longer seemed to have a self. I was a body, a wounded, battered body, lying in a bed. I had no past, and I could envision no future for myself. All that existed was the now, and frankly, the now sucked. Big time.

A psychiatrist came to see me. His name was Dr. Burger, and he was very pleasant. He did a number of tests, had me count backward by sevens from one hundred, wanted to know about my childhood. I told him I didn't even have an adulthood, let alone a past. He smiled and said, "You will. You will." I wasn't sure I believed him, but I wanted to.

One morning, I woke thinking that the thing I wanted most in the world was a decent cup of coffee, not the swill they'd been serving me from plastic mugs in this place. When my mother came in, I said, "I'd kill for a good cup of coffee."

She covered my hand and smiled. "See?" she said. "I told you you'd be back."

The next morning, Peter arrived bearing a Thermos pot of a Brazilian Santos blend. He poured it into real mugs, and helped me sip mine.

"Just like the old days," I said. "You used to make coffee and bring it to me in bed, remember?"

And as I said it, I knew it to be true. Peter just looked at me, a grin spreading across his face.

Slowly, slowly, I was beginning to feel like myself again. More to the point, I was beginning to feel that I *had* a self again. I savoured each returning memory, treasured them all like my children. The memory of sitting in the kitchen, drinking coffee and reading the newspaper while Dawn sipped one of her godawful breakfast drinks. Or perhaps walking along a tree-lined street, shuffling through the autumn leaves that covered the lawns and sidewalks. Each was as precious as the next.

When they discharged me from the hospital to a rest home, three weeks after I'd gone in, my body was in good enough shape that I could get myself up, even hobble around a bit on crutches. I couldn't go far, but I didn't really want to. The pain had subsided but not vanished. The rest home was ... well, restful. My room, overlooking the Rideau River, faced east, and the morning sun woke me later every day, as the last days of autumn took hold, turning the grasses by the river a pale, washed out yellow.

One evening, a week or so after I'd come to this place, Peter knocked on the door. He'd brought still more flowers, to refresh the collection accumulating on my window-ledge.

"How are you feeling?" he asked.

I made a noncommital noise. "I've been reading the newspaper," I said. "The series you wrote — about the Russian mob and so on. I keep getting more and more little flashes of memory, bits and pieces of things. One of them is this woman screaming something in another language — I wondered if it might be Russian?"

"I don't know," Peter said. "What does it sound like?"

"*Das* something." I closed my eyes and tried to conjure the voice in my mind. "*Da sveedanya,* that's it. She screams it, and then there's this bright white light."

"'Good-bye.' It means 'good-bye'," Peter said slowly. "Katy, I think you're hearing yourself. Screaming good-bye to Viktor and Sergei, right before you crashed the car. They were criminals, the men who died in the crash. Murderers."

"They were? Who had they killed?"

"A lot of people, probably. But most recently, a woman named Amanda Weatherburn, and a man named Geoffrey Acres. Oh, and Mike — the guy I was working with in Montreal."

"Mandy," I said slowly. "She died from wasp stings. On an island, in a shed. She turned purple. And the other one — Mr. Acres — he drowned, didn't he? Dawn thought he'd taken off with the class's trip money, but he hadn't."

Clunk. Pieces were raining into place now, fast and thick. I had an image of a woman lying on the ground, a torn and stained lime-green jumpsuit, a wasp crawling up the side of a purple, puffed cheek. A man, crouching over her, begging her not to be dead.

"What happened to Jimmy?" I asked. "Did they arrest him?"

"I don't know. I've been kind of busy, these last few weeks. This wonderful lady I know nearly got herself killed in a car crash, and then Ben, my little worm of an editor, decided I should go with what I had on the Russian mob stories. He decided we couldn't afford to wait."

"Money laundering. That's what Benjamin said Jimmy was doing. Money laundering for the mob. And he had something to do with that rabbi, too — what was her name?"

"Masha."

"That's right. Where is she? She's the one ..." My voice trailed off. Masha Streltsov, a Jew. We wish to speak with her. The voice echoed through my head, and suddenly my mouth was very dry. "Peter, I have part of it."

"Part of what?" He leaned forward, puzzled.

"The crash. I have part of it. There was a man. He had a gun, and he wanted me to take him to Masha. That's what this was all about."

"But what —"

"I wouldn't do it. I took them in the opposite direction. If I'd taken them to Masha, I would have taken them to Dawn and my parents. They all would have died. Instead of just me."

The car leaps forward with a roar, and there is a loud crack as the gun goes off, once, then again, we hit the grassy median, the men behind me are shouting and swearing, the concrete pillar is right there, we're going to crash, I'm going to die, it's coming, coming, I'm twisting the wheel, there's a flash of white light. It's over. All over.

Peter was crouched on the floor in front of me, gripping my hands in his. "Katy, what is it? You're shaking ... what's happening? Should I call the nurse?"

I shook my head. "No — I'm fine," I whispered. "The crash. It's coming back."

"Katy, you crashed into that bridge on purpose, didn't you?"

I nodded. "I had to. It was the only way. I couldn't let them near Dawn. I thought I was going to die, and you know what? I felt good. I felt happy. I wasn't letting those bastards anywhere near my family. You know how we used to read about the kamikaze pilots in the Second World War? Well, I always thought they were completely nuts, choosing to die like that. But I chose to die too, and it didn't feel nuts at all. It felt like the absolutely right thing to do, even when I realized that concrete pillar was going to kill me if Viktor's bullets didn't. I didn't care, as long as I killed those two bastards, those bastards ..."

I was crying, and I couldn't stop, even though my sobs tore through my bruised flesh like knives.

Peter sat patiently, waiting for the storm to subside, and eventually I caught my breath, wiped my eyes and blew my nose. That's when I made my decision.

"Peter, you remember Dr. Burger, the shrink who came to see me in the hospital? Do you think he takes on private patients?"

"We can only ask," Peter said.

26

Over the next several weeks, I rested, ate, went to physio to rebuild my mangled muscles, received countless cards, flowers and visitors, and saw Dr. Burger twice a week. He came to me, which I greatly appreciated. Turns out he was a friend of Greg's, and somehow this didn't surprise me. Neither of them believed in drugging away feelings, so I did a lot of crying in my sessions with Burger, and cursed him out on a regular basis, but each week, I felt myself rebuilding, regenerating, returning to my pre-shattered self.

One afternoon, my mother dropped by, as she did most afternoons. "Katy? Are you awake, *mamaleh*?" She popped her head round the door.

I'd been lying on my bed, trying to develop a taste for the afternoon soap operas. "Yes, come on in, Mama. How can people actually watch this dreck? I've been watching this show for three weeks running now, and I still can't tell Alex from Brooke from Erica from Phoebe. They all look alike to me; they must go to the same hairdresser or something."

Mama chuckled. "You sound better! Listen, I brought you a visitor — she's just in town for the day. I thought you might like to see her. Come in, come in," she told the person behind her, ushering her forward.

Masha entered tentatively, almost on tiptoe, as though afraid of what she might see. I didn't disappoint. The angry burns on my face and scalp had subsided to a dull red, but I still wore casts on an arm and a leg; my hair had begun to grow back, but it was patchy yet.

"Katy, I'm so sorry, you suffer." Masha smoothed a patch of rumpled bedspread and perched on the edge of my bed. "I hear from your mama, she tells me you have the ... danger? No, the accident because of me."

"Please, it wasn't your fault," I said. "But tell me — why were Viktor and his friend looking for you? They never explained that to me, and I've been wondering."

Masha stared out my window for several minutes, watching a flock of wild ducks skid gracefully onto the river's surface.

"Is a long story," she said finally. "In Russia — it was not always Russia, it was USSR. When it was USSR, I worked for the secret service. The KGB. I was very young, very foolish. I work there four, five years." She held up her fingers to illustrate. "Not long, but long enough. Then I leave, go to London, England, study for the rabbinate. I am, no, I was much happier there. I go back to Russia after communism falls, everything is changes. I think, I will teach my people what Jews do, how to be a Jew. I fill my mind with this only. Later, I come to Canada, work in Montreal with other Russians. I am happy, I have the life I want."

"But when you were in the KGB, didn't they have something to do with keeping Russian Jews from learning about their own religion? I had a friend once who was followed and arrested for trying to bring Torahs into Russia," I said.

Masha nodded, her face pink. "I pretend I am not Jewish, but I can only pretend this until I see other Jews, my people, getting hurt. I begin to think, am I not a Jew? I make a choice."

My mother, who had been rocking in the large chair next to the bed, nodded. "And a good choice, Masha. You did a brave thing."

A sad smile crossed Masha's smooth face. "I hope is good choice. Now I am in Canada, policeman comes to me. He tells me there are some Russians living here who say they are Jewish, use that to get into Israel, then come to Canada, no problem. He says these Russians are criminals, selling drugs, washing their money, killing ... then he tells me, some were in KGB."

"So they asked you to come and work with them, to identify former KGB members?" Carefully, I rolled onto my right side, the less painful of the two, and hoisted myself into a sitting position. This manouevre took me about five minutes, but I waved away offers of help.

She nodded. "I try to help. Zheemy, he is my contact, he brings me books of photos. We meet, go over them, I talk about people I know. One is Viktor — he came from my town. Zheemy says Viktor now lives in Canada, is running drug rings in Montreal, moving into Ottawa."

"And somehow, Viktor found out that you'd identified him, and decided to kill you," I finished for her. "But they didn't know where you were — and that's why they needed me."

She nodded again. "I never mean to put you, to put your family in danger. When your daughter saw me in car with Zheemy, I hide my head, thinking she will tell everyone I work for police. But now I think, if I tell you all before, none of this will happen. I am sorry." She looked imploringly at me.

"You couldn't have known," I said. "It wasn't your fault. Listen, when you say 'Zheemy', you mean Jimmy, right?"

"Yes! Zheemy. You know?"

"I know. Where is he now?"

Masha smiled. "He is no more a money changer. He is gone back to office, to make reports."

"So ... you're saying Jimmy really is a police officer?"

"No ... yes. National police, not city police. He work for months to set up foreign exchange office, build reputation, bring in many 'businessmen' who want their money made clean. He is getting ready to make big arrests, when Viktor begins to wonder if Zheemy is trying to set a trap. Viktor takes Zheemy's brother, who tells him the truth ... and Viktor kills him. Now, Zheemy knows that Viktor knows, and tries to hide his wife and sister. But his wife is very stubborn, thinks he is trying to trick her, that he wants only her money. So she dies too."

"The fishermen," I muttered.

"Pardon me? What are fishermen?"

"The fishermen who followed our water taxi to the island the day Mandy was killed. They were out in a boat, they must have been waiting for her to arrive. But — here's what I don't understand. If they were planning to exterminate Jimmy's whole family, why wouldn't they just follow Mandy and shoot her? Why go to all that trouble, with the wasps and all?"

Masha shook her head. "You do not understand. They are not just killing whole families. They want to make Zheemy know that his family dies in pain, in suffering. They send him a picture of his brother, sinking in the water. He got it the day his wife leaves for the island. This is how he knew he must try to stop her."

"Sick," my mother clucked. "Sick, sick people."

I had to agree. I was sure Dawn would be terribly disappointed to learn that Jimmy, her erstwhile archnemesis, was actually on the side of goodness and light.

She hadn't mentioned much about her obsession with Jimmy lately, but knowing her, it wouldn't be far from her mind. She probably just didn't want to worry me, in my weakened state.

That evening, I called Benjamin at home.

"Hey," I said. "It's me."

"Hey," he said. "How's it going? Sorry I didn't make it in today."

"Never mind. I think you owe me a chocolate-covered offering of some kind, don't you?"

"You got it. Are you sure they'll let you eat that kind of stuff, over there at Happy Haven? I've seen the way that scrawny little nurse looks when your mother brings you blintzes. You'd think she was trying to poison you."

"I'll hide them. And if they try to torture me to tell them who smuggled in the contraband, I won't talk. I'm tough. You can trust me, Benjamin."

"I never doubted it."

"Listen, I have a question for you."

"Shoot. Oh, sorry ..."

I laughed. "It's okay, my shrink is helping me get over my morbid fear of loud noises. Anyway, it's about Jimmy Healey."

Benjamin didn't say anything.

"Benjamin? You still there?"

"Yeah, I'm here. But ..."

"Did I say a bad word or something?"

"Not exactly." Benjamin seemed to be choosing his words with care. "It's just that we've had word from the top. We're not supposed to discuss the guy."

"Oh, I know all about his undercover activities," I said airily. "What I wanted to know was whether the charges against him ever amounted to anything."

"Katy!" Benjamin exploded. "How do you know

about Jimmy Healey? I swear, you are the most exasperating woman I've ever met!"

"I should hope so! So — were the charges dropped, or what?"

"No. They were never laid. In usual cop fashion, it took the RCMP a while to drop the word down to the OPP that they were barking up the wrong tree. But once they figured it out, they dropped any idea of going after him. And eventually, someone in the OPP thought to let us know what was going on, so now everyone's copacetic. Okay? You happy?"

"Well, good. I just wanted to make sure. You know, I think I actually saw the guys who killed Mandy Weatherburn. I've been going over and over it in what remains of my mind, and the only ones who could have done it were the fishermen."

"Pardon? What fishermen are we talking about?"

I told him what I'd told Masha.

"Katy, I hate to break this to you, but for once in your life, the police got there before you. Hendricks called me the day after your car crash, and filled me in."

"So ..." I thought for a moment. "The fishermen — they were Victor and Sergei, right?"

"That's our best guess so far."

"One more question?"

"Could I stop you from asking?"

"Probably not. I just realized something, though. The whole time between Mandy's death and my accident — whenever I talked to you about Jimmy Healey, you were always really vague, weren't you? You never came out and said you weren't really looking for him, and when Dawn told you stuff, you didn't discourage her. And it seemed like every five seconds, you were telling us to keep our mouths shut. You were managing us, weren't you?"

Benjamin coughed uncomfortably. "Well ..."

"Come on, out with it."

"Okay, yeah, I was. Word came down from on high that you two were butting in — again, I might add — and since I had a personal relationship with you, the brass figured I stood the best chance of keeping you quiet until some arrests were made. They were trying to protect Healey's operation, without telling anyone what was actually going on — it was one of those federal top-secret deals, need to know basis only. But it was for your own good, Katy."

"I'll bet." I made a rude noise. I wasn't really mad, but I had a role to play. "So basically, the reason this whole thing stretched out the way it did is that you cops couldn't play nice together?"

"You have to understand, it's a jurisdictional thing. There are longstanding rivalries — it's not right, but that's the way it is. We try to share information, but ... I don't know, there are communication gaps sometimes. What can I say? We're not perfect."

I snorted. "Typical males. Now, if women ran the police force ..."

"Katy, don't get me started," Benjamin warned.

"Why? What are you going to do? Come and break my legs? News flash — you're too late." I laughed, and he joined in.

A few days later, there was a timid knock on my door. A sleek brunette head peeked into my room. I nearly didn't recognize my visitor.

"My brother told me you might still be here." Her whispery little girl voice hadn't changed, but somehow she looked taller, more of a presence.

"Hey, Rowan. Come in, come in." I put aside one of the word search puzzle books that my mother insisted on bringing in by the truckload.

"If you're sure I'm not disturbing you." She slipped into the room and seated herself primly on the chair at the foot of my bed. "I just wanted to thank you. For all your help."

"No need," I said. "In fact, I sort of hoped you might drop by. I feel like I owe you an apology."

She looked startled. "For what?"

"Oh, just for being a bit impatient with you. I was too wrapped up in my own concerns, and ..." My voice trailed off. There really isn't a polite way to tell someone that they irritate you beyond belief, is there? So I went with the theory about not saying anything at all.

"Oh, that. I understand. You were scared. I was too — especially when I thought Jimmy might have had something to do with Geoff's death. I can't believe I was such a ninny about that."

"You weren't a ninny; you were going on available evidence. And everything was pretty confusing, wasn't it?"

She nodded. "I've never felt so helpless in my whole life. But you know, it's interesting. I learned a lot about myself from the experience. For one thing, I'm stronger than I thought I was. I used to think I needed crutches — Jimmy, Mandy, pills — to keep myself going, but out there in the wilderness, I figured out that I could help myself if I needed to, and I didn't need anyone else to prop me up or give me permission."

"Pills?" I echoed. "So you really were stoned out there on the beach that day, right?"

She looked embarrassed. "I'm afraid so. I was always so ashamed of it — and it's not like I was doing anything illegal, just using the Xanax my doctor prescribed for me — but when you asked me, I just couldn't bring myself to tell you the truth."

"We thought Jimmy must have drugged you and left

you there," I said. "Except I couldn't figure out why he'd do that. Why not just haul you off with him in the boat, or else tell you to stay put?"

"I know. I never meant to make him look bad, really. It just kind of ... came out that way. No, that's wrong," she corrected herself. "I've been seeing a counsellor lately, and one of the things we're working on is how I always thought things just happened to me. Now I know they happen because of my own choices."

I nodded agreement. "True enough. And good for you for taking responsibility. So what really happened on that beach, anyway? I've been wondering about that."

"Well, originally Jimmy wanted to take me with him to the mainland, get me to Aaron's, and get me out of town. I was happy to go along with him at that point, because I was pretty freaked out about Mandy's death. Then his cell phone rang, and he changed his tune completely. He decided I'd be safer staying on the island. He took off in the boat, and told me to head back up to the lodge. Said he'd contact me back in town. He never actually said so, but I think the guys who killed Mandy were in the vicinity, and he wanted to get past them without having to worry about me getting killed or something."

"Makes sense," I said. "So where did the pills come in?"

"That's the humiliating part. I was feeling good and sorry for myself — Mandy was dead, Jimmy was abandoning me, I was feeling scared and alone — so I took a handful of pills. I had some warped idea about committing suicide, showing Jimmy how badly he'd let me down. My counsellor says I was acting out a passive-aggressive fantasy. She calls it a suicidal gesture — I didn't really want to die, just let Jimmy know how mad I was. I guess that about sums it up."

"Wow," I said. A pivotal moment in history: Katy Klein at a loss for words.

Rowan smiled timidly. "I brought you something. I hope that's okay."

"Hey, you didn't have to do that." Now my guilt was in overdrive. I felt myself starting to flush.

"I wanted to. I called your daughter and asked what you might like, so you can thank her, too." Reaching into her Italian handbag, she pulled out a small box and handed it to me.

I undid the gold foil wrapping and opened the cardboard box. Inside, wrapped in tissue paper, was a small, perfect gold astrolabe. Tears started to form in the corners of my eyes as I held it up to the sun that streamed in my window. Years ago, when I first began studying astrology, my father had given me an astrolabe, which had occupied pride of place on my desk for a very long time. It had been lost last winter, and I'd felt its absence more keenly than anything else in my office.

"Thank you," I managed to whisper. "It's ... perfect. Thank you."

"You're welcome." She hugged me gently, careful not to disturb my bruises. "Maybe someday I'll come by and get you to read my chart."

"Please do," I said. And I meant it.

27

MONDAY, DECEMBER 8
Sun trine Saturn ✦
Moon trine Pluto ✦
Venus conjunct Neptune ✦

"So — how does it feel to be home?" Dawn asked, one early December morning.

Peter, who'd been carrying my suitcase and an armload of paraphernalia that I'd collected during my sojourn at the rest home, dumped the case on the floor, the cards and candies and stuffed animals and such on the kitchen table. I leaned against the doorframe of my tiny apartment, my tiny, cramped, wonderful apartment, and breathed deeply. The place had been shut up for several weeks now, as Dawn had moved in with her father upstairs, but there were traces of old smells — coffee and dust and the vanilla body lotion Dawn uses every morning when she gets out of the shower.

"You guys should have brought me back here when I had no memory," I said. "The smells alone would have brought it all back, guaranteed."

"Well, your shrink said it would all come back when you were good and ready," Peter said. "He said not to rush you. And you know, for someone who was at death's door eight weeks ago, you're not doing all that badly."

"I come from resilient stock. We're a family of survivors," I said.

Peter patted me on the back. "Listen, gang, I've got to get to work. Ben's been breathing down my neck lately ..."

"You're not doing another organized crime piece, are you, Dad?" Dawn sounded anxious, as well she might.

"In a manner of speaking," he said. "Only this time it's more or less legal. Do you know how little the major banks in this country pay in taxes? It's organized larceny. I've only just started the research, but already, I can tell this one's going to be big. Really big."

"Go." I shooed him out the door. "Off you go to make Canada safe for democracy."

I hobbled into the kitchen, which looked strange, somehow. All the dishes were done, the counters wiped down, the floor free from crumbs or detritus of any kind. "Wow, this place is spotless! I feel like I'm in some kind of weird alternative universe. What happened?"

"Dad did it. Well, he didn't actually do it himself. He hired this cleaning company to come in and take care of it. He thought it would be a nice homecoming present for you. Now, go sit down. I'll make you some coffee."

Obediently, I sat. Technically, I wasn't supposed to be on my feet at all—I'd only escaped from the rest home by promising my doctor I'd stay on bed rest. Well, couch rest, anyway. A few minutes later, Dawn handed me the coffee she'd made. Considering her feelings about my caffeine intake, I was touched.

"Oh, before I forget, Flavia sent you an e-mail yesterday. I printed it out so you wouldn't have to sit at the computer." She handed me a sheet of paper.

Dear Katy,
I've been trying and trying to phone you, and finally I got a call back from Peter, your ex. Man, what a cutey he is! Scrump-dilly-ish-us! Course, I couldn't see him, but his voice could melt stone!

Seriously, though, I was so worried about you. He says you're getting your health back, but I feel so guilty about having left you to cope with all that on your own. I knew when I left that you probably thought the worst of me — that I might actually have killed Mandy — and I felt bad about that, but I couldn't think of anything that would prove to you that I'd had nothing to do with it. It's a shame, really, because I just loved seeing you and Dawn — what a great kid she is, just like her mama — but I felt like we never really connected quite the same way we did by e-mail. Funny how the internet has created this whole new way of relating, isn't it? But I digress. As usual.

The point is that I cut out and left you when you could have used a helping hand, and I'll never forgive myself for that. It's not what friends do to one another. I hope you'll be able to find it in yourself to give me another chance. I'm not sure I could, if I were you, but your friendship means a lot to me.

Lots of love, Flavia.

I put the e-mail down and leaned my head back against the cushion Dawn had thoughtfully placed behind me. For a while I said nothing.

"I thought it was a nice e-mail," Dawn said. "Are you going to answer her?"

"I am."

"Are you still going to be friends?"

"I hope so," I said. "She's right — we've got some hurdles to overcome. I guess we'll just have to try to straighten things out between us as best we can."

"She was scared," Dawn observed. "People do stupid things when they're scared."

"That they do, *mamaleh*. That they do."

"Mom, I want to talk to you. I had a lot of time to think about things while you were away, and one of the things I realized is that I haven't been very fair. I decided way back when I first met him that I didn't like Detective Benjamin, and it really bugged me that you would go out with someone I didn't like. But you know, he came to see you every single day while you were sick, and he would just stand there, staring down at you."

"He did? I don't remember that."

"Mom, you were in la-la land at the time," Dawn said matter-of-factly. "Out to lunch. Wheel's spinning, hamster's dead."

"Okay, okay, I get the point." I laughed. "So what about Benjamin?"

"Well, I watched him come in every day without fail, and after a while I realized, hey, he really does care about her. He talked to Dad a lot, and I think they actually like each other now. Anyway, it just made me think. And I thought, well, what if I had a boyfriend that you didn't much like? So I just wanted to say, I'm going to try to be better about him, okay?"

I worked to still the twitching at the corners of my mouth. "Thank you, sweetheart. I appreciate it. But you know what? I had time to do some thinking, too, and I realized something important. Before the crash, I was scared. Too many bad things had happened, and I felt like the world was closing in on me. My whole life revolved around my fear. I was so scared, I tried to just hide myself away, to keep out of danger and not let it find me."

"I know. I could feel it, but every time I tried to talk to you about it ..."

"I know, I know, I shut you down. I'm sorry. I was shutting everyone out, and I couldn't figure out how to stop doing that. I was scared to be in a relationship with anyone, because I was sure I'd get hurt; but I was scared not to be in a relationship, either. And Benjamin — well, he kind of made me feel like I was protected, you know? He's a great guy, and I do care about him, but I think I've been going out with him for all the wrong reasons."

"Like what?"

"Like, that he could keep bad things from happening to me and the people I love. That was wrong, for a couple of reasons. For one thing, it's wrong to lead someone on. I feel badly about that. But the other thing is, no one else can protect me. I have to do that for myself."

"Mom, you nearly died! How is that protecting yourself?"

"It's not, I guess. I don't know if I can explain it to you — when I was in that car, driving along with a gun stuck in my ribs, I was terrified. I was the most scared I've ever been in my whole life, I won't lie about that. But all I could think was, I'm not going to let these bastards win. And I didn't."

"I think I see," said Dawn. "So, are you going to tell Benjamin?"

"Yeah." I sipped my coffee. "I am."

By mid-December, I was back at work again, at least half-days. Benjamin and I had our little talk, and he looked mournful, but not surprised, that I wanted to be friends and nothing more. We hugged, and he made me promise that if I were ever to change my mind, I'd call him. I don't think I'm going to change my mind.

Greg and I had a talk too, and I asked him whether

the offer of a consulting position still stood. He said it did. And so, one blustery January day, I got out of bed, gulped my coffee, donned a suit for the first time in nearly seven years, and took the bus to the Royal Ottawa Hospital for my first day of work as a forensic psychologist. I'm working there two days a week now, and it's gone a long way toward clearing some of the bills that accumulated while I was out of commission.

The fear is sometimes still with me. I feel it most at night, when I'm lying awake watching the headlights of passing cars on the wall of my bedroom. It slips into my mind softly, winding its way around my thoughts until I can no longer deny it. Don't drift off to sleep, it whispers. Who knows what might happen? And you know what? The fear is right: I don't know what might happen. Not now, not tomorrow, not ten years from now. And maybe, just maybe, that is as it should be.

ACKNOWLEDGEMENTS

As always, I could not have completed this book without the love and support of my family: Adrian, Rachel, and especially Mitchell — you are the wind beneath my wings.

My friends at the Coffeehouse have been there for me throughout, cheering me on and providing the kind of daily sustenance only friends (and other writers) can provide.

Lynn Henry, my wonderful editor, makes editing a joy; and the publicity team at Raincoast is a dream, as always. Thank you all so very much!

ABOUT THE AUTHOR

Karen Irving is the author of *Pluto Rising* (nominated for an Arthur Ellis Award) and *Jupiter's Daughter*, the first two books in the Katy Klein Mystery Series. She has been writing — and studying astrology — for twenty-five years. Karen Irving lives with her husband, son and daughter in Ottawa, Ontario.